MYSTERY OF THE MOSS-COVERED MANSION

A friend of Carson Drew's has been arrested and charged with sending a truck loaded with explosive oranges into the Space Center complex at Cape Kennedy. Knowing that Mr. Billington could not possibly be guilty of sabotage, Nancy and her father rush to the defense of the accused man.

During the Drews' investigation Nancy becomes suspicious of an old, spooky mansion. Behind a high, steel-mesh enclosure fierce African wild animals roam over the extensive grounds. Through a ruse the clever teen-age detective discovers that something besides the training of wild animals is going on at the mysterious moss-covered mansion estate.

Many dangerous moments await Nancy before she proves Mr. Billington's innocence and thwarts the plans of treacherous subversives bent on undermining the U. S. space program.

Orange trees were burning everywhere

NANCY DREW MYSTERY STORIES

Mystery of the Moss-Covered Mansion

BY CAROLYN KEENE

PUBLISHERS *Grosset & Dunlap* NEW YORK

PRINTED IN THE UNITED STATES OF AMERICA

Contents

CHAPTER I

The Crash

THE Drews' living room was in semidarkness as Nancy walked in. Only one lamp was lighted. Under its glow her father sat absorbed in a single sheet of newspaper which lay across his knees.

On the table next to him were a pad and pencil. Figures, letters, and symbols were scrawled on the top sheet.

Nancy stopped beside his chair. "Crossword puzzle?" asked the reddish-blond haired girl.

Mr. Drew, a tall, good-looking man, glanced up at his attractive, eighteen-year-old daughter and smiled. "No, it's not a crossword puzzle. Actually it's a message in a personal column from this Florida newspaper."

"A personal?" Nancy repeated. "But why are you making all these hieroglyphics on the pad?"

"Sit down and I'll show you," her father said.

Nancy pulled up the chair from the opposite

side of the table. Her father was the leading attorney in River Heights where they lived and she was sure he was puzzling over some problem in connection with his work.

She asked, "Dad, are you busy on a regular case or one with a mystery?"

Mr. Drew laughed. "A case with a mystery. I sent to Florida for newspapers of several weeks back, thinking I might pick up a clue from them."

He handed the paper to Nancy and pointed out an item in the personal column. "What does my detective daughter think?" he asked.

Nancy studied the unusual message. Finally she read the ad aloud:

" '*Son of fruit grower wishes forgiveness. Will return money.*' "

The young sleuth was silent for several seconds, then she frowned. "This could or could not be suspicious. Maybe some father and son had a difference of opinion and he ran away, taking some of his dad's money. He put this ad in the paper, expecting his father to see it and forgive him."

Mr. Drew did not reply. He picked up a sheet from another newspaper dated several days later. He pointed to it and said, "Do you think this one makes as much sense as the other?"

The second ad was longer. It said, "*Natural color oranges best antidote for grower's son's special kind of chronic asthma.*"

"This one sounds more like a code than the first," Nancy remarked.

Her father asked, "Do you see any connection between the two messages?"

"Yes, one. Both items contain the words son and grower." Nancy looked up at her father. "Dad, do you know what it means and are you teasing me to see if I can figure it out?"

Mr. Drew chuckled. "Such a thing would have been a temptation," he said, "but this time I confess I haven't the faintest idea what these personals mean. The fact that the words son and grower appear in both makes me suspect that they're code messages."

"And you have a hunch they may relate to your case?" Nancy inquired. Her father nodded.

Nancy picked up a sheet of paper and began to jot down letters and numbers. Mr. Drew watched her, always intrigued by the way his daughter tackled a code. Nancy had made a study of codes and he was sure she would soon find the answer to this puzzle.

There was silence for a minute, then suddenly Nancy exclaimed, "Here's a hidden message that makes sense!"

As she leaned across the table to show it to her father, they heard a terrific crash directly in front of the house.

"Oh!" said Nancy. "A car accident!"

She was already dashing across the room to the

front door. Mr. Drew followed her through the spacious hall and outside into the autumn night. They could vaguely see two cars locked together. The Drews raced down their curving driveway to the street.

Nancy and her father were appalled by what they saw. One car had smashed through the hood of the other. The lone occupant, a man, was slumped over the steering wheel, unconscious.

Looking into the other car, Nancy exclaimed, "Bess! George!"

Bess Marvin and George Fayne were cousins and Nancy's closest friends. Their parents had gone away together for a few days and Bess and George had come to the Drews to stay.

"Girls, how dreadful!" Nancy cried out. "We'll get you into the house right away and call a doctor."

George, who had been driving, was unbuckling her seat belt. The safety belts and shoulder straps the cousins were wearing had saved them from being thrown against the windshield.

Bess was quivering with fright, but George was angry. "That crazy driver!" she said indignantly. "He suddenly came whizzing across the street and smashed into us! I don't need a doctor! Just a new car!"

Mr. Drew said, "I'm sorry about this, girls, but fortunately you seem to be all right. Nevertheless,

"How dreadful!" Nancy exclaimed

I insist that you have your family doctor look you over. Nancy, suppose you take Bess and George inside and call Dr. Clifford."

By this time the Drews' housekeeper, kindly Hannah Gruen, had come from the house to see what the commotion was.

Recognizing Bess and George, she said worriedly, "My goodness! What happened?"

Mr. Drew answered. "George can explain later. Right now, will you notify the police to come at once? I'll go over and see if I can do anything for that man."

Hannah hurried into the house and called headquarters. Then she dialed Dr. Clifford's number. The girls had followed her. Bess, a blonde, was naturally pink-cheeked, but now she looked like a ghost. George nervously paced the floor, though she said her legs felt like rubber.

"Please sit down, George," urged Nancy, "and try to relax."

Just then a police car arrived. Nancy ran outside to join her father. He introduced officers Hampton and Russo.

"This young man," said Mr. Drew, "lost control of his car. He seems to be in bad shape."

Officer Hampton leaned over to examine the man. He straightened up and nodded. "You're right, Mr. Drew. I believe this guy is under the influence of some drug. Probably he passed out before he hit the other car."

A moment later Dr. Clifford drove up. The officers asked him to give his opinion about the victim. After a quick examination, the physician agreed with Hampton's diagnosis and declared the young man should go to the hospital at once.

"We'll take him there," said Russo.

Meanwhile Hampton had been making notes and snapping pictures of the two cars. He helped Russo lift the victim into the police car.

"Mr. Drew," he called, "will you phone a towing company to haul these cars away at once? They're blocking the street. If you have no luck, let me know."

"I'll be glad to," the lawyer replied.

Russo said they would return as soon as possible from the hospital, and get a statement from Bess and George.

When the others entered the house, the cousins greeted Dr. Clifford with hugs. He had brought them both into the world and they were very fond of him.

The doctor chuckled. "You girls don't seem very sick," he said, "but let me examine you." Mr. Drew left the room. In a few minutes the physician said, "No broken bones or sprains. Nevertheless, it's bed for you, Bess and George, as soon as the police talk with you. I'd say go now, but I suppose the law has to come first!"

Shortly after he had left, the two officers returned. Officer Hampton did the questioning while his partner took notes. The session was soon over and the men left.

Bess and George went to bed, but Nancy and her father stayed up to wait for the towing company truck. It was midnight when they turned out the lights and retired.

The evening's excitement had interrupted the discussion of Mr. Drew's case and the suspicious personals in the Florida newspaper. But immediately after church the next morning it was resumed.

"Nancy, what was it you were going to tell me last night about the coded message?" he asked.

"I think I've figured out the first one you showed me. The message in it is, 'Son wishes money.' "

"It could be," her father agreed. "What method were you using?"

His daughter smiled. "Words 1, 5, 9, and 13."

The other girls were intensely interested.

Bess had picked up the second personal and tried to make sense out of it. She wrinkled her forehead. "What in the world does 'Natural antidote special asthma' mean?"

"Nothing," Nancy replied, "but how about using only the first letters of those words?"

George exclaimed, "They spell NASA!"

The others looked at Nancy in astonishment, and Bess cried out, "NASA? The National Aeronautics Space Administration?"

"Yes," the young sleuth answered. "I believe it refers to the Kennedy Space Center in Florida!"

Mr. Drew looked grim. "Now I'm convinced the personals relate to my case," he said. "Explosives were shipped into the base hidden inside oranges in sacks. I must get down there at once! I was wondering if—"

As her father paused, a thought raced through Nancy's mind. Was he debating if he should take her along?

CHAPTER II

Suspicious Message

NANCY watched her father's face carefully as he stared out the window. She knew he was trying to make up his mind about something important. Finally he turned toward his daughter.

"I could use some help in solving the mystery of the explosive oranges."

"And," Nancy said hopefully, "you think I might be able to help?"

The lawyer nodded. "My client, Mr. Billington, was arrested for bringing explosive Hamlin oranges into the Space Center. He is out on bail but his case is coming up soon. He's innocent. Mr. Billington owns a grove on Merritt Island, which produces only Pineapple Oranges. Someone secretly borrowed a truck of his and delivered several sacks of Hamlin oranges to the Center. The person presented an official card bearing Mr. Billington's name, and signed a slip with his signature. Of course it was a forgery."

Mr. Drew went on, "Unfortunately I can't represent him in Florida because I have no license to practice in that state. My main reason for going down is to engage the services of a Florida lawyer. He and I will work together on the legal angle. I can't stay long this time because I have other urgent matters coming up. But the mysterious culprit must be found before the trial."

Nancy could not refrain from saying, "Dad, if you can't remain on Merritt Island, how about Bess and George and Hannah and I making the trip and staying there?"

"Just what I was thinking," her father replied. "Mr. Billington received special permission from the authorities to leave Florida and come North to sign for the purchase of some property. The buyer is going to Europe, so the transaction had to be made at once.

"Mr. Billington has offered me the use of his house and car and invited anyone else I would like to bring along. He and Mrs. Billington are on their way now but they have a caretaker and his wife who live in the residence. They're Antin and Tina Resardo. She takes care of the house and does the cooking. Antin is foreman of the grove and the sorting and packing house."

Bess and George said they would love to go but would have to obtain permission from their parents. George made the long-distance call. First she told her father about the accident and the wrecked car. "But Bess and I are okay."

"It's too bad about the car, but I'm glad you and Bess weren't hurt," he replied. "George, report the damage immediately to our insurance agent, Mr. Dowley."

"All right, Dad." George now told him about the proposed trip.

"That sounds great!" Mr. Fayne said. "I'll ask the Marvins." He came back to the phone, saying, "It's okay. Have a good time."

George spoke to her mother and Bess talked to her parents. When she finished, George phoned the insurance man and within fifteen minutes he was at the Drew house. She gave Mr. Dowley all the details and he promised to take charge of the matter.

"You go on to Florida and have fun," he said. "When do you leave?"

George went to find Mr. Drew and asked him. He smiled. "I'd like to hop a plane this afternoon," he said. "Do you think you could be ready?"

George looked at her watch. "It will take me about twenty minutes to pack some lightweight clothes and my swimsuit."

It was decided that the group would have an early lunch at the Drews' and leave immediately afterward. While they were eating, the telephone rang. Nancy answered it.

The others heard her exclaim, "Ned! How good to hear from you. Where are you?"

From there on Ned did most of the talking. He was an attractive Emerson College football player who dated Nancy exclusively.

When she came back to the table, her eyes were sparkling. "Great news!" she announced. "You know Ned's parents have had a house on Merritt Island for some time. Mr. and Mrs. Nickerson are there right now and they're going to have a house party. Bess and George, you're invited, as well as myself, and Ned will bring Burt and Dave along."

Burt Eddleton and Dave Evans were George's and Bess's favorite dates. They, too, went to Emerson College.

"Fabulous!" Bess exclaimed.

"Super!" George added.

Nancy remarked, "We'll have time to work on the mystery before the house party starts."

Mr. Drew chuckled. "Well, we'd better leave. I'll load your luggage in the car, while you girls tidy up the kitchen. Hannah, will you see that all the doors and windows are locked and the burglar alarm set?"

The housekeeper hurried off to do this. Then the travelers grabbed their coats and left the house. On the way to the local airport, Mr. Drew said they had a choice of flying either to Orlando or Melbourne, Florida. "Melbourne is a little closer to Merritt Island so I've chosen that one. We land at Kennedy Airport there. I phoned the Billington house and asked Tina if she and Antin would meet us. She agreed."

Hours later, when the Drews and their friends reached Melbourne, they looked everywhere for the couple. No one fitting their description was around. Finally only one elderly woman and a naval officer were left in the passenger waiting room.

"I think I'll telephone the house and see what happened," Mr. Drew said.

He closed himself into a phone booth and tried for ten minutes to get an answer. At last he came outside.

"No one was there, so maybe the Resardos are on the way. I guess we'll just have to wait."

An hour passed and still Antin and Tina had not arrived. Mr. Drew was annoyed. "We'll have to take a taxi," he said. "It'll be an expensive trip. I wonder what happened to the Resardos."

The group enjoyed the ride past the many beautiful homes and glimmering lakes and inlets, some small, others large. When they reached Cocoa the driver went across the bridge to Merritt Island, then along various winding roads. Finally the taxi pulled up in front of a large Spanish-type house on the Indian River. The ground floor had a patio across the front and on one side. There were several chairs under a small grove of shade trees.

While Mr. Drew was paying the taximan, Nancy went to the front door and rapped with the knocker. The visitors stood waiting but no one came to let them in.

George walked to the rear of the dwelling and pressed a buzzer at the back door. No response. She rejoined the others.

"Nobody home," she announced, and dropped into a garden chair. Her companions also seated themselves and waited. About twenty minutes later a car pulled into the driveway and a couple got out.

As they approached the visitors, the man said, "We are the Resardos. Where have you been?"

Mr. Drew looked directly at Tina. "Exactly where I asked you to meet us."

The woman rolled her eyes toward her husband but did not speak. He said angrily, "You told my wife we were to meet you at Orlando but you weren't there."

"I told her Melbourne," Mr. Drew replied, "but never mind. Just let us into the house, please. How much time do we have to unpack before dinner?"

Antin glared at the newcomers. "My wife has a bad headache and must lie down. You people will have to get your own dinner."

He unlocked the front door, ushered Tina in, and followed her.

"Warm reception," Bess whispered to the other girls.

"I can foresee trouble with that couple," George replied.

Tina went upstairs, but Antin stalked to the back door and went out. He walked off to the right into a large orange grove.

The newcomers climbed the stairs and chose bedrooms. They found that one was closed and locked and assumed this must lead to the Resardos' quarters.

After unpacking, Hannah and the girls located the kitchen and examined the contents of the refrigerator. There was plenty of food for a good meal and Hannah chose a big pot of chicken cooked with rice and gravy. The girls set the table in the flower-papered dining room, which had a large glass-top table and white wicker chairs.

When the meal was ready, Antin walked in. Without saying a word, he took one of the plates warming on the stove and helped himself to a very generous portion of everything. He then filled a second plate with food.

He said to Hannah, "I'm taking this up to my wife. We'll eat in our room."

The others assembled in the dining room and after grace had been said by Mr. Drew, they began to eat the delicious dinner. Before they had reached the dessert course, Antin came down the stairs carrying the empty plates, which he put into the sink.

The others heard him open a cabinet door and knew he was getting plates for the dessert, which was an apple pie. The visitors were aghast to see Antin going through the hall with at least half the pie on two plates!

After he had gone upstairs, George burst out, "What's eating him?"

Bess giggled. "Nothing. He's eating everything."

Nancy jumped up and went out to look at the pie. The portion that was left, if cut into five slices, would give each person a piece one-inch wide!

"That man is the limit," she complained to Hannah, who had followed her.

"He certainly is," the housekeeper agreed, "and I suppose he expects me to wash his dirty dishes."

A little later Antin returned and left two empty plates. Nancy stopped him. Eager to start work on the mystery at once, she asked him what he knew about Mr. Billington's case.

The caretaker scowled. "Nothing that you don't know," he replied and went outdoors.

From the window Nancy saw him go into the orange grove. Dusk had fallen and she could not see which direction he had taken.

After the dishes had been put into the washer

and the dining room vacuumed for crumbs, George said that she and Bess had promised to let their parents know of the girls' safe arrival.

"I'll do it," Bess offered and went to the rear of the hall. As she picked up the phone, the unfamiliar voice of a man was saying, "You know what to do next. Keep your eye on all visitors."

Bess hung up and came back to the living room to report the conversation. "Are the Billingtons on a party line?" she asked.

"No," Mr. Drew answered. He frowned. "I don't like this. There must be an extension phone and somebody in this place is talking on it."

"I'll check!" Nancy offered.

She knew there was no other phone on the first floor, so she started to climb to the second. Halfway up the stairs, she heard a door close softly. She ran the rest of the way and walked along the hall. There was an extension in Mr. Billington's bedroom but nobody was there. The Resardos' door was closed.

"Perhaps Tina was using the phone up here," Nancy thought.

What had the message meant? she wondered. And were she and her father and her friends the "visitors" that the man had referred to? Nancy went downstairs and told the others her suspicions.

"There's probably another extension outside somewhere," Nancy said. "Perhaps in the orange packing house! Let's see if anyone's there!"

CHAPTER III

Spooky Grounds

WHEN Nancy rushed from the rear entrance of the Billington home, she headed for the orange grove. A distance beyond she could see a wavering light and assumed that someone with a flashlight was walking among the trees.

"I wonder who the person is?" she asked herself. "Antin?"

When George and Mr. Drew caught up to Nancy, they said Bess had remained with Hannah. Nancy mentioned the light. They had not noticed it and now the beam had vanished.

The three had left in such a hurry they had neglected to bring flashlights. As they progressed deeper into the grove, the searchers could see practically nothing under the trees.

"We'll never be able to find the orange packing house," George remarked.

They went on for several seconds, then Nancy stopped. "I guess you're right. We'll come back in the morning and find out if there is an extension in the packing house. I'm inclined to believe it was Antin calling from there. What do you two think?"

Mr. Drew agreed, but George said, "It might have been Tina. Don't forget, Nancy, that you heard a door close softly."

Nancy made no reply. She had turned to go back to the house but suddenly realized she did not know which direction to take. She consulted her companions.

Mr. Drew laughed. "I should think a detective like you could find her way in the dark," he teased.

"Just for that," said his daughter, "I'll lead you right back to the Billingtons'."

She began to feel the tree trunks, saying to herself, "We came north and that would be the roughest side of the tree." Presently she found the south side and then said, "Follow me!"

The trees, though planted in straight rows, were not in lines parallel to the compass. Nancy felt the bark of each tree she came to and kept veering slightly eastward. In a little while the lights of the Billington house came into view.

"You did it!" George praised her friend.

Nancy laughed. "I played leader this time but either of you could have found the way."

When the three came into the kitchen they were greeted by Hannah and Bess. "Mission accomplished?" Mrs. Gruen asked.

"I'm afraid not," Nancy replied. Then she whispered, "Has Antin come in?"

Bess replied, "Yes. He rushed past the two of us without saying a word and went upstairs. He sure is a weirdo."

In low voices the group discussed the Resardos. While they had no proof the couple was dishonest, each of them had a feeling of mistrust. Hannah suggested that as a safety precaution the visitors lock their bedroom doors. Everyone looked at Mr. Drew. Would he agree to lock his?

To their surprise he did. He said no more, but the others were sure Nancy's father was taking no chances with the caretaker and his wife in the house. The night passed peacefully, however.

When the Drews and their friends assembled for breakfast, Antin and Tina had not yet come downstairs. Just as the group finished eating, the couple appeared. They said good morning but carried on no conversation. They helped themselves to the food Hannah had left on the stove and ate in the kitchen.

Presently Antin went out the rear door. Tina announced she was going shopping and did not offer to help with the housework. She hurried away.

Hannah Gruen was exasperated. "How long

does that woman expect me to wash her dirty dishes and prepare meals?"

"I'll speak to them later," Mr. Drew promised. "I'm leaving now in Mr. Billington's car to see Mr. Datsun, the lawyer I engaged to help me on the case."

Tina had already left in the Resardos' car. Was she going grocery shopping or on some errands of her own?

"I don't know whether to buy any supplies or not," said Hannah. "What do you think, girls?"

Bess, who was hungry most of the time, answered, "I vote we buy some food and not depend on that awful creature."

"But how are we going to get it?" George spoke up. "We have no car."

Mrs. Gruen sighed. "I guess we can make out until your father returns and you can borrow the car."

As soon as the necessary housework was finished, the girls set off through the orange grove to find the packing house. It was a good distance ahead. On the way Nancy and her friends saw many men picking oranges and putting them into baskets. A small truck would pick them up.

The packing house at the far end of the grove was a long, rectangular building. It contained machinery for sorting oranges by size, cartons for mailing fruit, and net sacks for local delivery.

Men and women were busy picking out defective fruit.

There was a glass-partitioned office in one corner. On the desk stood a telephone!

Nancy walked up to one of the men and inquired if Antin was around. She learned he had not been there all morning.

"I can't say when he'll be back," the workman continued. "He stays away from here a good deal nowadays. But that's all right. We get along without him."

The girls looked questioningly at one another but made no comment. Nancy asked the man, "Is the telephone here on a separate line or is it an extension of the one at the house?"

"It's an intercom system with four extensions on this one number. Two of them are in the house. A third is at the side of this building. Would you like to make a call?" he asked.

"Yes, I would," Nancy replied, glad of the chance to let her eyes roam around the office desk for a clue to the mysterious phone conversation.

She was disappointed not to find any, but Hannah Gruen had a message for her.

"Mrs. Nickerson called. She said something of interest has come up and she wants you to stop over as soon as possible."

"She didn't say what it was?" Nancy queried.

"No," Hannah replied.

Nancy said the girls would visit Mrs. Nickerson when they could use Mr. Billington's car. "We'll see you in a little while, Hannah."

She and her friends watched the sorting and packing operation. Nancy spoke to several of the workers. Not one of them could give any information about the identity of the man who had delivered the oranges with the explosives in them. All the men declared they knew nothing about it except what had been in the newspapers. One thing they were sure of—Mr. Billington was innocent. They hoped he would soon be exonerated.

The girls heard a truck arriving and went outside to watch it being unloaded. Baskets of oranges were lifted onto a belt which carried them to a chute where the fruit was dumped into the washing and sorting machine.

Nancy stood near the truck, gazing at the man who was lifting out the baskets. Suddenly one slipped from his hands and came tumbling directly toward Nancy's head!

"Look out!" cried Bess behind her.

Fortunately Nancy had seen the basket and leaped out of the way. The fruit smashed to the ground. Her first thought was that the man had dropped it on purpose, then she rationalized what possible purpose could he have in harming her? He did not apologize. Nancy went inside and asked a workman his name.

"It's Jackson," he replied. "We call him Old

Clumsy Fingers." Nancy smiled and said that explained why she had almost been hit with a basket of oranges.

Nancy, Bess, and George walked back through the grove, disappointed that they had learned nothing to advance their sleuthing.

As they approached the house, Nancy told the girls about Mrs. Nickerson's call. "But we can't go there without a car. It's too far. I hope Dad will be back soon."

When he had not returned by late morning, Nancy became restless. She was on the verge of telephoning Mrs. Nickerson, when George, who had been exploring the grounds, dashed into the house.

"Guess what I saw!" she explained. "The Billingtons' boat. It's neat! Why don't we go to the Nickersons in that?"

"Great idea!" Bess spoke up. "Let's see if it will run."

Nancy told Hannah where the girls were going, then the three hurried through the Billingtons' lovely garden to the waterfront. Only a few motorboats were purring along the shores of the Indian River.

The end of the garden was several feet above the water level and had a bulkhead to keep the soil from washing away. A boathouse extended into the river. Inside it was a sleek speedboat, the *Starbeam*. The key was in the ignition.

"What a beauty!" Bess cried out. "But it looks powerful. Nancy, would you dare take it out?"

The young detective smiled. "Of course."

She made sure there was sufficient fuel and familiarized herself with the various gadgets. Her eyes twinkling, she said, "Here goes!"

In a few seconds the motor was throbbing quietly and she steered the craft into the river. Twenty minutes later she pulled alongside a dock which bore the name Nickerson. The girls tied the boat securely and went up to the house.

Ned's mother was a very attractive woman. When greeting Nancy she showed the deep affection she held for the girl.

"What I wanted to tell you," Mrs. Nickerson said as they all sipped glasses of cola, "is that friends of ours who have gone North to live have put their house on the market. It's listed with Mr. Gilbert Scarlett, a local realtor. I was thinking how wonderful it would be, Nancy, if your father would buy the place."

"I'd love to see it," Nancy replied. "Is it far from here?"

"No, we can walk there easily."

Mrs. Nickerson led the girls to a charming place about a quarter of a mile away. The house stood halfway between the river and the road. It was a two-story building with attractive, well-kept grounds.

"How lovely!" Nancy exclaimed.

"The owner, Mr. Webster," said Mrs. Nickerson, "has all kinds of unusual trees and shrubs on the place besides an orange grove. He even has a sausage tree. It is rarely seen in this country."

The visitors were intrigued by the wide variety of trees and shrubs. Each had a plaque attached that gave its Latin botanical name and the English equivalent. Finally they came to the sausage tree.

It was about thirty feet tall with a profusion of leaves. From the branches hung greenish sausage-shaped fruit that resembled rough-textured melons. These were nearly six inches wide and twelve inches long.

George felt one. "Wow! This would make a real swinging weapon!" The others laughed.

Mrs. Nickerson said the fruit was not edible and the pollen was carried in the spring from one flower to another by bats.

"Ugh!" Bess exclaimed.

The tree was near a high wire-mesh fence which looked strong enough to stop a large, fast-moving truck.

Bess remarked, "That place next door sure is spooky with all those old oak trees dripping with Spanish moss. Who lives there?"

"I don't know," Mrs. Nickerson replied.

At that moment a chilling scream came from inside the grounds!

CHAPTER IV

Newspaper Clue

THE piercing scream was not repeated. Nancy and her friends peered through the wire-mesh fence for a glimpse of a house. The jungle of trees with their long streamers of Spanish moss concealed whatever buildings might be on the property.

Nancy turned to Mrs. Nickerson. "Have you ever been in there?"

"No," Ned's mother replied. "The place is so forbidding I never tried to get acquainted with the occupants. Besides, I suspect whoever lives there owns some wild animals!"

George said she was curious to find out what she could. "If this fence doesn't go around the whole property, let's look for an opening and go in."

Bess objected at once. "Not me!"

Nancy settled the matter. "Actually we don't have time," she said. "Dad will be home, I'm sure, and I want to see if he has any news for us. But we'll come here the first chance we have."

Mrs. Nickerson teased, "Now I understand how you girls become involved in mysteries."

Nancy smiled. "Sometimes we do stumble upon them."

The group walked back to the Nickerson home, said good-by, and hurried to their boat. When they reached the Billington house, Mr. Drew was there. He was smiling and Nancy was sure he had had a successful morning.

"I like Mr. Datsun very much. It didn't take long to talk over the case," the lawyer said.

Mr. Drew delved into a breast pocket of his sports jacket and pulled out an envelope. "Surprise for you girls," he announced.

He handed the envelope to Nancy. She opened it and took out six badges on which the word PRESS was printed.

Mr. Drew explained, "As an accredited writer I was given badges at the news center for you and the boys to watch the moon shoot next week."

Bess and George stared at Mr. Drew. "You are an accredited writer?" Bess asked.

He chuckled and nodded. "I have a number of publications to my credit. Of course they're all on legal matters."

"How exciting!" said George. "Now we can see the lift-off and be as close as anyone is allowed."

"Right." Mr. Drew asked Hannah and the girls

if they would like to make a tour of the Kennedy Space Center that afternoon. All were enthusiastic and Nancy said, "It will give me a chance to get acquainted with the place where the explosive oranges were taken. I might pick up a clue."

As soon as luncheon was over they set off for the vast, well-kept government grounds that stretched along the ocean for miles. Mr. Drew parked the car near a sprawling building with a large roofed-over patio area. Under it were benches. Nancy and the others sat down to wait for a bus while her father bought tickets.

"This is the Visitor Information Center," Mr. Drew remarked when he came back.

Nancy was impressed by the large number of European and Asiatic tourists who were there.

"The Kennedy Space Center means a lot to the whole world," she thought, then walked up to the adjoining building to peer inside. There was a room with illuminated wall pictures of the various types of missiles. Here visitors could purchase books, postcards and souvenirs. Nancy saw an intriguing miniature model rocket. "I must come back and buy that," she decided.

"All aboard!" called George, and Nancy hurried to join the others.

The two-hour tour began, and the driver announced that they would cover fifty miles. Nancy and her friends were fascinated by the mock-ups of missiles and rockets stretching ahead of them in long rows. Most of them were in the familiar cone shape.

The guide said that the very first missile sent up from the Cape was a two-stage Bumper.

"The first stage was a captured German V-2 missile and the second an army WAC Corporal rocket. It was launched in July 1950."

Mr. Drew whispered to his daughter, "Our country has certainly come a long way in rocket building since then."

As the guide indicated gantries and rockets, Nancy recognized the names Thor, an early antiballistic missile, Titan, Minuteman and Saturn.

Next, the guide talked about the artificial satellites orbiting in space. He explained that the man-made moons are classified according to the jobs they do: (1) communication satellites, (2) weather satellites, (3) navigation satellites, (4) scientific satellites, and (5) military satellites.

"You, no doubt, are familiar with the Tiros and other satellites that take weather pictures and track hurricanes. Communication satellites, like Early Bird and Telstar, make it possible to send radio messages, telephone calls, and television programs from one continent to another in a matter of seconds."

The tour continued on to the moon rocket, which stood majestically next to its gantry. The onlookers craned their necks to see the top where the astronauts would live and work.

"It's all so overwhelming!" Hannah Gruen exclaimed.

The next stop on the tour was at the mammoth Vehicle Assembly Building. George remarked, "This is a real skyscraper."

"And it covers eight acres," the driver said. "The ceilings in the wings of this building are twenty stories high. That's where the smaller rockets are put together. The center section is fifty-two stories high. The big Saturns for trips to the moon and other planets are assembled in this area. Each booster for them is brought here on a very long covered barge which resembles an aluminum Quonset hut, painted white. The capsules come by truck or air."

When the sightseers walked inside to the Vehicle Assembly section they gasped. The center section was tall enough to accommodate a 360-foot rocket standing upright. Around the walls of the huge structure were metal scaffolds on which men had worked to complete the latest rocket assembly. From the ground floor those who were busy high above the visitors looked no larger than small boys.

"This is absolutely fascinating and unbelievable," Nancy said.

Suddenly she realized that Hannah Gruen was not with them. She looked at all the visitors but did not see the Drews' housekeeper.

"Maybe she stayed in the bus," Nancy thought,

and went outside to look. Hannah was not there.

"Where could she have gone?" Nancy asked herself, then told her father and the girls.

All of them searched but could not find Hannah. The guide was already calling to his passengers to board the bus.

"I don't want to leave without Hannah," Nancy said to her father. "This building is so huge if she started to walk around it, she couldn't possibly be back by this time."

Mr. Drew said he had an appointment with Commander Nichol at the Base in connection with the case. "Suppose I go ahead," he suggested, "and you girls keep on searching for Hannah. You can catch the next bus."

He spoke to the driver, who agreed that this would be all right.

Nancy, Bess, and George went back inside the big building and began looking again for Hannah. Moments later the door to an office opened. Hannah Gruen walked out, followed by a young man. They came directly to the three girls.

"This is Herb Baylor," Hannah said. "He's a distant relative of mine but I didn't know he was here. I happened to see him walk into an office and followed."

After the pleasant young man had acknowledged the introductions, Hannah went on, "Herb's an engineer and works on the assembling of rockets."

Nancy asked him, "Of course you know about the oranges containing the explosives that were sent into the Base."

"Yes, and I hear you're on Merritt Island to solve the mystery and clear Mr. Billington." He smiled boyishly. "I'll tell you a possible clue that I gave to Security."

"Wonderful!" Nancy replied. "What is it?"

Herb said he happened to be near the truck when it was leaving. "Part of a newspaper blew out. I picked it up and noticed a pencil-ringed personal. It was a garble of words that made no sense."

"What did it say?"

Herb replied, " *'Son on board ship ready to be sailor for peaceful kind of action.'* "

Nancy took a pad and pencil from her handbag and asked Herb to repeat the message. Quickly she read words numbered 1, 5, 9, and 13. The hidden message was, "Son ready for action."

She thanked Herb, telling him that the girls would work on it.

"I wish you luck," he said, smiling. "Now I must go back."

When the next bus came Nancy and her friends climbed aboard. The tour continued, and Nancy listened attentively to the driver's descriptions.

"On a long flight, like to the moon," the guide said, "an astronaut gets about twenty-eight hundred calories of food a day. Seventeen percent of this is protein, thirty-two percent fat, and fifty-one percent carbohydrates."

Bess gave a low giggle. "That's the place for me!"

The guide went on to say that the men eat four meals a day and a series of menus are rotated every four days. "All the food is in bars, cubes, and powders sealed in plastic pouches, or pastes which are kept in tubes."

Bess called out to the guide, "Could you tell us what some of the menus are?"

The man smiled. "Yes. How would you like this for breakfast? Strawberry cereal cubes, bacon squares, peanut-butter sandwiches, and orange juice."

"That's great," said Bess.

"Here's a typical dinner menu," the guide told her. "Beef with vegetables, spaghetti with meat sauce, toast squares, fruit cake made with dates, and tea."

"That would suit me," Bess commented. "It sounds yummy."

When the bus returned to the Visitor Information Center, Mr. Drew was waiting for them and they walked to the parking area.

As soon as they were seated in their car, George said, "Nancy, don't keep us in suspense any longer. What did you figure out of that newspaper clue?"

Nancy told her and the conversation turned to a series of guesses as to what it meant. They could only surmise that someone, somewhere, was ready to strike a blow. But who and at what?

When the group reached the house the Resardos were not there. Hannah remarked, "I suppose they won't show up until dinner is ready."

The girls offered to help her prepare dinner. When Nancy went into the dining room to set the table she noticed that a photograph of her father which he had sent Mr. Billington was gone from the buffet. She asked the others if any of them had placed it elsewhere. No one had.

"How strange!" said Hannah. She hurried into the living room and called out, "A picture of Mr. and Mrs. Billington is gone too."

On a hunch Nancy rushed upstairs to her father's room. A photograph of her with Bess and George, which he always took with him when he traveled, had been removed from the bureau. Next the young detective went to her own room and pulled out a dresser drawer. She had left a wallet in it containing a snapshot of her father and one of Ned Nickerson. They were missing. But none of the other contents had been taken.

Nancy dashed down the stairs. "Every photograph has been taken!" she exclaimed. "I'm sure they were stolen to use as identification of us because we're trying to solve the mystery of the explosive oranges!"

CHAPTER V

Alligator Attack

WHEN Bess heard about the missing photograph of Mr. Drew, she ran from the living room and up the stairs. Deep in her suitcase she had left a snapshot of herself with Nancy, George, Ned, Burt, and Dave. Bess riffled through the clothes still in the bag but could not find the picture.

"That was stolen too!" she told herself and hurried back downstairs to tell the others.

George said angrily, "Nobody has been in this house. We locked all the doors and windows before we left and they were still locked when we came home. I'm sure the Resardos took those pictures!"

Everyone agreed but Mr. Drew warned them that they had no evidence to prove this.

"Why don't we search their room?" George asked.

Before anybody could stop her, she bounded up

the stairway to the couple's quarters. But the Resardos' door was locked and continuous knocking on it brought no response. Dejected, George returned to the first floor.

"Now what do we do?" she asked Nancy.

"Suppose I phone the orange sorting and packing house. Antin may be there."

The worker who answered said that Antin had not been in all day. "He didn't tell us he wasn't coming, so we have no idea where he is."

Nancy thanked him and hung up. The Resardos returned just as the group was about to eat dinner.

"Where have you been all day?" George burst out.

Tina and Antin scowled but replied they had received word a relative in a distant city was ill and had gone to visit him. The couple turned toward the stove and picked up two dinner plates which were warming. As they helped themselves from each of the pots, Mr. Drew approached them.

"One minute," he said. "What can you tell us about all the photographs missing from the house?"

The Resardos looked at each other, then Antin said, "What are you talking about?"

When Mr. Drew explained, Antin declared he knew nothing about the pictures.

Tina spoke up. "I don't either. Are you accusing us of taking them?" She began to laugh raucously. "What would we want with photographs of you people?"

Mr. Drew turned on his heel and walked into the dining room. The Resardos filled two plates, got out some silver, and sat down at the kitchen table to eat.

The others were surprised that they had not gone upstairs. Nancy, however, figured the couple wanted to hear the conversation in the dining room. In a whisper she warned the rest not to discuss the Billington case. If the Resardos had hoped to pick up any information, they were disappointed. The talk was general, mostly about the fascinating trip through the Space Center.

When everyone finished eating, the Resardos piled their dirty dishes in the sink as usual, and went up to their room.

"I won't wash them!" Hannah Gruen said firmly.

Nancy smiled. "Tonight you're not washing anybody's dishes. You go into the living room and watch TV. Bess and George and I will take care of everything."

While the girls were doing this, Mr. Drew telephoned the police to report the theft of the photographs. Two officers came to the house. They agreed that it appeared to be an inside job and asked to talk with the Resardos. The couple vehemently declared their innocence. As the police were leaving, they told Mr. Drew that without any clues there was little hope of apprehending the thief.

Tina and Antin cast black looks at the others, then went upstairs without saying good night.

In the morning, when Nancy and her friends came downstairs, she found that the Resardos had already eaten breakfast and left the house. Their dirty dishes were piled up in the sink!

Hannah Gruen stared at the dried egg on the plates and the stained coffee cups in disgust. But she said nothing and started getting breakfast for the others.

When Mr. Drew came down, Nancy said, "Dad, I haven't had a chance to tell you about a darling house that's for sale." She described the Webster property.

He smiled at her enthusiasm. "I'll look at it," he said. "I can see you've fallen in love with the place."

While they were eating, a telephone call came for Mr. Drew. After a few minutes' conversation, he returned to the table and said he must leave for River Heights. "Something important has come up and I'll have to return home at once. Will you girls drive me to the airport?"

"Of course," Nancy replied. "Do you want me to call and see about planes?"

"If you will, please."

Nancy found out that if they left the house within ten minutes, her father could catch a nonstop flight to New York from Melbourne and get another plane to River Heights soon afterward. She hurried upstairs to tell her father and help him pack.

When Mr. Drew and the girls were ready to leave, he said to Hannah, "Take care. Better lock yourself in." The housekeeper nodded.

Two hours later the girls were ready to return from the Melbourne airport. Bess spoke up, "Let's take a scenic route home."

"All right," Nancy agreed. She consulted a road map and figured out what direction to take.

As they neared the area of the Cape, Bess spotted a long, wide ditch of water choked with water hyacinths, with bluish-violet lily-type blossoms.

"Oh I want to get some of those!" she said. "Please stop."

"They are pretty," Nancy agreed and pulled up to the side of the road.

Bess jumped from the car and went over to pick some of the blooms. After plucking several, she laid them at the edge of the water.

"Don't lean over so far or you'll fall in," George warned her cousin.

Bess rested on her heels and reached for another beautiful flower. Just as her hand touched it, something rustled among the leaves. The next moment an alligator thrust its snout from among the leaves and opened its jaws wide!

Bess screamed, jerked back, and sat down hard

on the muddy bank. The alligator moved toward her! Terrified, Bess scrambled up and ran to the car. The alligator disappeared under the water hyacinths. Nancy and George had hopped from the car to help her in. Bess was trembling and now began to sob.

"He—he was going to bite me!" the frightened girl exclaimed.

Nancy and George tried to calm her. In a few minutes Bess was all right but her white slacks were wet and muddy.

To take her mind off the unpleasant incident, Nancy said, "As soon as you change your clothes, Bess, let's go see the real-estate agent who is handling the sale of the Webster house. I want to look at the inside. After that we'll work on the explosive orange mystery."

"Good idea," said George. "Who is the realtor?"

"Mr. Scarlett."

When they reached the Billingtons', it did not take Bess long to change to dark-blue slacks and a clean shirt. After a quick lunch the girls set off again. They drove directly to Mr. Scarlett's office. Nancy parked and they walked up to the one-story building, then stopped short. A sign tacked to the door read:

CLOSED FOR VACATION
WILL OPEN IN TWO WEEKS

The alligator moved toward Bess

"We can't stay that long!" said Bess.

"I know," Nancy agreed. "Wait here, girls."

She went to a nearby store and asked where Mr. Scarlett lived. She hoped the realtor was not out of town.

"He didn't tell me his plans," said the store-keeper, and gave her the address of Mr. and Mrs. Scarlett.

When the girls rang his doorbell, there was no answer. Windows were closed and blinds were down.

"Maybe they're only away for the day," George said optimistically.

Nancy was determined to see the inside of the Webster house and told herself, "I'll find a way!"

George remarked, "Normally a realtor wouldn't go away without making provisions for prospective buyers to see properties he has listed."

On the way back to the Billington house, Bess gave a tremendous sigh. "Can't we relax and play some tennis?" she asked. "Then we'll go sleuthing."

"Great idea!" said George. "I'll take on both of you."

Bess giggled. "How we hate ourselves," she teased. "Just for that, I accept. Nancy and I will whitewash you! Three love sets in a row!"

Bess came near being right. She and Nancy won the first two games. By the time the girls had finished three sets, the scores stood two sets for Nancy and Bess and one for George.

"I'll get even another time!" George vowed with a wide grin.

As they walked from the court, the cousins asked Nancy what was next on the schedule.

"You're so good at keeping your mind on two things at once," said Bess, "that half your brain was playing tennis and the other half conjuring up something."

Nancy laughed. "I was just thinking that if I call Dad's friend Commander Nichol at the Base he'll give me the name of the guard who admitted the driver with the explosive oranges."

"And after that—" George prodded her.

"After that," Nancy replied, "we'll try to talk to that man."

Commander Nichol said that the guard's name was Patrick Croft.

"He has been dismissed," the commander went on, "but hasn't left town. He's at home," and gave Nancy the address.

After she had said good-by, Nancy turned to the girls. "Let's go! Maybe by talking to Mr. Croft we can get a clue to the man who impersonated Mr. Billington and drove into the Base."

CHAPTER VI

Exciting Evening

PATRICK Croft lived alone in a small house. When Nancy explained why the girls had come, he invited them inside. Before he sat down the sad-looking man offered them some candy he had made. They learned he was a bachelor and liked to cook. Nancy surmised that Mr. Croft was reserved and not apt to defend himself when any trouble arose.

"That's too bad," the young detective told herself. "Maybe if Croft had been more aggressive, he wouldn't have been dismissed from NASA."

When Nancy queried him about the driver of the truck with the explosive oranges, Croft described him minutely.

At once Nancy thought, "It is true then that this man could have passed as Mr. Billington!"

Croft went on, "The driver said he was Mr. Billington, whom I don't know. He had all the proper credentials with him, so of course I let him in. The last I saw of him he was turning toward the food supply depot and I assumed that was where he went."

"And he didn't?" George asked.

Mr. Croft smiled. "A guard got aboard and took him there. Fortunately the explosive oranges were discovered before any damage was done. But it's my opinion he intended to blow up part of the rocket while it was still in the Vehicle Assembly Building.

"I'm mighty sorry about the whole thing, but I don't think I should have been dismissed. The explosives had been put in the oranges very cleverly and they looked innocent enough in the sacks.

"I hope someday I'll be reinstated." Mr. Croft heaved a great sigh. "By the way, I was taken to identify Mr. Billington. He and the impostor look enough alike to be twins."

The girls felt sorry for Croft. They realized his dismissal had been necessary. After the saboteur was caught, perhaps Croft would be exonerated.

Nancy told him that her father was the lawyer who had been retained to defend Mr. Billington, but that he in turn had engaged the services of Johnson Datsun.

Croft said he had heard of Mr. Datsun. "He's a very fine lawyer. If anybody can straighten out this case, I'm sure he can."

"But it's not just a legal matter," Bess spoke up. "It's a mystery too. Nancy's an amateur detective and—"

Nancy smiled. "And with the help of my two good friends here, I have solved some mysteries."

Mr. Croft's eyes opened wide. "That's wonderful," he said. "I always wanted to be a detective, but I wasn't cut out for that kind of work. The nearest I came to it was checking people's credentials when they entered the Space Center." He sighed again.

Nancy stood up. Bess and George took the cue from her and arose also.

"Mr. Croft," said Nancy, "if you should hear or recall anything that might help us solve this mystery, will you telephone me?"

"I'll be glad to," the man replied. Nancy gave him the Billingtons' address and telephone number, then the girls left.

Upon reaching home, they found Hannah Gruen quite excited. George asked, "Have the Resardos pulled another fast one?"

"No," the housekeeper replied. "I haven't seen them all day. But I think I've picked up a clue for you. If I'm right, it may spell trouble or danger for you, Nancy, and your father."

"What do you mean?" Nancy queried.

Hannah produced the day's newspaper. She pointed out a personal. It read:

"*Dorothy's son has just released trunk. It is empty. Advise at once where to find contents.*"

Immediately the three girls read words numbered 1, 5, 9, 13. These said, "Dorothy's released empty where."

Bess said, "They don't make sense."

Hannah was eager to tell her clue. "But put the first letters of those words together," she said. "They spell Drew."

"Wow!" George exclaimed. "What could this possibly mean?"

Nancy did not answer. She had not yet figured out the meaning of the personal but one thing was certain—someone was sending a message which could have dire consequences for her and her father and possibly her friends. She was worried but did not speak her thoughts aloud.

Bess admitted that she was scared. "I think we'd better give up our sleuthing and leave here," she declared.

George said, "Bess, you know as well as I do that the thrust of a hundred-thousand-pound rocket couldn't force Nancy to give up this case."

Nancy smiled. "A wild thought just occurred to me. Suppose this reference to Drew has something to do with our interest in the Webster house. We already know that Mr. Scarlett has gone on vacation. For some reason unknown to us, the people who use the code may not want us here and encouraged Scarlett to go away. What we must do is find out that reason."

Hannah Gruen reminded the girls that their dinner was ready. "The meal will be spoiled if you don't eat it now."

Nancy, Bess, and George washed their hands and combed their hair, then sat down at the table with Hannah. All had good appetites and thoroughly enjoyed the delicious roast beef. They were tidying up the kitchen when Bess remarked, "The Resardos missed a good dinner, but we certainly didn't miss them."

"Maybe they're not coming back at all!" George said with a grin. "It would please me if I never saw that couple again."

"I agree with you," said Mrs. Gruen.

That evening the phone was kept busy. First Nancy called her father and told him all she had learned that day.

After hearing the whole story, he observed, "It's evident that someone or a group is keeping an eye on us. The situation could become dangerous."

"But you're not going to let them scare us away, are you?" Nancy asked.

She was sure her father was going to say no and he did not disappoint her. He warned Nancy, however, to keep alert for trouble.

"I'll get back there as quickly as I can," he added.

Nancy had just put down the phone when it

rang. The voice at the other end said, "Well, I'm glad I got you at last. I've been trying for hours to get hold of you."

"Hi, Ned!" Nancy said. "We can hardly wait for the house party to start, but we haven't been idle. There'll be lots to tell when you boys arrive."

"No doubt," Ned said. "I've never known a time when you weren't doing as much as three people. I have just one favor to ask—that you have this mystery solved before Burt and Dave and I arrive. We want to have fun."

"Why, Ned," said Nancy, a teasing tone in her voice, "I thought you adored solving mysteries and tracking down villains."

Ned laughed. "You're right. Okay, Nancy," he added, "I'll help bring this mystery to a quick termination!"

"Actually there are two mysteries," said Nancy. "The explosive oranges and the spooky-looking grounds of an estate on this island. When I get a chance I'm going to investigate the place."

"I'll take the spooky one," Ned answered.

Nancy laughed. "I hope to have at least one of them solved before you arrive."

Ned chuckled, then became serious. "Watch your step. I don't want anything to happen to you."

After he and Nancy had said good night, she joined the other girls. Within seconds there was another call.

"Maybe it's Burt," George spoke up.

"And maybe you're both wrong," Hannah remarked. "The call might be for me—from Herb. He said he'd phone and make a date to call on us. I think he was very much impressed with you three girls."

As Hannah had predicted, the caller was Herb, who told her he had been put on special assignment. "I won't be able to come over to the Billington house until after the lift-off."

"By that time we'll probably be gone," Hannah said, "but give us a ring anyway."

The girls were giggling when Hannah returned. Bess teased her. "Did Herb want to make a date to take you up in a rocket?"

The housekeeper flushed slightly but joined in the banter. "Don't think I didn't catch on. He wanted to see you girls!"

Just then the phone rang again. Burt and Dave were calling. Both boys were eagerly looking forward to the house party at the Nickersons' and sent their best wishes to Hannah and Nancy.

By bedtime the Resardos still had not returned and everyone wondered if the couple would put in an appearance.

As the group was about to go upstairs the telephone rang again. Nancy, nearest the instrument, answered.

"Is this Nancy Drew?" a man asked.

"Yes."

"This is Patrick Croft. I've been trying to call you but your line has been busy. A man phoned me around eight o'clock. He sounded like the driver I let into the Base with the oranges. He told me I was to have nothing more to do with Nancy Drew or I'd be harmed."

"That's dreadful!" Nancy said.

The words were barely out of her mouth when Patrick Croft gave a cry of panic. "Someone's breaking in!" he shouted. "Help! Help!"

CHAPTER VII

False Information

THE phone connection remained on but there were no voices. Evidently Patrick Croft had run away from the instrument without hanging it up. Nancy could hear banging and shouting, then a crash, as if the intruder had broken open the door.

Nancy hung up, waited a few minutes for the connection to be broken, then called police headquarters. She told the sergeant on duty what had happened at Croft's house. He assured her that two officers would be sent there immediately.

Nancy rushed upstairs to tell Hannah and the girls of Croft's predicament. "I'm going over to see what happened!"

"Not by yourself," Hannah spoke up firmly. "We'll all go. This is shocking. Poor Mr. Croft!"

With Nancy at the wheel, they covered the distance to his house in a short time. A police car and an ambulance stood in front and sympathetic neighbors had begun to gather.

"Oh, he's been hurt!" Bess exclaimed.

Nancy pulled up to the curb and jumped out.

Patrick Croft was just being brought out on a stretcher. He was unconscious and his face the color of pale alabaster.

Two policemen followed. After the ambulance pulled away, Nancy spoke to the taller officer, telling him she was the person who had phoned headquarters.

"I'd like to explain to you in more detail what I know about the attack tonight."

"Come with me, miss," said the officer, and added, "My name is Regan."

He led the way back into the house, then took a notebook and pencil from a pocket. "Tell me everything you can," he said. "Sometimes a small detail that the average person considers unimportant can prove to be a valuable clue."

Nancy knew this very well from her own sleuthing experiences. She introduced herself and told where she was from, then said, "Mr. Croft was a security guard at NASA. He's the one responsible for allowing the truck with explosive oranges to come onto the Base."

"Oh you know about that," the officer replied.

Nancy nodded, then related Patrick Croft's telephone conversation verbatim.

"So Croft thought the caller might have been the truck driver," Officer Regan observed. "If he wasn't Mr. Billington, have you any idea who he is? And why did the person who phoned not want Croft to contact you?"

"I don't know the man's name," Nancy answered. "That's what I'm in Florida to find out. My father and a local lawyer are trying to solve this case and prove Mr. Billington innocent."

"I see," the policeman said. "Poor Croft was beaten into unconsciousness so it will be some time before he'll be able to answer any of our questions."

Regan told her that there was only one set of clear footprints but this was not a help in identification because the intruder had worn flippers.

"Also, the man must have had on gloves," the officer said, "because he left no fingerprints."

The word flippers caught Nancy's attention and she remarked, "The man you'll be looking for could be a snorkeler."

"You're right," Regan admitted. Then he asked, "By the way, have you and your friends visited the Real Eight Museum of Sunken Treasure yet?"

"No, we haven't."

"Do by all means. It's most interesting, even though a little terrifying if you visualize what happened during one of the worst hurricanes on record. Well," the officer said, "I must go. Thank you for your information."

He escorted Nancy outside. His fellow officer produced a padlock for the broken front door and pocketed the key. The police car pulled away. A

curious group of neighbors who had gathered finally dispersed.

Hannah and the girls started home. On the way
Nancy said she felt largely responsible for what
had happened to Croft.

Hannah asked, "How could you possibly be responsible?"

Nancy replied, "We know there are people who
don't want us working on Mr. Billington's case.
They're probably watching all our movements.
They found out I went to Croft's house today and
figured he had told me all he knew about the case.
That's why he was beaten up!"

"How terrible!" Bess said angrily.

"Here's another possibility," said George. "Suppose Croft is actually one of the gang? He might
have been the inside man."

Hannah spoke up. "If Croft is one of the gang,
why would they beat him up?"

"Because," George replied, "he was given a job
to do at the Base and he bungled it."

Nancy remarked, "That's good reasoning,
George. I don't happen to agree with it, though.
I think Croft was given the beating to keep him
from saying any more. He may suspect other people whom he didn't tell us about."

When she turned into the Billingtons' driveway, George said, "The Resardos' car is here."

"That Antin is a cheat!" Hannah burst out.
"Mr. Billington pays him for working in the grove

and taking care of these grounds. He hasn't touched the lawn or garden since we came. The grass is getting so brown I put on the sprinkler today."

The housekeeper unlocked the rear door and turned on the light. "How about a little ice cream before we go to bed?" She went to the refrigerator to take some out.

Nancy glanced at her watch. It was after eleven o'clock. "I wonder if it's too late to call Mr. Datsun," she said to the others. "I think I should tell him what happened tonight."

Hannah, Bess, and George agreed, so Nancy went to the phone and picked it up. Someone was using it!

As the young detective listened, a man said, "Got it straight? R-day."

George had followed Nancy to the hall. Nancy made motions indicating that her friend was to run upstairs and see who was on the extension phone.

As George took the steps two at a time, Nancy heard a man's muffled reply, "Okay." The connection was cut off.

George came down the stairs to report that she had found no one using the extension phone up there.

"The call must have been made from the orange packing house," Nancy declared.

Hannah had come to see what was troubling Nancy. After hearing about the conversation, she said firmly, "Nancy, you're not going to that place to find out. It's too dangerous. Anyway, the person who used the phone has probably left by this time."

Nancy agreed. "But I think Antin should investigate," she said. "I'm going upstairs and tell him."

George gave a sardonic laugh. "He won't thank you for waking him up."

"I don't care," Nancy replied, and mounted the stairway. She knocked on the Resardos' door. There was no response, but after a second knock, a woman's sleepy voice said, "Who's there?"

"It's Nancy Drew, Tina. I'd like to speak to Antin. It's very important."

There was a long pause, then finally Tina came to the door. "Antin can't see you now. He's taking a bath."

"Please tell him that some prowler is in the packing house. He'd better go find out about him."

"Okay, I'll tell him."

Nancy returned to the first floor. She and the others ate their ice cream, but Antin Resardo did not appear.

"Some more of his indifference," George remarked. "He's a surly person."

"Yes," Bess spoke up. "He's no help at all around here. I certainly think Mr. Billington should be told."

"You can bet he will be," Hannah informed her.

When they finished the ice cream, the girls washed and dried the dishes and spoons. Then they put out the lights and followed Hannah up the stairway. Suddenly Nancy turned back.

"What is it?" Bess asked her.

"Listen!" said Nancy. "I think someone is using a key to open the kitchen door."

Led by Nancy, the group tiptoed down the stairway and went toward the kitchen. The rear door opened just as Nancy clicked on the overhead light. They were astounded to see Antin Resardo coming in.

"You weren't taking a bath at all as Tina said!" George cried out. "You were in the orange packing house phoning!"

Nancy walked up to him. "What does R-day mean?" she demanded.

Antin gave a start, then suddenly his face flushed with anger and he glared at the young detective.

"You little sneak!" he yelled.

The next second he grabbed her by the shoulders and shook her so hard Nancy felt as if her head would snap off.

CHAPTER VIII

Doubting Workmen

"STOP that!" George yelled at Antin.

She grabbed his arm and as Nancy staggered away, George buckled the man's knees and flipped him over her shoulder. He fell to the floor with a crash.

"Good for you, George!" exclaimed Bess in glee.

Antin had been taken completely by surprise and had had the wind knocked out of him. Slowly he arose.

Meanwhile Hannah had rushed to Nancy's side and asked, "Are you all right? That was a contemptible thing to do to you!" she said. "Antin, hereafter don't you ever dare lay a finger on Nancy or any of the rest of us!"

Nancy assured Hannah she would be her normal self in a few minutes and flopped into a chair. Antin looked at her, then said grudgingly, "I didn't mean to hurt you. I'm sorry if I did. You make me see red when you act suspicious of me. You mentioned my taking a bath. By the time I finished, Tina was asleep.

"It worried me that since I'd been away all day the machinery might not have been switched off in the packing house. I went to investigate.

"While there, I decided to put in a phone call to a friend of mine who is giving a surprise birthday party for his wife. Her name is Ruth. We are calling it R-day."

The commotion had brought Tina downstairs in her robe and slippers. She looked at the group questioningly. Antin repeated his story about R-day to her and she nodded affirmation.

Hannah spoke up. "There may have been misunderstanding on all sides. Why don't we talk this whole thing out?"

"Good idea," said Antin.

Mrs. Gruen went on, "In the first place, I may as well tell you I resent your not helping in the house. You eat the food I cook and even leave your dirty dishes for me to wash."

Tina retorted, "Mr. Billington didn't tell me I had to wait on these extra people. He just told me Mr. Drew and his daughter might be down. I'm not strong and I'm not too well," she went on, "and I won't wait on so many people! That's final!"

"She's right," Antin burst out. "Between all the extra work and you people practically accusing us of being crooks, I think Tina and I will move to a motel until after you go home."

Hannah and the girls looked at one another. It would be a great relief to have the unpleasant Resardos out of the house. But if the couple stayed, they could be kept under surveillance.

Antin went on, "You think I had something to do with those explosive oranges. Well I didn't, and I gave the FBI an airtight alibi about where I was the day it happened."

Nancy did not like the man's defensive attitude. She knew that guilty people often play the part of aggrieved persons, trying to cover up the truth. Was this the case with the Resardos?

Again Hannah spoke up. "I'm glad we had this talk," she said. "Tina and Antin, I'm sure Mr. Billington would be very hurt if you leave and he might even decide not to let you come back."

This thought startled the couple. They looked at each other and finally Tina said, "All right, we'll stay. I'll help with the cooking whenever Antin and I are here. I guess all of us can keep the house clean."

Nancy sensed the Resardos were annoyed because Hannah had won her point. The couple wished the others good night and went to their room. George looked after them. Did she imagine it, or was Antin limping a little because of her Judo trick?

The atmosphere the next morning was a bit

strained, but Tina did help prepare breakfast. She did not serve the food, however. Instead she and Antin sat down in the kitchen to eat, while the others carried their plates of eggs and bacon to the dining room.

Immediately after breakfast Nancy and Bess went upstairs to make their beds. George was about to follow a few minutes later when she saw Antin leave the house. On a hunch she trailed him, keeping well out of sight.

The foreman went directly to the packing house and George started back through the grove. Suddenly it occurred to her that she might get a clue to the orange mystery from some of the pickers. Seeing two of them a little distance away, she walked toward the men.

When George came near, she heard one man say, "I wouldn't trust that guy any place."

His companion replied, "Me neither."

The other man said laughingly, "I'll bet you the boss is making a killing for himself!" Were they talking about Antin or Mr. Billington?

Puzzled but suspicious, George hurried back to the house. By the time she arrived Tina had gone upstairs and Bess and Nancy had come down. George told them what she had heard in the grove.

"Which boss do you think the men were talking about?" she asked.

Nancy smiled. "I'll try to find out."

She went to the phone and called the packing

house. When a man answered, she said, "I'd like to speak to the boss."

"Okay. I'll call him," the worker replied. He yelled. "Antin, you're wanted on the phone."

Noiselessly Nancy put down the receiver and reported to the other girls.

"Shall we go tackle him?" George asked. "I'm sure he's doublecrossing Mr. Billington."

Nancy agreed but said, "I have a feeling that today Antin will be on his good behavior. In the meantime let's try once more to get into the Webster house. I can't wait to see the inside."

"How are you going to accomplish that without a key?" Bess queried.

Nancy said she would start by going back to Mr. Scarlett's office. She might be able to learn something from nearby store owners.

When the girls reached the realtor's office, they were surprised to see the door open. Lovely, low singing was coming from within. Wondering what was going on, the three callers walked inside. A stout, pretty woman was singing a lullaby as she dusted the furniture.

Upon seeing the girls she smiled broadly and said, "You want Mr. Scarlett?"

"Yes we do," Nancy replied.

The pleasant woman jerked her thumb toward a closed door. "He's in there."

Nancy was surprised and delighted. Now she could get the key!

She knocked on the closed door. A voice said, "Come in!"

As Nancy walked in, she said, "Good morning. I'm Nancy Drew."

"Oh yes. Mrs. Nickerson left a note you might come. Why did you?"

"To have you show me the interior of the Webster house," she answered.

The realtor scowled. "Don't you know I'm on vacation?"

"Your sign said so, but you seem to be right here," the young detective replied with a smile.

"Well, I am on vacation. There were certain papers in my files I had to pick up."

Nancy pretended not to notice he was trying to evade her. She said pleasantly, "I'm lucky to have found you. If you can't show me and my friends the Webster house, then, since you know the Nickersons, will you please lend me the key? I'll return it through your mail slot, unless my father decides he wants to buy the place. In that case I'll keep the key."

"You'll do nothing of the sort," Mr. Scarlett said unpleasantly. "The house is not for you. You wouldn't like it and there are lots of things the matter with the place."

"Like what?" Nancy asked.

Mr. Scarlett frowned. "It's not necessary for me to go into that."

Nancy was not ready to give up yet. She smiled.

"Why are you so anxious to keep us away from the Webster property? If I were a suspicious person, I would think something wrong was going on there."

Mr. Scarlett's eyes narrowed angrily. "Nonsense."

"Then why are you refusing to let me see it?"

Mr. Scarlett bit his lip. "Oh, all right," he said. "I don't have time to show you the place myself." He opened the drawer and took out a key with the letter W cut into it. A tag marked Webster was attached. "Here you are," he said icily. "But if anything is missing or disturbed, you'll be held responsible."

"I understand," Nancy said.

She took the key and joined Bess and George. They said good-by to the cleaning woman and went out to the car. Nancy drove directly to the lovely house on the Indian River and the three girls went in.

"How wonderful!" Bess exclaimed, after looking around. "It's even nicer inside than outside."

Nancy too was charmed by the place, which was attractively furnished. The walls of the modern Spanish-type rooms were artistically decorated. In this warm climate the whole place had an air of coolness and true hospitality.

"I don't see anything the matter with this house," said George. "Mr. Scarlett's opinion is for the birds." The others agreed and all of them wondered why the realtor had tried to discourage them.

Suddenly they were startled by the same chilling scream they had heard when looking over the grounds with Mrs. Nickerson.

"There it is again!" Bess murmured. "Ugh! I wouldn't want to live here with that gross thing next door."

"Let's find out what it is!" Nancy urged.

"Not me," Bess said firmly.

"Don't be chicken," George chided her cousin. Reluctantly Bess went outside and Nancy locked the door. The girls hurried toward the heavy wire-mesh fence. There was another scream, followed by a snarl.

"It's a wild animal!" Bess whispered. "We'd better run!"

CHAPTER IX

Jungle Threat

"No, Bess," said Nancy. "If Dad decides to buy this place, we must know what's going on next door. And I plan to find out right now. Let's walk along the shore and investigate."

Though Bess was fearful, she followed the others along the fence. It ran onto a peninsula beyond the Webster property. At the riverfront the fence turned left abruptly.

There was no bulkhead along the water and the earth was muddy and slippery. After a few steps Nancy, Bess, and George decided to take off their shoes and carry them. They rolled up their slacks knee-length and started across the swampy ground.

"Watch your step!" Bess warned. "No telling what we might step on—a lizard, snake or—Oh!"

She lost her balance but managed after a few gyrations with her arms to right herself. "I knew I shouldn't have come," she complained.

Moments later the girls reached the corner of the steel-mesh fence near the far side of the peninsula. It turned left again. The three trekked alongside through the mass of trees and bushes. They found it helpful to use the steel wire for support.

The girls had not gone far before they realized this was a real jungle. Going barelegged and barefoot did not seem safe, so the three friends put their shoes back on and rolled down their slacks.

"When will we get to the end of this?" Bess asked impatiently. Nancy said she judged it could not be much farther to the street.

The next moment the girls stood stock-still. From inside the grounds had come a loud roar.

"That's a lion!" George exclaimed. "Maybe this is a zoo."

Nancy said it was certainly not a public one.

"If it were," she surmised, "I'm sure Mrs. Nickerson would have known about it and told us. Besides, we'd have seen signs posted."

She and George pushed ahead, with Bess at their heels, terror-stricken. She suddenly gave a cry and pointed inside the fence.

A group of large African animals was galloping among the trees toward the girls. Roars, growls, and hisses filled the air. The big beasts, having scented the newcomers, pawed and clamored at the fence to get at them. A huge black leopard eyed the intruders, then began to climb the steel mesh.

Bess screamed and cried, "Look out, George!" Her cousin stood by the fence, fascinated, as Bess ran.

Nancy backed away quickly, but through the moss-draped oaks she could see a powerful-looking man running toward them, snapping a long whip.

The cracking of it finally had an effect on the animals. All of them slunk back except the leopard. He had almost reached the top of the fence and might spring over at any second!

"Get down!" the man thundered at him.

He wore a khaki suit and helmet like those used on African safaris. Now he swung the whip against the fence. It made a ringing sound and vibrated the wire mesh.

The leopard looked at his keeper balefully, then slowly climbed down. The man kept cracking the whip in the air and against the ground until all the animals loped off among the trees.

Their master turned his attention to the girls. He asked angrily, "What are you doing here?"

"Just looking," Nancy replied.

The man stared hard at each one of them before speaking again. "I guess I don't have to tell you this is a dangerous place. Stay away!"

From a little distance Bess called back, "You bet we will."

George said nothing, but Nancy asked, "Why do you have such dangerous animals here?"

"I train them and sell them to a circus."

The young detective was surprised to hear this. She knew that few circuses own the animals which are shown. They belong to the trainers who perform with them.

"What circus do you sell them to?" she queried.

Once more the big man stared at the girl until his eyes were only slits. Finally he opened them wide and said, "Tripp Brothers."

"Thank you," said Nancy. "How do we get to the main road from here? Follow this fence?"

The trainer replied shortly, "Go back the way you came."

Nancy would have preferred walking alongside the enclosure all the way to the street, but the man stood watching.

After they had traversed the full distance to where the fence turned, Nancy looked over her shoulder. The trainer was gone. She said eagerly, "Let's turn around and follow this side to find out what we can."

"Oh please don't!" Bess begged. "Those animals may come after us again and the leopard jump over the fence!"

"I'm willing to take the chance. George, are you?" Nancy asked.

"Sure thing."

Nancy took the key to the Webster house from her pocket. "Bess," she said, "if you don't want to come with us, why don't you go on and wait in the house?"

"Look out, George!" Bess cried out

Bess could see that there was no talking Nancy and George out of learning more about the jungle-like property. With a great sigh she said, "Oh, all right. I'll tag along. But if anything happens, don't say I didn't warn you."

The girls began their trek up the peninsula through the woods, following the fence. A distance ahead it suddenly turned to the left.

"The fence ends at a house!" Nancy whispered.

She and the others approached carefully and stared at the building. It was a very old mansion but large and well preserved. The walls were covered almost entirely with clinging vines and green moss. Great oak trees with long streamers of Spanish moss surrounded it, giving a weird and forbidding effect.

"A real spook house!" Bess said in a low voice. "Well, Nancy, have you seen enough? Let's go!"

Nancy inched closer to the wire fence and peered through. She could see several large cages attached to the rear of the house. The animals that had tried to attack the girls were now in them and sleeping. At the moment the breeze was blowing toward the girls, and the animals could not pick up their scent.

Bess tugged at Nancy's arm. "Let's not tempt fate," she begged. "Please come on."

Nancy could feel Bess trembling and nodded in agreement.

Nancy wondered how far it was to the street.

There seemed to be no road leading out, but she concluded there must be some way for cars and people to get in and out of the grounds.

Presently she spotted a truck off to one side. There was no name on it but she jotted down the license number.

"Here's what I've been looking for," she whispered, and pointed to a narrow road which zigzagged among the moss-covered trees.

As the girls walked along it silently, they listened for sounds of anyone approaching and watched the ground to avoid any holes. George, however, sank down in a soft spot. Her feet were sucked in so quickly she could not pull them out.

After trying for several moments she called out, "Girls, come and help me! I'm stuck!"

It took the combined efforts of Nancy and Bess to pull George out of the oozy mass. She looked down at her shoes which had changed from white to brown.

"I'm sure a mess!" she said. "The sooner I can get into a tub the better I'll like it." She thanked her rescuers who could not help laughing at George's appearance. Mud was splattered over her clothes, hair, and face.

A few feet farther on, the ground was harder and the girls quickened their pace. As they zigzagged along the curving road, the three grew careless about being watchful.

Nancy suddenly pulled back and bumped

against George. The others looked to see what had startled her. A snake had begun to unwind itself from a tree branch and was trying to reach Nancy with its forked tongue!

She recovered her wits quickly and said, "He won't harm us if we don't bother him."

"I hope you're right," said Bess, and took a circuitous route to avoid the reptile.

In a few moments the girls came to a small orange grove. As they hurried through it, Bess picked one of the luscious-looking fruit and put it into her pocket.

"In case I get hungry," she explained to the others.

A few minutes later the girls reached another bit of jungle-like area. If it had not been for the roadway, they would have found it hard going through stout reeds and brier bushes. At last the street came into sight.

Nancy, in the lead, suddenly called back in a whisper, "Hide!"

CHAPTER X

Disastrous Fire

"Quick!" said Nancy, ducking behind a brier bush. "Mr. Scarlett is just outside in a car!"

Bess and George squatted down too. The three remained very still, not making a sound.

Mr. Scarlett got out of his car and walked up and down, looking and listening. The girls were puzzled by his actions. Perhaps someone had seen them going toward the moss-covered mansion and had reported this to him.

In a few minutes the realtor seemed satisfied about something. He got back into his car. Then, to the girls' amazement, he drove toward them along the winding path. They crouched lower behind the tall bushes. His car soon disappeared but they could hear the motor. Seconds later it was shut off approximately where the house would be.

"He must know the animal trainer," Nancy thought.

She and her friends came from hiding. Nancy wanted to go back to the moss-covered mansion but Bess objected. "I think we've had enough adventures for one day. Besides, George is a mess. Please, let's return to the Billingtons."

As they walked down the street toward the Webster house to get their car, the girls discussed Scarlett's furtive behavior. Why had he come to the mansion with the wild-animal enclosure?

"He's hiding something, that's sure," George declared. "Nancy, if you see him again, are you going to ask him why he was here?"

"No, George. I believe we can find out more by having him think we didn't see him."

When they reached home Hannah Gruen met them at the kitchen door. "My word, George, where have you been?" she cried out. "Did you fall in the water?"

"I wish I had," said George. "I'd have been better off." Quickly she explained about their sleuthing trip to the moss-covered mansion.

The housekeeper was aghast. "The place sounds dreadful. You had better not go there again."

Bess said, "You can bet I'm not going to."

She pulled the orange from her pocket, and told Hannah she had taken it from a tree at the strange house.

"This isn't the same kind as Mr. Billington's,"

Bess said. "Do you suppose it's a Hamlin, the same as the oranges that were delivered to the Space Center?"

The thought intrigued Nancy. On a bookshelf she had noticed a volume marked *Oranges* and went to get it. The book was filled with color pictures and one by one she compared Bess's orange with those in the book.

"This is not a Valencia," she said, "because it's the wrong time of year for that kind of tree to be bearing. The fruit's ripe in the spring. Mr. Billington's, as you know, are Pineapple Oranges. Remember their bright-orange skin and pineappley shape?" Nancy turned the page and exclaimed, "Here it is! The oranges at the moss-covered mansion are not Hamlins but Parson Browns. Hamlins have a smooth skin while the Parson Browns are pebbly-skinned."

George sighed. "I guess we'll have to ride around looking for Hamlin groves to see if we can pick up any clue to the ones that were brought into the Space Center."

The girls decided to start their search directly after luncheon. They hurried upstairs to take baths and put on fresh clothes.

By the time they came down again, Tina was in the kitchen helping Hannah. The three girls winked at one another and began to set the table.

The menu called for baked chicken with a special kind of cream sauce. Tina said she had never heard of it and did not know how to make the sauce.

"Nancy does it very well," Hannah said proudly, and called, "Nancy dear, will you come and make cream sauce for the chicken?"

Smiling, Nancy hurried to the kitchen and prepared it.

When everything was ready, Hannah and the girls went to the dining room. They invited Tina to eat with them, but the woman refused, saying she was not hungry. Perhaps by the time Antin came in, she would be ready for her lunch.

Instinct told Nancy not to talk about the moss-covered mansion within Tina's hearing. The group were relieved when she went outdoors and walked into the grove.

The telephone rang. Nancy answered it. Mr. Datsun, the lawyer, was calling. He wanted to know if Nancy had anything to report. She gave a quick account of her sleuthing but admitted she had learned little about the explosive oranges.

"No one has been able to track down any clue except to Mr. Billington," the lawyer said.

On a hunch Nancy told him about the old mansion. "Do you know who lives there?"

"No," the lawyer replied. "Why?"

Nancy explained about the possibility of her father buying the Webster place and the strange behavior of Mr. Scarlett. "Are you acquainted with him?"

"I know there's a realtor of that name," said Mr. Datsun, "but I can't tell you anything about him. I'm afraid I'm no help to you, but I'm hoping you can help me.

"Nancy, a very odd note was left under my office door. Maybe you can figure it out. This is what it says:

" *'Can a mouse with a brain of jelly capture a lion with nerves of steel?'* "

"How strange!" Nancy remarked. "Would you mind repeating it?"

Mr. Datsun read it again and Nancy quickly wrote down the words and read those numbered 1, 5, 9, 13. Neither the words nor the first letters of them made any sense.

"Are you still there?" Mr. Datsun asked.

"I'm sorry," said Nancy. "I was trying to see if there might be a code in this message. I think not. But it occurs to me that it could have been written by some sarcastic person interested in the case of the explosive oranges. The message might imply that you and my father are as helpless as a mouse against a lion."

"That's a very good guess," the lawyer remarked.

Nancy went on, "Whoever the lion is, we'll catch him!"

"Indeed we will!" Mr. Datson agreed.

After the conversation ended, Nancy continued to think about the message. She suddenly remembered the lion at the moss-covered mansion. Suppose that by some chance this was the beast referred to in the mysterious note! It could mean that the strange setup of the animal enclosure and the odd behavior of Mr. Scarlett are connected with the explosive oranges!

"It would explain why the girls and I aren't wanted at the Webster house," Nancy told herself.

At this moment Bess came to warn her that Antin and Tina had come in. The caretaker was taciturn. Not only did he not speak to anyone but did not wait to eat lunch. Instead, the couple went up to their room.

"What's the matter with him?" George asked.

Before anyone could hazard a guess, an alarm bell began to ring.

"What's that for?" George asked.

There was pounding on the stairway and Antin came rushing down. "Fire!" he shouted, and rushed out the rear door.

Everyone followed. He sped through the grove to the packing house.

Suddenly Nancy stopped. "I wonder if anyone notified the fire department," she said. "I'd better go back and phone them anyway."

"I'll go with you," said Bess. "This might have been a ruse to get all of us out of the house." They had left the doors and windows open.

"We'll soon find out," said Nancy.

Hurrying inside, she dashed to the telephone

and called the fire department. They had not been notified but said they would come at once.

Quickly Nancy and Bess locked all the doors and windows, and took the kitchen door key with them. As they ran through the grove toward the packing house, the girls noticed that blazes had sprung up here and there among the trees.

"This fire has been deliberately set!" Nancy declared. "Someone started it while the workers were at lunch." Immediately she wondered where Antin had been. Could he possibly be the arsonist and if so why?

When they caught up to George and Hannah, Nancy told them that the firemen were coming. She rushed up to a burly picker and asked how she could help.

"You're a girl," he said. "What can you do?"

Nancy was angry. She turned away. There was nothing she could do to save the orange packing house which was now a mass of flames, but she might be able to do something to preserve the trees. She ran over to Tina, who was sobbing, and asked her.

The woman pointed toward the river. "There's a hose and a pump down there," she replied.

Nancy did not wait to hear more. She quickly told Bess and George, and the three rushed off toward the river. It seemed as if trees were burning everywhere. They found the pump and hose, quickly unwound it, and turned on the nozzle.

Within minutes they were able to put out the fire in the nearby trees.

"Let's try another section," George suggested, and began lugging the hose forward.

Just then they heard the fire engines arriving. The girls, however, kept on with their own work.

In a short while two of the firemen came into the grove dragging a large hose. Suddenly they realized that the trees were already being hosed, and were astounded to see the job being done by three girls.

"Good work!" said one.

With the two steady streams of water, the rest of the fires in the grove were soon extinguished.

"Who's in charge here?" one of the firemen asked Nancy.

"The foreman, Antin Resardo. I think he's at the packing house."

"Let's get out of here," Bess suggested. "This place smells horrible."

The scent of scorched oranges mixed with burning wood was bad enough, but added to this was rank-smelling steam. The girls' eyes were smarting and they were covered with soot.

"We'll take care of your hose," said one of the firemen. "You'd better go to the house and bathe your eyes."

"We will," Nancy replied.

On the way back they met Hannah, who reported that the packing house was a complete wreck.

"It's a shame," she said. "The fire chief is convinced this was the work of a firebug."

Nancy said she thought the arsonist might be the enemy of Mr. Billington who had used his name to deliver the explosive oranges. "Whoever the person is he knows he's being pursued. He hopes to intimidate Mr. Billington into dropping the hunt by ruining his orange business."

The others agreed. Hannah said a neighbor had offered to let Mr. Billington use his packing house until he could build a new one. "Only I'm afraid there aren't many good oranges left."

When they reached the house Nancy said she must telephone her father at once. "I'll tell him what has happened so he can pass the word along to Mr. Billington."

Fortunately he was in his office and she quickly told the story. Mr. Drew was astounded.

"I'll get in touch with Mr. and Mrs. Billington immediately about coming down. Please stay there. I'll call you back."

Within half an hour Mr. Drew phoned. He and the Billingtons were leaving River Heights at once in order to make a quick plane connection in New York.

"We'll get to Melbourne about ten tonight," he said. "Please meet us, Nancy."

"Bess and George and I will be there," she promised.

Nancy reported the conversation to Hannah and the girls, then said, "I'd like to go back to the packing house and look through the ruins if they're cool enough. Maybe we'll find a clue to the arsonist."

Bess and George were eager to join her.

"Setting those fires was a wicked thing to do," Bess declared.

When the girls arrived at the water-soaked ruin, they walked around it, their eyes alert for any clue. Suddenly, in a heap of half-burned papers, Nancy spotted something that could be a clue. She bent down and picked up a scrap of paper.

"Look at this!" she exclaimed excitedly.

CHAPTER XI

Off the Market

THE partially burned newspaper which Nancy showed to Bess and George was a copy of the edition which held the name *Drew* in the code message.

"It's ringed with red crayon!" Bess burst out. "What does that mean?"

George made a guess. "I think the person who set the fire is a member of some gang out to ruin Mr. Billington's reputation and business. He's worried because Mr. Drew and Nancy have been brought in to solve the mystery."

Nancy agreed. "We have very few clues," she said, "and everything seems to be so disconnected. What we must do is find a motive for the whole thing."

Bess suddenly caught her breath. The other girls looked at her and asked, "What's the matter?"

Bess's reply was upsetting. "Suppose that fire-bug takes it into his head to burn down the house we're staying in!"

There was silence for a few moments. Finally Nancy said, "Perhaps we'd better go back and talk this over with Hannah."

When they reached the house, Tina and Antin were with Mrs. Gruen. Hannah became alarmed at the thought of another fire.

"I wish we had a good watchdog here," she said.

Tina was fearful of the house being set on fire, but Antin shrugged off the idea.

"What reason would anyone have for doing such a thing?" he asked Nancy.

She replied, "What reason would anyone have for burning down the packing house and setting fires in the grove?"

As she spoke, Nancy watched the caretaker's face intently. He showed no change of expression.

Nancy thought, "He certainly is a strange person." Aloud she asked, "What do you think is going to happen to Mr. Billington's orange business?"

Antin set his jaw. "That's up to Mr. Billington. I know what I'd do if it belonged to me—forget the whole thing. But of course I'll follow whatever orders he gives me." The foreman stalked from the house.

As it neared time for the girls to leave for the Melbourne airport to pick up Mr. Drew, Hannah confessed that she felt uneasy about staying alone. The Resardos had already left, saying they were going to Ruth's birthday party.

When George suggested that she come with the girls, Mrs. Gruen said, "I don't think I should go along and leave this house unprotected."

"You're absolutely right," said Bess. "Nancy, I'll stay here with Hannah."

Nancy and George set off. On the way George remarked, "Wouldn't you think after what happened here today Antin and Tina would have stayed home and waited for the Billingtons? They didn't even offer to pick them up at the airport!"

Back at the Billington house, Hannah and Bess were startled by loud knocking on the front door. Hannah went to answer it.

"Don't let anybody in!" Bess called out.

Hannah asked, "Who's calling?"

"Mr. Scarlett."

Mrs. Gruen opened the door and the man stepped inside.

"Where's Nancy Drew?" he asked abruptly.

"She's not here."

"Where did she go?"

Bess started to tell him, but Hannah gave the girl a warning look and answered for her.

"Nancy has gone on an errand. Do you have a message for her?"

Mr. Scarlett said indeed he did—a very important one. "Mr. Webster has taken his house off the market. It's no longer for sale. I must have the key to the house at once. Get it for me."

Hannah said she had no idea where it was. He would have to wait until Nancy returned.

"I can't wait," the realtor snapped. "I must have the key now." He turned to Bess. "She probably told you where it is. Bring it to me!"

"I don't know," the girl replied firmly. "When Nancy returns, I'll tell her you want the key. She can bring it to you in the morning."

Mr. Scarlett seemed nonplussed as well as angry. Before he had a chance to make any further demands, Hannah said to him, "That's all. Good night, Mr. Scarlett."

She held the door for him and reluctantly he went out.

Immediately Bess said, "Nancy's going to be dreadfully disappointed about the Webster house being taken off the market. I wonder what the reason was. I gathered from Mrs. Nickerson that Mr. Webster was eager to sell the place."

As they continued to discuss the strange turn of events, Nancy and George were bowling along the road toward Melbourne. When they were about halfway there, George remarked that a car was racing up behind them.

"That driver certainly is in a hurry," Nancy remarked, glancing into the rear-view mirror.

Instead of whizzing by, the car suddenly drove up alongside and the driver yelled, "Stop!"

Nancy suddenly recognized the driver and stopped her car.

"Mr. Scarlett!" she exclaimed. "What do you want?"

"The key to the Webster house," he replied. "Hand it over."

Nancy said she did not have it with her. She changed the subject abruptly and asked Mr. Scarlett who lived in the moss-covered mansion next to the Webster home.

"I don't know," he replied. "I've never been in there."

Nancy and George looked at each other but said nothing. Why had Scarlett lied?

The realtor came back to the subject of the key. "Give it to me!"

"I told you I don't have it with me," Nancy replied. "But tell me why you want the key. My father is coming down tonight and I need it to show him the house tomorrow morning. I'm sure he'll buy the place."

"It's no longer for sale," Mr. Scarlett snapped. "Mr. Webster has taken it off the market."

"What!" George exclaimed. "I understood he wanted to sell it as soon as possible."

"Not any more. Tell me where the key is and I'll go back to the house and get it from your friends."

Nancy had no intention of doing this. It had occurred to her that this whole story might be false. She would ask her father to get in touch with Mr. Webster direct and learn the truth.

"Hurry up!" Mr. Scarlett shouted.

Before Nancy had a chance to answer, a trooper on a motorcycle whizzed up and stopped. He pulled out a pad and pencil and said to Mr. Scarlett, "You were going way beyond the speed limit."

"I was in a hurry," the realtor replied.

George nudged Nancy and whispered, "Now's your chance to get away."

Nancy thought so too. Putting the car into gear, she drove off down the road.

George glanced back several times to see if Mr. Scarlett was following them. There was no sign of his car.

As they neared the airport, George said, "It seems strange he knew where to find us. Do you suppose he was at the house and Hannah or Bess told him?"

"Even if he were there, I'm sure they wouldn't tell him. Besides, they could truthfully say they didn't know where the key is because I hid it and forgot to tell you all the place."

Nancy parked and glanced at her watch. Ten minutes to ten.

"Dad should be in soon," Nancy said, a smile crossing her face. "It will be so good to see him again."

As the girls walked into the terminal building,

they noticed that people waiting to meet relatives or friends looked tense and worried. One woman was pacing the floor nervously, wiping perspiration from her face, though the night was cool.

As she came close to the girls, she said, "The New York plane is in trouble."

"What's wrong?" Nancy asked her.

The woman looked at the girl, terror in her eyes. "The landing gear jammed. The wheels won't come down. This means a crash landing!"

CHAPTER XII

Frustrated Thief

THE girls gasped and rushed outside to watch the plane carrying Mr. Drew and the Billingtons. It was circling the field. The runway had been sprayed with foam. A fire truck and an ambulance stood nearby. Soon the great jetliner began to descend.

"But the landing wheels aren't down!" murmured the woman who had followed the girls outdoors.

With Nancy and George she watched breathlessly. Upon landing the plane might spin around.

Fortunately the pilot made a skillful belly landing and all the waiting friends and relatives gave sighs of relief. Mr. Drew and the Billingtons were among the first to get off. The pilot had already come out and the two men hurried to catch up to him.

"Congratulations on your fine work!" Mr. Drew called. Mr. Billington also complimented the pilot.

"It's all in a day's work," the young captain answered with a smile, then disappeared into the offices of the airline.

Mr. Drew introduced the Billingtons, who said they had been looking forward to meeting Nancy and her friends. As soon as they were seated in the car, Mr. Billington requested that the girls tell him about the fire.

Nancy reported on it in detail and told him the arsonist had not been caught. "Mr. Billington, we have found Tina and Antin a complete mystery. Do you think it possible that he had anything to do with the fire?"

"Not Antin," Mr. Billington said quickly. "I always thought he loved my orange grove and would be heartbroken if something happened to it."

Nancy and George made no comment. Antin had certainly not shown this kind of regret about the burned trees and packing house.

George told about the girls' experience on the way to the airport. "Mr. Scarlett was positively contemptible, and he said that the Webster house had been taken off the market."

"Dad," said Nancy, "could you find out if it is really true?"

When he nodded, she added, "The girls and I

have wondered if Scarlett is acting in collusion with the owner of the moss-covered mansion." She told the men about the wild animals they had seen. "The trainer was very hostile to us. I suspect he doesn't want any new neighbors."

Mr. Drew asked, "Have you talked to the police about the place?"

"No, I haven't," Nancy replied, "but I'll do so first thing in the morning."

When the Drews and their friends arrived at the Billington house, they were amazed to hear of Mr. Scarlett's rude behavior toward Hannah and Bess.

Mr. Drew scowled. "I don't like his actions. I doubt that he is to be trusted. You say he went into the grounds of the moss-covered mansion furtively?"

"Yes," Nancy replied. "Suppose I call the police right now and ask if they can tell us anything about who lives there."

She phoned at once but was told she would have to wait until morning when the office with the local records was open.

The next day Nancy lost no time in getting the information. The old house had been purchased by a man named Fortin. He had been a trainer of wild animals for a circus. Fortin had received a permit to have the beasts there as long as they were properly caged. Nancy thanked the clerk and hung up.

"I wonder if Fortin was that tall heavy-set man with the whip," she said to Bess and George.

Nancy was more convinced than ever that Fortin was in back of the move to keep the Drews from buying the Webster house. He might have found out she was an amateur detective and did not want her so close. She might report that he allowed the dangerous animals out of their cages.

"I wish I could get inside that mansion," Nancy said. "I have a strong hunch there's something going on between Scarlett and Fortin which has a direct bearing on the Webster property."

Bess spoke up. "You'd better forget it, Nancy. We came down here to solve the mystery of the explosive oranges. Why don't we forget that place with the wild animals and go hunting for Hamlin orange groves as George suggested?"

"I'm ready to start," Nancy said.

The girls set off in the Billingtons' car. Nancy drove up one road and down another. Many people had small groves, others large ones, but none had Hamlin oranges. Most were apparently Valencias.

At last the girls spotted a big grove of smooth-skinned Hamlins. Nancy turned into the long driveway and went to the packing house. She introduced herself and her friends to the foreman, saying they were from the North and were interested in solving the case of the explosive oranges.

"My father is the attorney for Mr. Billington," she said. "I'm eager to find out which grove those particular oranges came from. Can you help me?"

The foreman, who told them his name was Tom Seever, smiled. He looked up at the darkening sky and said, "We'd better run into the packing house. I'll tell you what I know. Looks like a heavy shower coming any second."

The girls hurried after him and went into the shelter. Pickers from the grove and a visitor who had just driven in began rushing inside too. By the time the rain came down hard, the place was so crowded that moving around was impossible.

Suddenly the lights went out. A few seconds later Nancy felt a rough hand against her arm. She realized that someone was trying to cut the strap of her handbag.

Quickly she clutched the bag in one hand and with the other grabbed the man's wrist. Finding it, she pinched the flesh so hard that the purse snatcher cried out in pain. Instantly she could feel him moving away.

A few seconds later the lights went on. Nancy craned her neck to look at all the people who had taken shelter in the packing house. It was hopeless to try identifying the suspect, but she saw the visitor dash to a car and drive off. Was he guilty and had he followed her here?

The rain had stopped and the men had begun to file outside. Nancy and her friends were the last to leave the building. After talking to Mr. Seever for a few minutes about the mystery, she was convinced that there was nothing he could tell them which would cast any light on the case. All his oranges were sold to trustworthy buyers he knew well, and no fruit had been stolen.

The young sleuth asked if he would give them directions to another Hamlin grove.

He told her of one about a mile away and the three girls headed for Owen's Grove.

It was a large grove and there were many pickers at work. Nancy was directed to the office of the owner, Mr. Owen. It was in a small building that stood a short distance from the packing house.

She went to the door and asked, "May I come in?"

The owner rose, smiling, and said, "Yes, indeed. Won't you sit down?"

Bess and George had stayed outside to look over the packing house.

The young detective introduced herself. "My father is working on Mr. Billington's case. Since the explosive oranges that were brought into the Base were Hamlins, I wondered if you might possibly have a clue to help solve the mystery."

Mr. Owen said he did. "The FBI were here, of course, and I told them a suspicion of mine. One of my workers never showed up here after the affair. He was a strange, uncommunicative person by the name of Max Ivanson. We tried to get in touch with him where he boarded but were told that he had disappeared."

"Did he take anything from here with him?" Nancy asked.

Mr. Owen nodded. "Several sacks of oranges were missing. We think he took them. I've forgotten the number now but it corresponded to the count which the NASA authorities had listed in their report about the delivery."

Nancy was intrigued by this information. "What did Max Ivanson look like?"

Mr. Owen opened a desk drawer and pulled out a photograph. "This is the man. I just came across it."

Nancy tried not to show her surprise. Ivanson looked enough like Mr. Billington to be a brother!

"Can you tell me anything more about him?" Nancy queried.

"A little. Ivanson's a bachelor. He was a good picker but would never stay to work overtime."

Nancy arose. "You have been most kind and helpful," she said, putting out her hand.

Mr. Owen shook it warmly and wished her luck in solving the mystery. "I'm glad if I've been of help," he said.

Bess and George were excited when Nancy told them what she had found out, and discussed the clue as they started for home. A shortcut led them past the Nickersons' house.

"Let's go in," Nancy suggested, and turned into their driveway.

Both of Ned's parents were home and were amazed at all Nancy had accomplished, particularly her last clue. Then the conversation turned toward the Webster house and the moss-covered mansion.

"I certainly wish I could get inside that weird-looking place with the wild animals," said Nancy.

Mr. Nickerson grinned. All three girls thought how much Ned looked like his father when he smiled broadly.

"I think I just might arrange such a visit," Mr. Nickerson said. "I know a man who is an animal control officer in the Public Health Service. Perhaps he could make a routine inspection of the moss-covered mansion and"—he winked at Nancy —"perhaps he could take a secretary with him!"

CHAPTER XIII

Eerie Inspection

"WHAT an exciting suggestion!" Nancy exclaimed. "Think of going inside the moss-covered mansion!'

All the others agreed it was a good idea except Bess, who looked worried.

"Nancy, please think this over. You know the trouble we almost got into with those wild animals on the outside of the house. No telling what may happen if you go indoors."

Nancy turned to Mr. Nickerson. "Surely it can't be dangerous if the Health Department goes there regularly to inspect the place."

Ned's father nodded. "I can soon solve this," he said. "My friend Mr. Wilcox, the animal control officer, will know whether or not it's possible and also safe for you to go into the moss-covered mansion."

He went to make the call. While waiting, George said she was envious of Nancy's visit to the place. Bess remarked timidly, "Well I'm not. I don't mind telling you those animals frightened me half to death."

Mr. Nickerson soon returned, a wide smile on his face. "Everything is arranged. Mr. Wilcox will be here tomorrow morning at ten to pick you up."

"That's wonderful!" the young detective exclaimed. "I think we'd better dash home now. I'll see you at ten o'clock tomorrow morning. By the way, Mr. Nickerson, will you request Mr. Wilcox not to introduce me at the moss-covered mansion?"

"That's a good idea," he agreed. "If they know your name, you might not get a friendly greeting! Anyway, since you are not a regular member of the Public Health Service staff, let the people at the mansion think of you as Wilcox's Girl Friday."

This reference to the Robinson Crusoe story struck Bess funny and she began to laugh. "You'll be Mrs. Robinson Crusoe," she remarked. On the way home, however, Bess sobered again. "I just hope nothing happens to you!"

"I promise to keep my eyes open," Nancy told her friend.

She could hardly wait for the following morning to come, but during the remainder of the afternoon, Bess kept referring to the possible dangers Nancy might encounter.

Once she said, "Suppose that leopard mauls you!"

George looked at her cousin severely. "Will you

be quiet? Nancy is determined to go and I don't blame her. There's no point in trying to scare her away."

Bess said no more but Hannah Gruen did. She was inclined to agree with Bess. "I know Mr. Wilcox will be with you, but what protection would he be against an angry lion?"

When Mr. Drew and Mr. Billington heard what the plan was, they took a different attitude. Both were sure Nancy could not be harmed if Wilcox was with her.

The lawyer added, "I know you will keep alert, Nancy, and look in all directions at once."

Nancy bent to kiss her father and patted him on the cheek. "Are you trying to make me into some kind of a wonder of science?" she teased. "I've never learned to swivel my head!"

He chuckled, then said that he and Mr. Billington were going out to have dinner with Mr. Datsun.

"See you in the morning," he told the others and the two men set off.

The three girls went up to Nancy's room to help her pick the outfit she would wear the following morning. The choice was a white dress and shoes. Nancy would arrange her hair in a bun so she would look older.

Bess announced she was suffering with hunger pains so the trio went downstairs to have dinner with Mrs. Billington and Hannah. Once more the

Resardos were not there. The rest of the evening was spent reading the latest reports of the forthcoming flight to the moon.

"I see that there are going to be many celebrities here," Mrs. Gruen remarked. "Even the president may come down!"

The newspaper carried pictures of well-known press correspondents who had arrived to report the shoot. There were photographers by the hundreds and a sprinkling of visitors from other countries.

"It's going to be fabulous!" Bess exclaimed. "Aren't those astronauts who are on the mission handsome?"

"Yes, and remarkably brave and intelligent," George added.

Finally it was time for the group to retire. Nancy was too excited to drop off to sleep but eventually she did and woke up refreshed and ready for the day's adventure. After breakfast the girls drove to the Nickerson home. A few minutes later Mr. Wilcox arrived and was introduced to them. He wore a khaki smock-type suit.

"So this is the young lady who will accompany me," he said, smiling at Nancy, "and act as secretary for the trip." He handed her a stenographer's pad and a pencil. "Take lots of notes," he added with a wink.

Nancy laughed. "I understand. Some for you and some for me."

The two went to the car. Nancy noticed a pair of asbestos gloves on the seat.

"I wear those whenever I have to go inside a cage," he explained.

When they arrived at the moss-covered mansion, Wilcox turned into the narrow path that wound through the orange grove and the jungle to the house. He parked and they walked up the steps of the old-fashioned house.

The Public Health officer rang the bell. He and Nancy stood waiting but there was no answer.

"Maybe the bell doesn't work," Nancy suggested.

Her companion pounded loudly on the door. After a long while it was opened a crack. Nancy's heart began to beat a little faster. Would the huge man with the whip open the door?

Wilcox called into the crack, "Mr. Fortin?"

"Yes," came the answer. "No visitors allowed!"

"I'm Wilcox from Animal Control of the Public Health Service," he told him. "I have an order to inspect your place again. Here are my credentials."

All this time two dogs had been yelping and barking in the background. Mr. Fortin certainly had protection, Nancy thought.

"Wait until I tie up these animals," the owner said.

He closed the door and was gone so long that Nancy thought perhaps he was not going to let them in. Finally the door opened.

"No visitors allowed!" Fortin said sharply

Fortin was a slender man about fifty years old
with a reddish complexion. It flashed across
Nancy's mind that he did not give the appearance
of an animal trainer. His hands were rather soft-
looking, not like those of a person used to heavy
work. He escorted the callers through the center
hall and out to the kitchen. He opened a rear door
which gave a view of the many cages backed up
against the house just beyond the kitchen door.
Nancy got her notebook ready.

"These cages look very clean and the animals
well-kept," Wilcox remarked, and Nancy wrote
this down.

She followed him outdoors and around the
three sides of the cages which seemed to be well-
constructed. Each had a sheltered area.

"Very good," said Wilcox.

All this time Nancy's eyes had been roaming
around the jungle. She could not detect anything
suspicious.

Fortin led the way back inside the house and
headed for the front door. At once Wilcox spoke
up. "I have orders to look over the whole mansion."

The owner frowned and said, "Why is this necessary? A license issued to me to keep the animals
certainly doesn't permit the Public Health Service to pry into my private life!"

Wilcox replied, "Those are my orders. There

could be vermin in the house from those wild animals." Before Fortin could object, Wilcox started up the stairway. Nancy followed, then Fortin.

After a quick inspection of the second-floor rooms, Wilcox said, "Everything seems to be all right." He turned to Fortin. "I thought maybe you had some small animals up here."

"Well I don't!" Fortin snapped.

He started down the stairway, but Nancy held the health officer back. She whispered, "See that door over there? It probably leads to the third floor."

Her companion nodded. "I want to take a look upstairs, Mr. Fortin," he called and walked over to the door.

As Wilcox opened it, the owner's face turned red with anger, but all he said was, "You'll find nothing up there. It's an old tower."

Nevertheless, Wilcox climbed the stairs, with Nancy at his heels and Fortin behind her. The tower had windows which looked out on the ocean. In front of one stood a powerful telescope.

"That came with the house," Fortin explained. "It's so old I guess it was put in soon after the people built the place. They probably watched the ships at sea."

Nancy had walked over and looked through the telescope. She could plainly see the Space Center and the rocket that would take the astronauts to the moon.

"Everything okay?" Fortin asked in a sarcastic tone.

"Everything's okay," the Public Health officer replied, and Nancy wrote this down, along with her observations relating to the telescope.

As the visitors were coming down from the second floor, Nancy noticed a man in the lower hall. He was the big fellow with the whip! Instinctively she held the notebook partly across her face so that she would not be recognized.

When they reached the foot of the stairs Fortin ignored her. He introduced his associate to Wilcox as Joss Longman, saying he was the best animal trainer in the world.

Wilcox nodded, then checked through the first floor with Nancy. They found nothing suspicious. Back in the hall the two men were waiting for them sullenly.

"That's all now," Fortin said sharply and walked toward the front door, but Wilcox did not move.

"We haven't seen your basement yet," he said.

Hearing this, Longman turned quickly and hurried toward the kitchen. Nancy saw him open a door at the back of the hall and disappear.

Once more Fortin began to argue that the Public Health Service had no right to intrude on his privacy.

"Orders are orders," Wilcox said firmly. "Take me to your basement."

Fortin glared at the visitors, then he slowly walked to the kitchen. When they came to the door at the rear of the hall through which Nancy had seen Longman disappear, she put out her hand toward the knob.

"Don't go in there!" Fortin shouted at her. "That's a clothes closet."

Nancy doubted this but she followed him into the kitchen. Fortin began to talk about how old-fashioned the room was.

"That's only a coal stove," he remarked. "It's pretty hard learning to cook on it. As soon as I get more money, I intend to replace it with a modern range."

Nancy suspected that the man was stalling for time. He went on talking about the outmoded plumbing and what trouble they had with it. She was convinced that Longman had gone ahead to conceal something in the basement.

"What is it," she wondered, "that they don't want us to see?"

Finally Fortin opened a door in the kitchen and clicked on a light in the basement. He led the way down a steep flight of wooden steps. Longman was not in sight. Nancy was sure he had used a secret entrance to the place.

Wilcox had already started walking around the basement which contained nothing but old furniture and piles of rubbish thrown against the walls. This seemed odd to Nancy. The Public

Health officer did not act as if he suspected anything.

Fortin asked, "Well, are you satisfied now with your inspection?"

Wilcox looked stern. "I don't think much of your housekeeping," he replied. "Please see that the trash is cleaned out of here."

"Okay," Fortin growled.

The two men started up the stairway. Nancy, pretending that she was writing down what Wilcox had said, purposely leaned against a pile of old furniture. Presently the load shifted. Nancy grabbed a child's desk for support.

The next moment the whole conglomeration of furniture came tumbling down on her!

CHAPTER XIV

Outsmarting a Liar

THE racket caused by the falling furniture sent Wilcox and Fortin running back to the basement.

The animal trainer, instead of asking if Nancy had been hurt, said to her angrily, "What were you trying to do? You have no right touching anything around here! You were snooping, that's what. Talk!"

Wilcox said icily, "I'm sure she meant no harm. Are you hurt?"

By this time Nancy had picked herself up and though her clothes were dusty from the furniture, she had not been injured.

"I'm sorry, Mr. Fortin," she said. "I used to have a desk very much like this one. When I touched it, the whole pile came tumbling down."

Fortin's face was grim. Nancy thought he was going to say he did not believe a word of her story. Quickly she asked, "Is this desk for sale?"

"No!" the animal trainer almost shouted at her.

"And I'd appreciate your leaving. I have work to do."

Mr. Wilcox spoke up. "We'll go at once and I'll give the Health Service an excellent report about your animal operation here."

While Nancy brushed dust from her clothes, she took in every detail of the wall behind the pile of furniture. She had spotted a steel door. Evidently Longman had rushed downstairs to try hiding it with the pile of furniture. Something secret must be inside!

Nancy had also noticed heavy cables in the basement. One of them ran through the wall next to the half-hidden door.

Fortin said sarcastically, "Listen, miss, you're delaying my work. Please go at once."

"Oh I'm sorry," Nancy apologized and scooted up the stairway.

She was puzzled by what she had seen. The young detective had a strong hunch that something besides the training of wild animals for a circus was going on at the moss-covered mansion.

Mr. Wilcox and his "secretary" left the house and rode off. Nancy told him what she had seen in the cellar. "Why do you think Fortin was trying to conceal that door?"

Wilcox smiled. "I'm no detective, but I suspect he had something hidden behind it. Since I insisted upon seeing everything, he was probably afraid I might want to look in there. I'm sure no wild animal was inside. Otherwise it would have picked up our scent and made some kind of noise."

Nancy said no more and in a short time she and the health inspector reached the Billington house. She thanked him for his help and jumped out of the car.

Bess and George met her at the front door. "Thank goodness you're here in one piece," said Bess.

George asked, "Did you learn anything exciting?"

Nancy related her experience to the girls, Mrs. Billington, and Hannah Gruen. All of them tried guessing what might be beyond the steel door where the furniture had been piled up.

"Even though Mr. Wilcox doesn't think so," Bess put in, "I'll bet there's some kind of an animal behind that door."

"You could be right," Mrs. Billington said, frowning.

George had a different theory. "I'm sure Fortin only keeps those wild animals to scare people away and isn't training those beasts to perform. There's some other reason he and Longman are living at the moss-covered mansion."

"Like what?" Bess asked.

"There could be all kinds of secret rooms," her cousin replied.

Nancy was intrigued by this idea. "They might even be storing explosives!"

Bess stared at her friend. "Are you hinting that Mr. Fortin might have been responsible for the explosive oranges that were shipped into the Space Center?"

George answered. "I wouldn't put it past him."

Mrs. Billington looked worried. "If you're right and anything should go wrong, the whole of Merritt Island could be blown up!"

Nancy turned to Hannah. "You haven't said a word. What do you think?"

Looking worried, the housekeeper replied that their suspicions about the moss-covered mansion should be reported to the FBI.

Nancy pointed out, "But it's mostly speculation —we haven't any constructive evidence."

She also reminded the others that the FBI had a good lead about the person responsible for stealing the oranges and delivering them to the Space Center. He was Max Ivanson. The man had disappeared and not been found yet.

When Mr. Drew and Mr. Billington came in, the results of Nancy's visit to the moss-covered mansion were reported to them. The men were as interested in the story as the others had been. They had no solutions to offer.

Mr. Drew said that he had obtained a postponement of Mr. Billington's trial. "I have some other news, too," he added. "I found out there's no Tripp Brothers Circus listed. Of course that doesn't mean there isn't one. It may be too small and unimportant to be in the police information files."

"I'm sure," Nancy said, "that the whole thing is a cover-up for something sinister."

Bess sighed and changed the subject. "While you were out, Nancy, we had a call from Mrs. Nickerson. Ned and Dave and Burt will be down tomorrow."

Nancy's face broke into a smile. How glad she would be to see Ned! "And it will be great to have him help on the mystery," she thought.

Bess told Nancy that she and George had been busy laundering the girls' clothes, including Nancy's. "So we're all ready for the Nickersons' house party," she told her.

"You were sweet to do that," said Nancy. "Thanks."

She learned that Tina and Antin had the day off, so all the work had fallen on the others.

"Would you mind doing the marketing?" Mrs. Billington asked Nancy. "We need a number of things. Perhaps you three girls could go and divide the shopping list."

"I'd like to," Nancy replied. "By the way, do you have the Websters' new address?"

"No, I'm sorry I don't."

Nancy decided to stop at the post office on the chance she could get it. She said, "Mrs. Billington, I don't trust Mr. Scarlett and I'd like to check his story with the owner."

The girls drove to town and each went in a different direction to buy meat, vegetables, fruits, paper napkins and various other items.

As soon as Nancy finished her shopping, she walked to the post office. There she asked if she might have Mr. Webster's other address, and told why she wanted it.

The postal clerk smiled but said he was not allowed to give out such information. "If you wish to write a letter and mail it, I'll be glad to forward it."

"I'll think about that," Nancy replied and turned away.

A woman who stood nearby had heard the girl's request. Now she came up to her and said, "I'm a friend of Mr. and Mrs. Webster. I know their city address. Would you mind telling me in more detail why you want it?"

Nancy explained the complication about the couple's Merritt Island home and that she wanted to speak directly to Mr. Webster about its being taken off the market.

The woman smiled. She took an address book from her handbag and flipped the pages to W. Then she wrote down the address of her friends, the Websters, and handed it to Nancy.

"Thank you very much," Nancy said. "As soon as I get home, I'll phone them."

As the young detective was about to leave the

post office, she saw something that made her step back quickly. Walking along the street and carrying on an animated conversation were Mr. Scarlett and Mr. Fortin!

"They *are* friends," she decided. "I wish I could hear what they're talking about."

This was not feasible because Scarlett would identify her and tell Fortin. Perhaps Fortin had already described her to Scarlett and he in turn had told who she was!

Nancy waited until the men were out of sight, then went to the Billingtons' car where the girls had arranged to meet. When Bess and George heard about the men, they agreed with Nancy that no doubt she had been identified.

"This means more trouble!" Bess prophesied.

As soon as Nancy reached home she telephoned Mr. Webster long-distance. He answered immediately. Nancy introduced herself and told why she was calling.

"I'm certainly glad you got in touch with me," Mr. Webster said. "I can't understand Mr. Scarlett's actions. He has had no instructions from me to take my Merritt Island house off the market. I'll call him at once and set him straight."

"You may have a hard time finding him," Nancy remarked. "He says he's on vacation, and no one answers the doorbell at his house. However, I've seen him several times. Mr. Scarlett even chased me in his car while I was on my way to the airport to meet my father. He demanded that I return the key which he had lent me."

"You have the key?" Mr. Webster asked. "In that case, you keep it and go into the house as often as you please."

Nancy told him about her experiences at the moss-covered mansion. "Didn't the wild animals bother you?" she asked.

"No. In fact, I doubt they were there then."

Nancy mentioned the friendship between Fortin and Scarlett. Mr. Webster was amazed.

"It certainly sounds as if something phony is going on. I'll give your father a long option on the house and notify Mr. Scarlett he no longer has it on his list."

"That's very generous of you," said Nancy. "My father will be in touch with you."

Mr. Drew and Mr. Billington had gone out again. They did not return until dinnertime that evening.

"I have nothing new to report, Nancy," her father said. "How about you?"

Nancy told him of her telephone talk with Mr. Webster. The lawyer was delighted to hear of the long option on the Webster house. "I know that if the mystery of the moss-covered mansion can be cleared up, you'd like me to buy the place."

His daughter laughed. "I guess I'd like it anyhow, but I admit we'd certainly have strange neighbors."

"Who could be very dangerous," Bess put in.

Suddenly Hannah Gruen said, "Oh, I forgot!"

All eyes turned in her direction. She went on, "There was a personal in today's paper that caught my eye. Using the code words 1, 5, 9, and 13 the message read, 'Beam ready for action.'"

Each one at the table pondered the words. "What do they mean?" George asked. "This message is the hardest one yet."

The others agreed but no one had an interpretation to offer. After dinner Nancy sat down in a big chair in the living room and stared straight ahead of her.

Mr. Drew said, "That brain of yours is cooking up something. How about telling us what it is?"

Nancy told them she had come up with a daring idea to help solve the mystery. "Using the numbered words code, I'll run a personal in Sunday's paper. It will arrange a meeting for the people who are communicating through the personal column."

"That's a clever idea!" her father said. "I wish you luck."

Nancy found a notebook and pencil. She drafted message after message but was not satisfied with any of the combinations of words. The whole sentence must make sense as well as the code words.

Finally the others said good night and went upstairs. An hour later Nancy heard the Resardos' car pull into the driveway.

"Oh dear! I don't want them to see these papers," she thought and quickly gathered them up.

When she reached her room, the young detective sat down to continue her work. Just as sleep was overtaking Nancy, a new idea for the wording of the personal came to her.

"I have it!" she told herself.

CHAPTER XV

Stolen Car

NEXT morning nothing was said about the personal which Nancy wanted to put into the newspaper. The Resardos hung around, so the others kept their conversation to inconsequential matters.

Finally Antin went off to the grove, presumably to see what fruit might still be saleable. Tina was unusually talkative. She assisted with all the work and even offered to help make the beds.

"Thank you but that won't be necessary," Hannah Gruen told her.

She was as eager as the girls to hear what Nancy had worked out on the code message. She kept Mrs. Resardo on the first floor, however, so the rest could go upstairs and talk out of earshot.

They gathered in Nancy's bedroom. Bess, bursting with curiosity, asked, "Nancy, did you finish the coded message?"

"Yes," she replied, and took a sheet of paper from her handbag. The others crowded around to see it.

"Does that sound innocent enough?" she asked her father.

"Very good, my dear," he replied. "I see you have underlined the vital words." He read it aloud:

" *'Meet round ship museum Monday twelve.'* "

"Where is that?" Mr. Drew asked.

Nancy explained it was in Cocoa Beach. "The museum has a replica of one of the Spanish Plate Fleet vessels which went down in 1715 off the coast of Cape Kennedy, then known as Cape Canaveral.

"One of the worst hurricanes on record drove the ships onto the rocks. Nearly everyone on board was drowned. Only one ship escaped and returned to Spain to tell the story."

Mr. Drew nodded. "At that time the Spaniards had conquered the Aztecs in Mexico and were robbing them of all their exquisite gold objects. These in turn were made into Spanish coins and packed in boxes and shipped to Spain."

Mr. Billington added, "Some of this treasure has been salvaged. The museum contains many gold coins and pieces of eight as well as other treasures. You'll be intrigued when you see them."

"Sounds great!" George said. "Nancy, I take it that you hope the coded message will be seen by the men involved in the explosive oranges mystery, and they'll gather outside the museum."

Nancy nodded. "Once we see who they are, we can report them to the authorities."

"That's right," Mr. Drew said. "Don't try capturing them yourself!"

Nancy laughed and said she would like to put the ad in the paper at once. "May I borrow your car?" she asked Mr. Billington.

"Yes indeed."

Mr. Drew smiled. "I have a surprise for you girls. Yesterday I rented a car for you to use during the rest of your stay here. It had to be serviced, so I said you'd pick it up this morning." He took the receipt from his pocket and handed it to Nancy.

"Wonderful, Dad!" she exclaimed, and kissed him. "Thank you loads. George and Bess can bring your car back, Mr. Billington."

"No hurry, Nancy. Your father and I have some work to do here on the case. We'll be around until after lunch."

The three girls left the house and drove directly to the newspaper office. Nancy handed in her coded message for the personal column and paid for it. She was assured it would appear the following day.

As Nancy and the other girls strolled outside, Bess asked, "What's next?"

Nancy said she wanted to tell Mr. Scarlett that

she had Mr. Webster's permission to keep the key, in case the realtor had not already been informed.

"We're not far from his office. Let's see if he's there."

She drove to it but found the door locked. She went to his home. No one answered the doorbell.

A woman in a neighboring yard called out, "The Scarletts aren't here. They drove off early this morning."

"Thank you," Nancy said. "I'll leave a note for Mr. Scarlett."

She took a sheet of paper from her bag and wrote down the message. Then she slipped it through the slot in the front door.

"When do we get our car?" George queried.

"Right now."

Nancy headed for the center of Cocoa Beach and drove to the rental agency. Bess and George waited for her while she went into the office. Nancy showed the receipt and the clerk led her to a parking lot at the back of the building. He pointed out an attractive tan station wagon.

"It looks new," Nancy said, delighted.

"It's practically new," the man told her. "I don't know why the owner wanted to sell it. Normally we don't buy private cars but this was such a good bargain we couldn't pass it up."

Nancy eagerly got behind the wheel and waved to the girls. George started the Billington car and headed for home. Nancy chose a different route.

She was making good time along the highway when suddenly a motorcycle roared up behind her. Riding it was a policeman.

"Pull over!" he ordered. "Let me see your license."

Nancy was sure she had done nothing wrong but did not question the officer. She showed him her license.

"Where did you get this car?" he asked.

Nancy gave the name of the rental agency and showed the receipt. The officer looked at her sharply, then said, "Are you aware you're driving a stolen car?"

The young detective gasped. "I certainly wasn't."

"Follow me!" the motorcycle policeman said. "We'll go back to that agency and see what it's all about."

The man in charge was shocked when he learned about the theft. He assured the policeman he was innocent, and explained that his company had purchased the car from an individual.

"What was his name?" Nancy asked.

"Rimmer," the clerk said. "Robert Rimmer."

The policeman said, "I suggest that you give this young lady another car and a new receipt."

The exchange was made and Nancy went on her way. When she reached home and told about the incident, Hannah Gruen began to laugh. "Nancy

Drew," she said, "it seems as if you can't go any-where without having an adventure."

"But I just love it," Nancy replied with a broad grin. "Dad, have you any news?"

"No, I've been checking to find out if there has been any word on Max Ivanson. It certainly looks as if he's the one who carried the explosive oranges into the Base."

Mr. Billington spoke up. "And there's no clue to who set fire to the packing house and started the blazes in the grove. Ivanson might have done that too."

He added, "I'm well-covered by insurance, but a lot of time will be lost in building up a grove. You can construct a packing house fairly quickly, but you can't make an orange tree grow over-night!"

All this time Tina had been buzzing around, setting the table and going up and down the hall. Nancy suspected that the woman was not missing a word of the conversation.

Presently the Drews and their friends sat down to luncheon. Mrs. Billington asked, "Nancy, what time are the boys arriving?"

"We're to meet them at the airport at four o'clock," she replied. "By the way, we're not offi-cially starting the house party until tomorrow. We girls thought it would be nice to give Ned a chance to visit with his parents before we all move in there. And Mrs. Nickerson agreed."

Soon afterward the girls began their long drive to the Melbourne airport. The plane was on time. Ned was the first of the boys to alight. Seeing Nancy, he rushed up to her.

"How's my little sleuth?" he asked, kissing her.

"I'm fine and have a million things to tell you."

Bess and George had found Dave and Burt. On the way to the Nickersons' the boys plied the girls with questions.

"We're going to start you working on the mystery Monday," Nancy told them. "At noontime we're to station ourselves at the Real Eight Treasure Museum and see if we can spot a few criminals."

"You mean it?" Dave asked.

Nancy explained her plan and the boys were eager to help.

Ned remarked, "Thinking up that coded message was pretty clever, Nancy."

"I only hope it works," she answered.

The boys were dropped off at the Nickerson home. They said they would come over to see the girls after dinner. "Is there some place we could all go and have fun?" Burt asked.

"I have an idea," said Nancy. "The Billingtons have a neat motorboat. Why don't we make use of it?"

"Good idea," Dave remarked. "I'll bring my guitar."

The three boys arrived at eight o'clock. Nearly

an hour was spent talking with Mr. Drew and the Billingtons. Since the Resardos were out, the mystery could be discussed freely.

"It sounds complicated to me," Dave remarked. "I'd like to have some time free from mystery. May we borrow your boat?" Mr. Billington nodded.

"I'll get the *Starbeam's* key," Nancy said. She had noticed it on top of the TV set.

The young people excused themselves and walked down to the dock. Nancy turned on the boathouse lights, then she and her friends climbed into the motorboat.

"Which way?" asked Ned, who had taken the wheel.

Nancy suggested that he turn right and cruise around a while, then come back and go past the Webster property.

Half an hour later they pulled up to the Webster dock. "The house!" Bess exclaimed. "It's all lighted up!"

Everyone was puzzled. Had Mr. Drew stopped in? Or was an intruder there?

"We'd better investigate," Nancy said quickly. "Ned, let's tie up at the dock."

He pulled alongside and the group scrambled out. While the boys secured the boat, the girls ran ahead. They had not gone far into the small orange grove when the lights in the house were extinguished one by one. When the visitors reached the back door, the place was in total darkness.

"Watch to see who comes out," Nancy called to Bess and George. She herself ran around to the front entrance. No one emerged from the house. By this time the boys had caught up.

"Do you suppose someone's hiding in there?" Bess asked Dave.

"Could be," he replied.

Nancy turned to Ned, who had found her. "Will you go back and use the phone in the boat? See if Dad is there and whether he has been here."

Ned hurried off. The others continued to watch the house, but nobody appeared.

Finally Ned returned. "Your father hasn't been here, Nancy," he reported. "But Mr. Drew said he'll be right over."

In a short time the lawyer arrived with Mr. Billington. "Did you bring the Websters' house key, Dad?" Nancy asked.

"No. None of us knew where you had hidden it," he answered.

"In my raincoat pocket," she said. "It's in my closet."

Mr. Drew had brought several flashlights which he distributed among the three couples.

"Let's look through the windows," Nancy suggested, and beamed hers through a front window.

"Oh!" she exclaimed. "The place is flooded with water!"

CHAPTER XVI

Misfit Shoes

"A PIPE must have burst!" Nancy cried out. "Oh dear! I wish I'd brought the key. We must do something fast!"

Mr. Drew decided to break a windowpane and crawl inside the house. Ned offered to do it and Nancy's father nodded.

"But go around to the back where the break won't show," Mr. Drew suggested.

Ned dashed off with the rest of the group following. As if about to punt a football, Ned made a run of several feet, lifted his right foot, and aimed it at a kitchen window.

Crash!

Ned reached inside, opened the latch, and raised the window frame. He pulled himself through the opening and unlocked the rear door. The others trooped inside. Nancy, making sure she was standing in a dry spot, clicked on the kitchen light.

Less than two feet away water was slowly flowing toward her! The faucets in the sink had been turned on full and water was pouring out. It was spilling over the edge and cascading onto the floor. George jumped forward and turned off the faucets.

At once a search for the intruder began. Mr. Drew called out, "Don't touch any switches if you are standing in water!"

"I won't," Bess assured him. "I don't want to be electrocuted."

Water had already flowed into the other first-floor rooms. It was also spilling down the stairway. Burt and Dave rushed up to shut off faucets in the bathrooms.

"Ned, let's look for the main valve and turn off the water," Nancy suggested. "I think it may be in the utility room."

The two dashed into the room adjoining the kitchen. They found that the faucets in a sink and a laundry tub had also been opened. Ned closed them, while Nancy looked for the main valve. She located it and turned off the flow.

When everyone assembled in the living room to compare notes, each declared he had seen no sign of the intruder.

"I guess he escaped by the front door before you got there, Nancy," Burt stated.

Bess gave a great sigh. "I'd say we have an all-night mopping job ahead of us!"

Dave grinned at her. "You forget I'm mop-up man for the Emerson football team. It won't take long. Let's go!"

Every broom, mop, and rag in the house was put to use. George and Burt found a couple of electric fans and plugged them in.

"Operation Dry-out is in good hands," Mr. Drew said with a grin.

He and Mr. Billington returned home ahead of the young people. The front light was on. As the two men walked up to the door, Mr. Drew bent down and picked up a shiny object.

"What is it?" Mr. Billington asked.

"A key. Someone must have dropped it."

Mr. Billington took the key. "This isn't ours," he said. "Why, look, it has the letter W cut into it."

"W?" Mr. Drew repeated. "Do you suppose it could stand for Webster? Maybe this is the key Nancy hid. Someone may have stolen it, then had no opportunity to replace the key, so he left it here."

When the men entered the house, Mr. Drew told Hannah Gruen about the find.

"That's strange," she said. "Nobody has come here this evening except the Resardos and they've been in their room all the time."

"Nancy hid the Webster key in her raincoat pocket," Mr. Drew remarked.

"I'll get it," Hannah offered.

Mrs. Gruen was gone only a couple of minutes, then returned holding the key. They compared it with the one Mr. Drew had found. It matched exactly.

"Queer things happen everyday," Hannah remarked. "I wonder what will be next."

Mr. Drew did not answer. He went to the telephone and spoke to the police captain about the flooded house and the key he had found on the doorstep. The officer promised to send a couple of men to the Webster house immediately.

Over at the soaking wet home the mopping-up operation was almost finished.

Nancy and Ned searched the house but found no clues to the intruder. While they were still hunting, the police car came in. Nancy spoke to the two men.

"The intruder must have had a key to this house," she said.

The police identified themselves as Needham and Welsh. They told of Mr. Drew's having found a key with a W on it near the Billingtons' front steps. Nancy and Ned looked at each other. Had Scarlett dropped it—or perhaps Antin?

As she and Ned walked to the rear of the house with the two officers, Nancy beamed her flashlight toward the river.

Suddenly she exclaimed, "I see some shoe prints!"

They stepped forward to examine them. "The

guy sure has big feet," Needham commented. "I think we should take plaster impressions of these." He requested his partner to drive back to head-quarters for the equipment.

Nancy knelt on the ground and examined the prints, which went toward the water. Did she imagine it or were they wobbly looking as if the person was unsteady on his feet?

"Or," Nancy thought, "did the intruder de-liberately put on shoes much bigger than his feet to disguise his size? He even took long strides and that too could account for the wobbliness."

She and Ned and Officer Needham followed the prints. Possibly the vandal had hidden a small boat among the bushes along the shore. The three made a thorough search but the only boat around was the Billingtons'.

The officer stopped to look at it. "She's a beauty!" he said. "It's a good thing that intruder didn't help himself to it!"

"It's locked," Ned said, "and I have the key in my pocket. Apparently the vandal escaped in his own boat."

By the time the searchers had returned to the house, Officer Welsh had come back with the plaster cast kit. While he was working, Nancy and Ned took his partner through the house, pointing out the damage.

The officer made a lot of notes and said the case would be put on the police blotter at once and a search started for a tall man with long feet. Nancy mentioned her own theory about his wearing over-size shoes and Needham was impressed.

"That's an idea," he said. "I'll jot it down."

Just then Officer Welsh came in. He said he had completed his work and if Needham was ready they might as well leave. House lights were turned off and the front door slammed shut.

As Nancy and her friends trudged through the orange grove and down to the river, Burt remarked, "We boys didn't have to wait long after our arrival for some excitement."

"It always happens," Bess added. "I vote that for the rest of the evening we forget about detective work."

She had hardly said this when George and Burt, who had started ahead, cried out in dismay.

"Our boat's gone!" George exclaimed.

The others ran to the dock. They could not believe their eyes. Mr. Billington's motorboat had been securely tied and Ned had locked the motor.

"There's only one way it could have been taken," Nancy spoke up. "It was towed away!"

"By whom?" Dave asked.

No one had an answer. A few seconds later Bess gave one of her great sighs. "It's a long trek from here to the Billingtons' house."

"It sure is," George agreed, "but let's get started."

Nancy said, "You all go and ask Mr. Billington

to call the police about the stolen boat. Ned and I will stay here a while. I want to hunt for clues to the thief."

The other four hurried off. With her flashlight Nancy searched for footprints.

"Here they are!" she cried gleefully. "The thief was the same person who was up at the house!"

Ned looked at her, puzzled. "But how could he have been? We were down here after he'd gone and our boat was still at the dock."

Nancy pointed out that the man could have towed the boat away when the police and everyone else were in the house.

"Or he might have been hiding up the shore a distance and a pal came to pick him up. Together they tied Mr. Billington's craft to a motorboat and went off."

Just then they heard a motorboat in midstream. "Let's hail it!" she said. "Maybe the pilot passed our boat."

Ned shouted lustily. The pilot heard him and slowed his motor. He steered for the Webster dock and called out, "Somebody need help?"

Quickly Ned explained. The pilot said he had not seen the stolen craft, but added, "How about hopping in here and we'll look for it?"

Nancy and Ned did not need a second invitation. As soon as the motorboat pulled up to the dock, they climbed in.

CHAPTER XVII

Tear Gas

NED introduced Nancy and himself. Their teen-age pilot said his name was Bud Musgrove. As his small motorboat sped along, they looked into every cove and indentation of the river, going up one side, then starting down the other. So far there had been no sign of the Billingtons' craft.

"I'm sorry," Bud said. "You say you have the key to the motor, Ned. Then the person who took your boat might have known about it and has a duplicate. Have you any idea who he is?"

Instantly Nancy thought of Antin, but said nothing. Was he accustomed to borrowing the craft whenever he pleased?

She asked herself, But why should he have gone to the Webster home? As Nancy was trying to puzzle this out, Ned suddenly exclaimed, "I think I see our boat! Over there at that rickety old dock."

Bud headed for the spot. A house on the property had burned down. The area was secluded.

"It's a good place for someone to hide a stolen boat," Nancy thought. "And for a thief to hide too!" Aloud she said, "Cut the motor! Quick!"

Bud obeyed. In the sudden silence Nancy spoke softly. "The thief may be hiding there, too. Let's go quietly and take him by surprise!"

The momentum of the craft carried it along quietly as Bud steered toward the dock. He pulled alongside the stolen boat.

"No one's in it," Ned announced. He looked around. "I guess this has been abandoned." He pulled the key from his pocket and jumped in.

Nancy was about to follow, but Bud held her back. "Better wait and see if the *Starbeam* starts."

Ned turned on the motor but there was not a sound. He tried again and again without result.

"That thief probably tampered with the boat and now it won't run," Nancy remarked. "Is the motor warm?"

"No," Ned replied, "so the *Starbeam* must have been towed here."

Bud jumped into the craft and together he and Ned examined the engine while Nancy beamed a searchlight on it.

Finally Bud said, "Several parts are missing. You won't be able to run this boat until they're replaced. I'll tell you what. Let's tie it to the back of my motorboat and I'll tow you home."

"Great! Thanks," Ned replied.

When they arrived at the Billingtons' dock Nancy invited Bud to come in.

The young man smiled. "Sorry, but I'm supposed to be on my way to a party. My date will think I've fazed her out."

The group at the house was amazed when they heard Nancy and Ned's story. Mr. Billington called the police to report that the boat had been found.

He said to the others, "I'm certainly burdening the authorities lately. We make at least one call a day to the police!"

Everyone smiled and Nancy thought, "We've come up with a few clues for them, too!"

Bess told Ned that his mother had phoned and was preparing a midnight snack for the young people. She was hoping the girls would move over there at once to start the house party officially.

"I'm all for that," Bess added, "Tonight's adventures have given me a tremendous appetite."

George teased her cousin. "You'd have had an appetite without any adventures."

The three girls hurried upstairs and packed the clothes they would need for the next few days. When they were ready to leave, Nancy promised her father she would keep in touch with him and the Billingtons to exchange news about the case. Mr. Drew said he would contact Mr. Webster and tell him of the vandalism.

"I'll ask him if he wants to have someone in town take care of it or if he'd like me to."

As he kissed his daughter good night, Mr. Drew wished her luck in getting results on Monday to her personal advertisement.

"Maybe you'll find out who the members of the gang are. Anyway, my dear, watch your step."

Nancy and Ned rode in the rented car, while the others took the Nickersons'. Despite the fact that the official opening of the house party lasted until almost two o'clock, none of the young people slept late the next morning.

After they had attended church services, Dave suggested that the whole group take a tour of the Space Center that afternoon. The others agreed.

Nancy was just as intrigued by her second visit to the Base as she had been before. The boys were especially fascinated by the rocket soon to lift off for the moon.

George, who had been silent for several minutes, said, "I'd like to be an astronaut. What do you think my chances are?"

"Oh no!" Bess exclaimed. "Suppose you went to the moon and got stranded there!"

Smiling, Nancy remarked that she too would like to become an astronaut.

Ned grinned and said, "How about letting us boys go first? We'll tell you how it is."

The bus driver, who had overheard the conversation, seemed to be amused. He turned slightly and said, "You boys had better get started on your training. While you're here, why not go for a physical checkup and briefing?"

"Great!" Burt replied with a wink.

George leaned forward in her seat. "What about me? Could I get the same treatment?"

"I think so," the driver answered, grinning broadly.

The others looked at Nancy. "How about you?" Ned asked.

"Perhaps," she replied, knowing they were kidding her. "After this case is over."

In a short time the bus reached the Vehicle Assembly Building. The tourists went inside. They were told about the immense structure and what took place there.

Then the guide said, "The space vehicle that will lift-off for the moon Tuesday was transported from here to its launch pad several weeks ago."

Nancy and her friends were the first to leave the building. They wanted to get a better view of the huge spaceship.

As they were coming out the door, two men, heavily bearded, came up to them. "Pardon me," said one. "We're doing an article on the moon flight for a science magazine. Would you mind if

we take your picture, and quote what we overheard you say on the bus about wanting to be
astronauts?"

The six young people looked at one another but
did not answer.

"Over here," said the second man who had a
large camera. "We won't use your names."

He led the way around the corner to the side of
the building away from the tourists.

"I guess there's no harm in it," Ned whispered
to Nancy.

She nodded and followed the two men down
the far side of the building. While one arranged
the group against the wall with the girls in front,
the other man focused his camera.

"All ready," he said.

His companion dashed out of the way and the
photographer clicked his camera. Instantly a
stream of tear gas shot toward them. Nancy and
her friends tried to run, but their eyes began to
smart and they could not see.

In the distance the guide was calling out, "All
aboard!"

Nancy heard running footsteps and assumed
their attackers had fled. As the fog of tear gas dis-
sipated, Nancy was able to see dimly, but not well
enough to move very fast for fear of bumping into
something. She realized, however, that a man was
coming toward her.

He proved to be one of the guards from the

A stream of tear gas shot toward them

Vehicle Assembly Building. Rushing up, he asked, "What happened?"

Nancy choked out the answer. "Tear gas! Two men with beards. One man had a camera that shot the stuff at us."

"Follow me!" the guard said. "We'll give you something to soothe your eyes."

"My friends too!" Nancy told him.

She could vaguely make out the rest of her group. Nancy called to them to follow her.

By the time they reached the front door of the Vehicle Assembly Building, the bus had gone. Nancy said there was a chance the attackers were on it.

"Hadn't you better phone the Visitors Center and have the bus checked?" she asked the guard.

"I'll do that at once—that is, as soon as I find someone to take care of your eyes."

Suddenly Nancy remembered the young engineer who was a relative of Hannah Gruen's. She asked, "Is Herb Baylor around? I know him."

"I'll get him," the man promised, and hurried off.

When Herb Baylor saw Nancy and the rest of the group and heard what had happened, he instantly took them to the infirmary where a young doctor gave them first aid. He put a few drops of a soothing solution in their eyes which soon relieved the burning sensation.

There was a knock on the door and the same

guard walked in. He was holding two wigs with beards attached and a box camera. "I found these at the side of the building," he said.

Nancy gasped. "The men who used the tear gas must have been wearing them!"

Ned added, "Now we can't describe those villains and they'll get away easily!"

"Too bad," Herb remarked. "What was their motive?"

George answered, "To scare us into dropping our detective work. But they can't do it!"

CHAPTER XVIII

A Ruse Works

HERB Baylor thought Nancy and her friends should return to the Nickersons at once. "Take it easy," he advised.

The young people were glad to and went to bed early. By morning everyone felt fine. A few hours later they set off for the Real Eight Museum of Sunken Treasure, reaching Cocoa Beach by five to twelve. Quickly Ned parked out of sight of the front entrance. Nancy and her friends took up positions behind posts on the covered patio of the octagonal-shaped building.

Exactly at twelve o'clock a car pulled in near the entrance. A few moments later a second one drew up behind it. Then a third and a fourth automobile stopped. A man got out of each car and the four assembled on the broad walk leading to the building.

Nancy's heart was pounding. One of the men was Scarlett, another was Antin!

"So Antin *is* one of the gang," she thought.

There was a heavy-set stranger. "That must be Max Ivanson!" Nancy decided. "He looks very much like that photograph I saw."

The last person to come toward the building was a young man.

Nancy thought, "Could he be the 'son' in the personals? His face looks familiar. Why do I think I know him?" Then it suddenly dawned on her. He strongly resembled Mr. Fortin, the owner of the moss-covered mansion.

The men came closer and then stopped to talk. Nancy could hear them plainly. Each inquired about who had written the personal in Sunday's paper. When all of them denied having done it, looks of fright spread over the men's faces.

"I'll bet the FBI found out about our code," said the heavy-set man. "I'm leaving!"

He ran to his car and the others fled to theirs. Moments later they roared off.

"Shall I chase any of them?" Ned asked.

Nancy replied, "Try Ivanson."

Ned and Burt rushed off and soon were out of sight.

Meanwhile Nancy had raced inside the museum to telephone her father. She paid the admission fee and dashed into a booth. Mr. Drew was astounded at what Nancy had discovered.

"I'll inform the police of this development," he told her. "They will certainly question Antin and search his room. I'll also clue the authorities in on who the other men are that may be responsible for the explosive oranges."

Nancy had remembered to jot down the license numbers of the men's cars and now gave these to her father. "Good work!" he said.

When Nancy emerged from the phone booth, Dave and the other girls stood waiting and demanded to know what was going on. In whispers she told them.

"Oh, Nancy," said Bess, "you've all but solved the case!"

Nancy did not think so. George was eager to go to the Billington house to learn the climax.

"But we have no car," Nancy replied. "We don't know when the boys will be back. Meanwhile, since we've all paid our admission, let's look at the exhibits."

A young woman came up to them and said, "You forgot to take your tapes and earphones. The tapes tell you all about the exhibits. Start on the left."

They went back to a counter where she handed each of them one of the little boxes to hold. They plugged in the tiny earphones. The tour began.

In the center of the room stood a replica of one of the ships dashed to pieces on the Florida coast in 1715. The old-time vessel had sailed entirely under canvas and for this reason was no match for a violent tropical storm.

Around the circular wall was a panorama of the history of cargo carried aboard these Spanish vessels that sailed between the homeland and the New World. The treasures on display were from ten of the eleven vessels in the ill-fated Plate Fleet.

As Nancy listened to the tape she learned that the Spaniards had subdued the Aztec Indians and made slaves of many of them. They were forced to work their gold and silver mines and fashion the metal into Spanish coins, jewelry, and other objects. Overseers were often cruel and the slaves worked long hours.

Other scenes showed gold ingots being packed into boxes, and gold and silver coins in others. Moving on, Nancy and her friends listened carefully to the running account on their tape recorders. Many of the objects on exhibit, such as sabers and sword handles, dishes and bracelets, were encrusted with coral.

Nancy found Bess rooted to one of the glass cases. "Isn't that pathetic?" she asked, pointing to a small wedding ring imbedded in coral. "It's so little a tiny woman must have worn it. Maybe she was the wife of one of the captains."

George walked up. She had heard Bess's remark and said, "I can't find much sympathy for those people. They were just plain thieves."

Nancy commented, "They certainly ruined the

Aztec civilization, which in many respects was far above that of their conquerors."

Before leaving the museum, Nancy and her friends went into the gift shop. The articles for sale fascinated them. Everyone bought pieces of jewelry made from gold or silver dug from the bottom of the ocean.

Nancy purchased a lovely necklace of pieces-of-eight coins for her Aunt Eloise in New York. She decided on a bracelet made of silver coins for Mrs. Billington, and a large piece-of-eight pin for Hannah Gruen.

After the young people had looked at everything in the shop, they left the building. Ned and Burt were just returning.

"Any luck?" George asked.

"No," Ned answered. "All the men disappeared in the next town. We couldn't find them or their cars."

"Let's go home," Nancy urged.

Bess insisted that they eat lunch before going to the Billingtons'. The boys found a lunch stand. Everybody was ravenously hungry except Nancy. She tried to hide the fact that her curiosity was getting the better of her but her friends sensed it.

"I'll eat this hamburger as fast as I can," Bess told her.

Nancy laughed. "Don't get indigestion!"

She ordered a lobster-salad sandwich and declared it was the best she had ever eaten.

"No dessert!" Ned spoke up. "I know Nancy's itching to leave and I am too!"

When they pulled into the driveway of the Billington home, a police car was there. Nancy and her friends hurried into the house.

There was wild confusion in the living room. Tina was screaming at a policeman that her husband was innocent of any wrongdoing. Antin was shouting that he was the victim of a frame-up.

At that moment a policeman and an FBI agent came down the stairs. The FBI man was carrying a bomb which he said had not yet been activated. The officer held supplies used in constructing homemade bombs. Nancy and her friends were told that Tina and Antin were attempting to move their possessions out when the officers arrived.

After advising the couple of their constitutional rights, the agent asked, "Mr. and Mrs. Resardo, if you're innocent, how do you account for these things?"

Instead of replying, the couple tried to make a dash for the front door. They were quickly stopped and brought back, but refused to admit anything.

Nancy whispered to the detective, "May I ask the prisoners a question?"

"Yes, go ahead. But of course they don't have to answer without having their own lawyer present."

The young detective looked directly at the Resardos. "Who set the fire in Mr. Billington's grove?" There was no response.

She tried another approach. "Is Max Ivanson a pal of yours?"

This question startled the Resardos, but they remained silent. Seconds later the prisoners were taken to jail.

Hannah Gruen gave a great sigh. "I'm glad they're gone," she said. "Imagine their making bombs right in this house!"

"Please don't talk about it!" Bess begged. "It makes chills go up and down my spine."

She wandered outdoors, more upset than she wished to admit. Dave had followed her and suggested that they all do something pleasant and get away from the mystery for a while.

"Like what?" she asked.

Dave thought for a moment, then said, "How about going to the Webster house to see if it has dried out yet?"

Bess liked this idea and so did the others. They climbed into the rented car and Ned slid into the driver's seat.

When they reached the Webster place, Burt said, "We couldn't see much of the grounds in the dark last night. Let's walk around now."

The boys were intrigued by the unusual trees in the garden, particularly the sausage tree. Everyone went over to it.

Suddenly they heard snarling in the jungle on

the other side of the fence. The young people shrank back just as the leopard came running from the direction of the cages.

"He's loose again!" Bess cried out.

Directly behind the animal was Longman with his whip. He kept snapping it against the ground and shouting to the beast. The leopard paid no attention. Snarling and hissing, the agile beast climbed the fence.

The next moment he made a flying leap across it and landed in the sausage tree next to the young people.

CHAPTER XIX

The Mansion's Secret

BRANCHES of the sausage tree broke from the leopard's weight. They crashed to the ground, together with several of the hard, twelve-inch melons.

Screaming, Bess dashed toward the Webster house. She kept urging the others to follow her. "Run! Run!"

Longman, on the other side of the high fence, seemed stunned for a couple of seconds. Then he cried out, "Catch this and slash that beast!" He tossed the whip to the boys.

Nancy, to avoid being recognized by the animal trainer, turned and ran to the house. In the meantime Burt and Dave had each grabbed a broken branch with the heavy sausage-shaped fruit and were ready to ward off the animal if he should attack.

As Ned caught the whip, he yelled to Nancy and

George, "Open the garage door! We'll chase the leopard in there!"

This was easier said than done. At first the leopard refused to come down from the tree. Then, responding to Longman's commands, he made a great leap toward the fence, but missed it and dropped to the ground.

Ned cracked the whip in the air and on the ground. The beast started to make another leap, then stopped. Lowering his head, he looked balefully at Burt and Dave and crouched as if about to spring at them. The two boys waved their tree-branch clubs in the air. By now the leopard was thoroughly confused.

With Ned working the whip and his friends flourishing their fruit-laden branches, the frightened beast was finally driven into the garage. Quickly George and Nancy yanked down the door.

Inside, the leopard set up a fearful racket. Above the loud snarls, the young people heard Longman call, "Keep him there! I'll get my van!"

While they were waiting for the trainer to come, an idea suddenly came to Nancy. She said to Ned, "This is our chance to get into the basement of the moss-covered mansion and find out what's behind the steel door. Will you go with me?"

Ned's eyes opened wide in amazement. "You mean ride in the van with the leopard?"

"Of course not," Nancy answered. "After the

animal is inside and Longman is in the driver's seat, you and I can quickly climb up to the roof of the van and lie flat. He won't know we're there and we can get off before he opens the van door."

Ned replied, "You know you're taking a terrible chance, Nancy. But I'm game to go with you."

To the surprise of everyone, Bess came speeding up the driveway in their car. They had assumed she was in the house.

She jumped out and said excitedly, "I brought some meat with a tranquilizer in it."

"You what?" George asked.

Bess explained that she had noticed a doctor's sign on a house in the next block. She had driven over there and explained to him what had happened. He could not come himself but had given her the chunk of raw meat with a tranquilizer pill imbedded in it.

The others stared at her in amazement. Finally Nancy said, "That's wonderful, Bess. It was quick thinking."

Dave took the chunk of meat. As the others carefully lifted the garage door a couple of inches, he poked the food inside. Then the door was shut tight again.

The enraged animal apparently sniffed at the meat, then ate it, because for a few minutes there was silence. Again he began to howl objections, but this time they did not last long.

"Bess, you're the heroine of the occasion!"

George told her cousin. She grinned. "And you know I don't say that often."

The others laughed, heaving sighs of relief. When they saw Longman's van coming, Nancy and Ned moved to another side of the house, so she would not be seen by the animal trainer. Bess and George followed.

As he jumped down, Burt told him that they had tranquilized his leopard. He looked at the boy disbelievingly. "How?" he asked.

Burt explained what Bess had done. "That tranquilizer should keep your animal quiet for a while."

"Very good." Longman looked around and asked, "Where are your friends?"

No one answered his question. But Dave said quickly, "Let's get to work. You'd better move the leopard to your place before the tranquilizer wears off."

"That's right," said Longman, and opened the rear door of his van.

The young people saw that a cage had been fitted inside. Longman opened the gate to it.

Burt and Dave rolled up the garage door gradually, in case the leopard was not asleep as they thought. This precaution was unnecessary, for the beast lay peacefully on the floor. It took the combined strength of Longman and the two boys to lift the leopard into the van. Then the cage gate and the van door were locked. The animal trainer murmured something that sounded like "thanks," and swung himself up into the driver's seat.

Instantly Nancy and Ned came from hiding. In a jiffy they had climbed to the van's roof and lay face down. By holding onto each other with one hand and grabbing bars along the sides with the other, the couple felt reasonably secure. Silently their friends watched them leave, hoping for safety and success.

Fortunately there was no one on the road to observe the two stowaways. The van turned into the grounds of the moss-covered mansion. When it reached the fence at the house, Longman got down and unlocked a gate. Then he drove through. The gate swung shut and locked itself.

Nancy saw a clump of bushes which would make a good hiding place. She whispered to Ned, "Here's where we get off."

The van was going so slowly toward the animal cages that the couple accomplished this easily without being injured. Instantly they dodged behind some bushes.

After Longman had unloaded the leopard, he secured the beast's cage with a double lock. Then he drove off.

"Now what?" Ned asked Nancy.

"I'm sure there's an outside entrance to the basement," she said. "Let's see if we can get in."

Luck was with them. They found a narrow door on the opposite side of the house. It was unlocked!

"Someone may be in there!" Ned cautioned in a whisper. "Let me go first."

Carefully he pushed the door open. It made no sound. The couple stepped inside. They were in the large basement room where Nancy had come with Inspector Wilcox.

The first thing she noticed was that all the debris had been moved away from the walls. Several doors were revealed. On tiptoe she and Ned walked toward the first one and Ned opened it. The place was well lighted and before them was a swimming pool filled with steaming, boiling water!

Nancy and Ned looked questioningly at each other. What was the pool used for? they wondered. Ned quickly closed the door. They moved to the steel door where the load of furniture had fallen on Nancy two days earlier.

In the room beyond, also well lighted, was an amazing laboratory. A complicated-looking machine with a dish-shaped parabolic reflector stood in the center of the floor. It faced the outside wall, which was made of glass building blocks.

"What is it?" Nancy whispered.

Ned walked around the machine, squinting at the various parts. He came back to Nancy and said, "Unless I'm all wrong, it's a very powerful transmitting antenna—a beamer."

"You mean some kind of signal is sent out from down here?" Nancy asked.

"Yes," Ned replied. "The telescope you told me about that's in the tower may act as a sighting device. It could locate the exact bearing and elevation of an object to be destroyed by the beamer."

Nancy was horrified. The telescope was aimed directly at the rocket scheduled for lift-off the next morning. She also thought about Antin's phone message regarding R-day. Instead of meaning Ruth, it could have referred to Rocket day.

"Ned," she said quickly, "would you know how to deactivate this machine?"

"I can try," he said. "But Fortin would have time to fix it before the launch."

"Meanwhile we could send the police here," Nancy told him.

Ned found some tools on a workbench near a series of wall cabinets. He worked with the tools for several minutes.

Presently she and Ned heard voices. To their amazement they were coming through a loud-speaker in the ceiling.

While listening, Nancy felt that no doubt Fortin, if it was necessary, could barricade himself in the laboratory and listen to conversations taking place upstairs. It would be a means of finding out how trustworthy his fellow conspirators were.

The couple recognized two voices as those of the tear-gas assailants at the Space Center. Nancy and Ned learned that Fortin was a clever and well-known scientist who had once been connected with NASA. He had become imbued with the ideology of a foreign power and was now using an assumed name.

He had entered into a conspiracy to undermine the U. S. space program and had agreed to cause great damage at the Center and to wreck the moon rocket. To accomplish this he had a spy working with the men in top-secret procedures. From this traitor Fortin had obtained the secret signals for the exact frequency and modulation for lift-off. In this way he could set his beamer to destroy the rocket.

Nancy whispered tensely to Ned, "He'll be murdering the astronauts!"

Just then Fortin spoke up. "Scarlett," he said, "I'm paying you off but not so much as I promised if you had done a good job."

Scarlett whined, "I did the best I could. I discouraged people from looking at the Webster house, but when Nancy Drew arrived, she was determined to see it. I pretended to go on vacation but she found me. I flooded the place to keep the Drews away, but she discovered it in time to avert any great damage."

"That's enough," said Fortin. "Ivanson, you certainly bungled that explosive orange deal. You were supposed to put those oranges around in strategic spots, so the lift-off would be delayed until my beamer was perfected. Luckily I have it ready in time."

Ivanson said belligerently, "You don't know what it feels like passing yourself off as somebody else even if I look like him. Fortunately they didn't examine the oranges while I was there. I guess Billington delivers lots of oranges to the Base, and since I had his truck, they must have thought the delivery was all right. I had no chance to drive around, though. A guard got aboard and directed me to the Space Center food supply depot and made me leave the sacks there."

"Here's your money," said Fortin. "Get out of here and never let me see you again."

A younger voice spoke. "Dad, I want to leave and go far away. I'm through!"

Fortin laughed. "You couldn't take care of yourself, son. You haven't been able to hold a job. I kept you away from here and even forbade phone calls so you wouldn't be involved if anything went wrong. You did think up that great father-son code but that backfired. We don't know yet who figured it out. But you came here to hide in case it was the FBI."

Young Fortin was not to be put down so easily. "If you expect me to stay, you've got to get rid of every one of those wild animals. You know they scare me to death."

Longman shot back, "We need those wild animals here to protect us."

"What's the latest news on Antin?" Fortin asked.

His son replied that a newscast had reported both the Resardos were in jail.

"What!" the scientist shouted. "There's no telling what they'll say to the authorities!"

"I can assure you," said one of the tear-gas attackers, "they won't talk. I made it pretty plain that if they ever did, their lives wouldn't be worth a nickel. And don't forget, boss, the Resardos did some good work. They stole those photographs and passed them around to us so we'd recognize Mr. Drew and the girls and their boy friends.

"Antin found out where they were going so we could watch them. Stevie here and I fooled them completely at the Vehicle Assembly Building and knocked them out with tear gas."

During the ensuing conversation Nancy and Ned learned that it was Max Ivanson who had started the fires in the Billington grove.

"Another stupid idea," complained Fortin.

Ivanson defended his actions. "I thought Drew would get scared and send his daughter and her friends home, but nothing shakes that bunch loose."

Scarlett grumbled, "Until Nancy Drew came along, we had the charge of the explosive oranges pinned neatly on Billington."

Nancy whispered to Ned, "I think we'd better go before some of those men come down here. Besides, we should notify the authorities at once!"

The two tiptoed to the door through which they

had entered. They were taken aback when the huge form of Longman appeared in the opening.

"You!" he cried and reached up to push a button on the wall. An alarm sounded upstairs.

"Let us out!" Ned demanded.

The towering Longman looked at the couple in amusement. "We have a special treatment for snoopers."

Nancy and Ned tried to break past him, but his huge, powerful body blocked the doorway like a stone wall.

Within seconds footsteps pounded down the stairway from the kitchen. Fortin appeared, leading the rest of his gang.

He glared at Nancy. "So you finally found out my secret. But you won't have a chance to tell anyone else. Ivanson, you and Stevie take these young detectives,"—he sneered—"and put them in the room with the steaming pool!"

CHAPTER XX

Countdown

EXERTING every bit of resistance they could, Nancy and Ned tried to escape from their captors. But their efforts were futile. They were shoved toward the room with the boiling pool and put inside.

"That's what happens to snoopers!" Fortin shouted excitedly. "I won't be thwarted in what I intend to do!"

The heavy door was swung shut and locked. The captured couple was forced to hug the wall since the ledge around the water was only six inches wide.

"Oh, Ned, I'm so sorry," Nancy said. "It's all my fault. I never should have asked you to come to this place with me."

"I certainly wouldn't have let you come alone," he replied. "Let's not give up hope of rescue."

Nancy nodded. Surely as soon as their friends realized Nancy and Ned had been gone too long, they would make a search.

"Only I hope they won't be captured as we were!" she worried.

Nancy and Ned tried changing their positions but almost tumbled into the water. To keep their balance they stood as straight and immovable as wooden soldiers.

"Something's got to break soon!" Ned remarked. "Maybe some of our captors will be afraid of a worse charge if they're arrested and the authorities find us in this pool. One of them may open the door."

No one did, however. Nancy and Ned assumed the men had left the basement. As the couple shifted their gaze, they noticed two tiny barred openings in the walls near the ceiling. One evidently admitted fresh air from the outside, the other from the basement.

Meanwhile, back at the Webster house the other young people were becoming more and more alarmed about their missing friends. Burt and Dave paced up and down the front yard. Bess nervously rumpled her hair, then smoothed it out and in a few seconds repeated the operation.

Finally George burst out, "We've got to do something! I just know Nancy and Ned were caught in a trap!"

The rest agreed. "We've waited long enough," said Burt.

Bess offered to drop the others off at the moss-

covered mansion. "I'll drive over to the Nickersons and get help."

When they reached the entrance, George and
the two boys got out of the car and set off along
the winding road that led through the jungle.
They listened and watched carefully.

"Do we dare pound on the door?" George asked.

Both boys vetoed this idea. "We'd surely be
captured," Dave replied.

By this time Bess had reached the Nickersons.
When Ned's father heard her story, he immediately rushed to the telephone. First he called Mr.
Drew and Mr. Billington, who notified NASA
headquarters. He reported the group's suspicions
regarding the activities of the occupants in the
moss-covered mansion, and the disappearance of
Nancy and Ned.

"We'll send men at once," the man at NASA
promised.

Mr. Billington telephoned the local police, who
also said they would rush to the suspected house
immediately.

Twenty minutes later, just as Nancy and Ned
felt completely discouraged, they heard a loud
commotion outside.

"Open up!" came a shout.

The couple heard no reply, but moments later
there was a stampede of footsteps on the stairway
to the basement. Fortin's voice rang out, "Police!

NASA agents! FBI! Open the secret lock, Longman! Let the animals loose!"

The pounding on the front door became more insistent and a voice cried out, "Open in the name of the law!" Inside the house the two dogs were barking madly.

The noise, coupled with Fortin's orders to release the wild animals, made chills go up and down the spines of Nancy and Ned.

"This is horrible!" she wailed.

Her remark was followed by screams from outside the house. Then came a roar. Had the animals attacked the law-enforcement men?

Suddenly there was silence in the basement. Moments later a voice called out, "Nancy! Ned! Where are you?"

Mr. Drew!

"Oh, Dad," Nancy cried out, "open the door that's below the vent near the ceiling."

Within seconds the heavy door was unlocked and opened. Nancy and Ned had inched along the ledge of the steaming pool and now literally fell into the arms of their waiting friends.

Bess gave a scream of horror. "Oh, you might have fallen into the boiling water!"

Nancy and Ned were pretty shaken by their experience, but recovered in a few minutes.

"Who's with you?" Nancy asked.

"FBI and NASA men and the police," George replied.

Quickly the couple reported what they had overheard before being captured. "I think I've deactivated the machine in the laboratory, but a NASA expert had better check," Ned said.

He walked over to open the heavy steel door to the laboratory. It would not budge. They all looked for a way to unlock it but could not find any.

"Let's go upstairs," Mr. Billington suggested. "I want to see what's happening."

They hurried to the kitchen and watched from a window. There was a great deal of excitement on the grounds of the moss-covered mansion. Tranquilizer guns were being used on the escaping animals. Finally all of them quieted.

Longman came from the house with a policeman and one by one they dragged the beasts into their cages, then locked the gates. Looking around furtively, Longman tried to escape but was caught and taken indoors.

The Drews and their friends found that the suspects, handcuffed, had been herded into the living room. Nancy and Ned were asked to come forward and tell the officers what they knew.

Before beginning, Nancy looked over the assembled crowd. Fortin was missing!

"The ringleader—the scientist—isn't here!" she exclaimed.

Nancy was assured that the man could not have left the house because it had been surrounded.

"Then I believe he's hiding in his laboratory," she stated.

Nancy led the NASA and FBI men downstairs, while the police stayed to guard the other prisoners. Engineers from the Space Center tried to unlock the steel door but concluded it must be fastened inside.

Nancy and Ned pleaded with them to break in. "I tried to deactivate the beamer that's going to destroy the rocket," he said, "but I can't be sure I was successful."

One FBI man suggested that they use a steel drill, but a NASA engineer said, "No. Vibrations might set off the beamer."

Nancy caught her breath. Suppose Fortin had decided not to wait until the next day to use his nefarious machine! He might blow up the rocket at any minute!

Quickly she told about the telescope in the tower which she and Ned believed was part of Fortin's setup.

Ned added, "Perhaps it's a sighting device to locate the exact bearing and elevation so Fortin can aim the parabolic reflector antenna in his workshop."

"We'll go right up there," one engineer stated. He and the two FBI men hurried to the third floor.

Meanwhile, the other NASA man put a radiation detector against the steel door. The results were negative.

Nancy and Ned returned to the living room. The saboteurs waived their constitutional rights to have a lawyer present and confessed their guilt. All were taken to jail except Longman.

"He will remain here with two detectives until the authorities can make arrangements for the wild animals to be moved," said one of the policemen.

The trainer told them he had become involved in Fortin's sabotage plan after forging the scientist's name on some bank checks. To avoid arrest, he had acceded to Fortin's demands that he care for the animals and keep intruders away.

"Fortin is a brilliant man," Longman went on as the other prisoners were led off. "But Fortin became obsessed with some dangerous political ideas and joined a radical group. I'm glad he's going to be prevented from doing the terrible thing he planned."

George asked Longman about the boiling pool. "Did Fortin build it?"

"Yes. It was one of his cruel ideas to dispose of intruders in case his animals didn't get them."

The trainer was questioned about how the authorities could get into the laboratory but he declared he did not know. They also asked him if Fortin could destroy the rocket from his basement laboratory. Again Longman insisted he did not know.

Guards were left at the moss-covered mansion inside and out. Two FBI agents had been stationed in the basement. Periodically they tried to persuade Fortin to give himself up but there was no response from inside the laboratory.

The Drews and their friends had mixed feelings about the mystery. It had been solved, but the instigator of the dreadful plot might still be able to destroy the rocket and possibly the three astronauts as well.

When they reached the Nickerson home, the young people were bombarded with questions by Ned's mother. She took a sensible view of the whole matter.

"I'm sure that if there is the slightest bit of doubt about the safety of those astronauts, NASA will not allow them to climb into the rocket."

Harboring this comforting thought, everyone went to bed feeling a little better. They were up and dressed by six the next morning. During breakfast they watched the television news. According to the report the moon shoot was planned for nine o'clock and at the moment all systems were go.

When the young people reached the building where the news media offices were located, they signed in. Together they walked out to get into buses and were taken to the Press Site.

"What a huge place!" Bess remarked.

The structure was really a large covered stadium. On each tier were long counters containing telephones. Behind them were rows of chairs, each one numbered. Nancy's group climbed the steps and found seats which had been assigned to them.

Men were bustling about, many with cameras, some with tape recorders, others with portable typewriters. Nearly everyone had binoculars.

In front of the Press Box was a long open lawn beyond which the Banana River gleamed in the sunlight. Near the shore, television and newspaper cameras had been set up by photographers. Across the river on Merritt Island stood the rocket, about three miles away, with condensed moisture, caused by the liquid oxygen, pouring from the base of it.

Every few minutes there would be an announcement and the young people would hold their breath. Was the countdown still on and would the rocket take off?

"Oh I hope Fortin was captured and had no chance to use a secret device to hurt the astronauts!" said Bess.

"I hope so too," Nancy replied.

There was a long wait before lift-off time. Nancy asked Ned if he would go with her to inspect the various trailers she had noticed off to one side of the Press Box. They went down and were told that these contained the broadcasting stations. Stepping across numerous cables, the couple walked along the row, then turned back. Behind the Press Box they found a snack bar.

"Let's grab a bite," Ned suggested.

While he bought hamburgers and milk, Nancy tried to phone the Billington house, but all the circuits were busy. When she and Ned returned to their seats, they learned that their friends had also been down to get a second breakfast.

As the countdown drew nearer zero, everyone who had been wandering around came to take their seats. Typewriters were clicking everywhere and cameras with telephoto lenses were busy.

Nancy wondered if ever again she would be so excited. Some time later she encountered another mystery, *The Quest of the Missing Map,* which also brought her some harrowing adventures.

It was five minutes to nine. The countdown for the moon shoot proceeded. Finally the announcer called out the final seconds:

"Three . . . two . . . one . . . zero!"

There was a burst of orange, green, and yellow gases from the base of the rocket. As it zoomed upward, enveloped in a varicolored cloud, the noise was ear-splitting and the grandstand shook as if a giant hand were shaking it violently.

"It's off!" someone shouted.

Nancy and her friends were holding hands, their nails pressing into one another's palms.

"Nothing is wrong so far!" Nancy thought, as

a white vapor trail formed behind the spaceship. "Oh, I hope—I hope—"

The rocket curved slightly and in a few moments disappeared among the clouds. Bess said shakily, "Ev-everything's A-OK!"

Seconds before this, a shout of triumph had gone up from the onlookers. Nancy and her friends did not cry out. Instead they were silently saying prayers of thankfulness.

When Nancy was breathing normally again she picked up the telephone in front of her. The main switchboard connected her with the Billington house.

Mr. Drew answered. "I knew it was you," he said. "Everything's A-OK here too. Fortin finally gave himself up, and his spy was caught. The transmitting antenna was ruined. The news was immediately telephoned to the Cape. This is why the astronauts were allowed to climb into the rocket and it was able to lift-off on time."

"Oh, Dad, that's wonderful!"

The lawyer chuckled. "You'll be interested to know that Fortin blames his failure on your detective work. But I'm terribly proud of you!"

THE QUEST OF THE MISSING MAP

"No! No! I won't go there!" seven-year-old Trixie Chatham cries out. "The Ship Cottage is haunted!"

Prompted by her concern for the frightened child, Nancy investigates the small studio on the Chatham estate. What the astute young detective discovers leads her to believe that there is a connection between the mysterious occurrences at Ship Cottage and her search for a treasure island.

With only a few slim clues to guide her—a half map and Tomlin Smith's vague memories—Nancy sets out to find Mr. Smith's long-lost twin brother, who possesses the rest of the map that will pinpoint the location of buried treasure willed to them by their father.

Constantly beset by danger and intrigue, Nancy courageously outwits her enemies and solves one of the most challenging cases in her career as a teen-age investigator.

"Leave here at once and never come back!"
the stranger warned

The Quest
of the
Missing Map

BY CAROLYN KEENE

PUBLISHERS   *Grosset & Dunlap*   NEW YORK

Contents

CHAPTER I

The Haunted House

HER golden red hair flying in the wind, Nancy Drew ran up the porch steps and opened the front door of her home.

She could hear Hannah Gruen, the Drews' housekeeper, saying to someone in the living room, "Why don't you tell your mysterious story to Nancy? She's a really clever young detective."

The mere mention of a mystery quickened the pulse of eighteen-year-old Nancy. She dropped her art books and portfolio on the hall table and glanced into the living room.

"Come in, dear," said Mrs. Gruen. "You're home early."

"Art school was dismissed at two-thirty today," Nancy replied.

Seated on a couch beside Mrs. Gruen was an attractive, dark-haired girl about twenty.

"Nancy, I'd like you to meet Ellen Smith," the

middle-aged, kindly housekeeper said. "You've frequently heard me speak of her."

The girls greeted each other, then Ellen said, "I was hoping Mrs. Gruen might accompany me to Rocky Edge this afternoon. I just dread going alone." She glanced at Hannah.

"Rocky Edge?" Nancy asked. "Isn't that the estate along the river?"

"Yes, it is," Hannah Gruen replied. "Ellen says she has been offered a summer position there with the owner. If she takes it, the salary will help tremendously toward her tuition at Blackstone College of Music."

Ellen added, "My parents have suffered some serious financial reverses. They can't afford to send me and recently my father was injured in a car accident."

"I'm terribly sorry," Nancy said sympathetically. After a pause she asked, "Are you taking piano lessons?"

"No. I'm studying voice, but I do play the piano."

"Ellen has a lovely voice," Mrs. Gruen put in. "A few weeks ago she sang on TV, and her teacher is urging her to devote all her time to music and become a soloist."

"If only I could!" Ellen murmured wistfully. "But already I've borrowed a lot of money and I'm worried about how to pay it back. I want to take the position at Rocky Edge because it pays well, but the place and the people have an air of mystery about them that scares me. Besides, I'm afraid I won't be able to get along with Trixie."

"Who is she?" Nancy inquired.

"Trixie is Mrs. Chatham's seven-year-old daughter," Ellen explained. "I've never met her but I understand she's unruly."

"Your job would be to look after her?"

Ellen nodded. "Mrs. Chatham wants me to live there and give Trixie piano lessons. The mother is a strange person, a widow, and frustrating at times." Ellen turned to Hannah Gruen and said, "Won't you please go with me to see Mrs. Chatham and talk about the position?"

The housekeeper smiled. "Why not take Nancy? She's had a lot of experience meeting strange people. If Nancy thinks it's all right for you to accept the position, I'm sure it will be."

"I'll be glad to go," Nancy said.

She was eager to help Ellen, and curious about the wealthy and eccentric Mrs. Chatham.

"I don't like to put you to so much trouble," Ellen protested. "But I would appreciate having you with me."

"You're not afraid of Mrs. Chatham?"

"Not exactly, and I'd try to get along with her and Trixie. I love children and enjoy working with them. At Rocky Edge I'll have time to practice my vocal work. I was told there's a small studio on the estate."

As Ellen talked, Nancy could not help but wonder, "Is Ellen's decision difficult to make because of the mysterious story I heard Hannah mention? Is it connected with the position at Rocky Edge? Or is some other mystery haunting Ellen?"

As the two girls left the Drew house and walked toward the driveway, Nancy remarked to Ellen, "I heard Hannah say something about a mysterious story."

"It has to do with a map and a buried treasure," the other girl replied as they stepped into Nancy's car.

Nancy hoped to hear more about the buried treasure as they rode along, but Ellen turned the conversation toward the two girls' interest in art: one of them in music, the other in drawing and sketching.

"What are you specializing in?" she asked Nancy.

"Drawing figures and faces," Nancy replied. "As a child I always filled in the capital o's in magazines and newspapers with eyes, nose, mouth and ears, so I guess Dad thought it might be a good idea if I turned my doodling to good account!" She laughed.

Ellen said, "I hope to do the same with my music. When Hannah Gruen worked for my family years ago, she taught me lots of children's songs. Hannah was really wonderful to my family. I was always sorry she left, but when Mother and

Dad returned from their trip around the world, Mother took charge of our home herself."

"My mother," said Nancy, "died when I was only three and Hannah Gruen has taken care of me ever since. She's like a member of the family."

Ellen nodded. "I know what you mean."

The car sped on past the outskirts of River Heights. Halfway to Wayland, Nancy turned into a shady road and presently drew up near a sign which read *Rocky Edge*. She drove slowly up a curving tree-lined lane toward the house.

It was a large rambling structure, half hidden from the road by masses of high, overgrown shrubs. The driveway led to a pillared porch.

"It's creepy here, isn't it?" Ellen remarked nervously.

"Oh, not really," Nancy replied. "No trimming has been done on the grounds, but that gives the place atmosphere."

"I could do without it," Ellen said uneasily as they got out of the car.

She went ahead of Nancy and pressed the bell. Almost at once the door was flung open. The two callers found themselves facing a little girl.

"I don't know what you're selling!" the child cried out. "Whatever it is we don't want any! So go away!"

"Just a minute, please," Nancy said. "We came to talk with Mrs. Chatham about Miss Smith giving her daughter music lessons."

The little girl's dark eyes opened wide as she stared first at Nancy, then at Ellen. She wore her hair in two long braids, and her short dress made her thin legs look like toothpicks.

"I don't want anyone to teach me!" the child exclaimed. "There are too many now. If another one comes, I'll—I'll run away!"

"Trixie!"

Mrs. Chatham, a stout woman dressed in a bright-blue silk dress, had come to the door. Seizing the little girl by an arm, she pulled her away.

As Trixie began to cry, her mother said contritely, "I didn't mean to hurt you, dear, but sometimes you are impossible."

Ellen introduced Nancy to Mrs. Chatham. The woman invited the callers into a living room furnished with bizarre modern tables, chairs, and paintings. She began a lengthy account of her daughter's shortcomings, regardless of the fact that the child was listening to every word.

At the first opportunity Nancy rose from her chair and asked Trixie to show her the grounds. As they walked down a shady trail, Nancy smiled at the child, recited a funny limerick, and soon had the little girl laughing gaily.

"I wish you were going to be here instead of Miss Smith," Trixie remarked. "I like you."

"You'll like Ellen too," Nancy assured her. "And I'll come to see you sometimes."

"All right. But I hope she won't try to boss me like the others did. No one can tell me what to do!"

"I'm afraid you've heard your mother say that to you so often you believe it." Nancy laughed. "Now let's forget about being naughty. Suppose you show me the rest of the grounds. Shall we go first to that little house?"

Through the trees at a spot that overlooked the river, Nancy could see the red roof of what appeared to be a tiny cottage. To her surprise Trixie held back.

"No! No! I won't go there!" she cried out.

"Why not?"

"Because the place is haunted, that's why!" The child's freckled face was tense. "I wouldn't go inside the Ship Cottage for anything!"

"The Ship Cottage?" Nancy repeated. "Is that its name?"

"It's what I call it. Please, let's go the other way."

Trixie tugged at Nancy's hand but could not make her turn in the opposite direction.

"I'm sure there's no reason why you should be afraid," Nancy said gently. "If you won't come, then I'll go alone. I'll prove to you that the place is not haunted."

"Please don't go there," the child pleaded frantically. "You'll be sorry if you do."

"What makes you so afraid of it?"

The little girl would not answer. Jerking free, she ran off in the opposite direction.

"Poor child," Nancy thought, shrugging. "I do feel sorry for her."

Nancy was sure that Trixie was watching her from a distance as she walked slowly down the path to the quaint little house. The door was unlocked and Nancy went inside. The one-room cottage was pleasant though dusty, and was lined with shelves of books. In the center of the floor stood a very old grand piano. The ivory keys had turned yellow and cobwebs festooned the mahogany case.

"It's probably out of tune," she mused.

Nancy crossed the room and ran her fingers over the bass keys. Not a sound came from the instrument. Nancy was bewildered, and played a series of chords. Although she depressed the keys again and again no notes came out.

"That's strange!" she thought.

Nancy bent to examine the pedals to see if the piano had a spring lock that prevented the strings from being struck. There was none.

As she was about to lift up the lid of the piano Nancy noticed several ship models on the mantelpiece and others on tables.

"So that's why Trixie calls this place Ship Cottage," Nancy murmured, taking down one of the fine models from the mantel. "Undoubtedly this is the music studio Ellen mentioned."

*"I won't go there! It's haunted!" Trixie
called out*

After carefully replacing the small ship, Nancy heard a sound behind her. At the same moment she caught a reflection in the mirror above the fireplace. What she saw sent icy chills down her spine. A wall panel behind her had slid open. A bearded man with cruel, beady eyes was watching her every move.

"Leave here at once and never come back!" he warned in a rasping voice.

CHAPTER II

Curious Revelation

NANCY wheeled around and caught a fleeting glimpse of a long row of brass buttons down the front of the man's coat. The next instant the panel closed noiselessly.

As Nancy dashed toward the spot, one hand brushed the piano keys. A crash of chords broke the eerie stillness of the cottage.

Nancy tried to be calm but her heart was thumping madly. "I mustn't let myself be frightened," she told herself.

Deciding it might be dangerous to investigate the cottage further at this time, she hastily left it. Once outside, she gazed about the grounds. No one was in sight.

"I'm glad Trixie didn't come with me," she said to herself. "I've never believed in ghosts and I refuse to do so now. All the same, there's something very queer about this place."

Nancy had inherited an inquiring mind from her father, an eminent criminal lawyer, but she knew the wisdom of using caution in all investigations. Since solving *The Secret of the Old Clock*, Nancy had built an enviable reputation as an amateur sleuth.

Now, as she stood staring at Ship Cottage, Nancy wondered why the piano had made no sound when her fingers had moved over the keys the first time.

"It wasn't imagination," she reflected. Just then Nancy heard her name called. Turning, she saw Ellen motioning to her from far up the path.

"Coming!" Nancy answered.

"I'm ready to leave whenever you are," Ellen announced, joining her new friend. "What became of Trixie?"

"She ran off. You know, Ellen, I rather like her," Nancy declared with sincerity.

"Mrs. Chatham speaks so harshly to her daughter," Ellen remarked. "Then the next minute she's as sweet as honey. I can't understand her."

"You've decided not to take the position for the summer?"

"I told Mrs. Chatham I'd think it over."

Nancy said slowly, "There's something about Rocky Edge I don't quite like. Ellen, I wish you wouldn't come here—at least not until we've made a complete investigation of the place."

"Why, Nancy," Ellen exclaimed in astonishment, "have you learned something about Mrs. Chatham?"

"Not a thing," Nancy answered. "It's mostly a feeling I have. I'll explain it later. When must you give her your answer?"

"Mrs. Chatham didn't say, but I imagine she wants to know soon."

During the ride back to River Heights, Ellen sensed that Nancy was keeping something from her, and asked if this was true. Smiling, Nancy refused to divulge what she had learned.

"I'll tell my secret when you tell yours," she joked. "But seriously, please don't accept Mrs. Chatham's offer until after I talk with my dad."

"All right, I won't," Ellen promised.

Nancy drove the girl to a bus which would take her back to Blackstone College, then went to her father's office. Nancy frequently asked his assistance in solving mysteries.

Although Mr. Drew was unusually busy, the tall, handsome man laid aside his papers, kissed his daughter affectionately, and listened attentively to her story about the mysterious Ship Cottage.

"You're certain you saw the open panel close again?" he asked when she had finished.

"Yes, Dad. Also, the piano was mute at first. Then later it played. How do you account for that?"

"I can't," the lawyer replied soberly. "However,

I think it would be unwise for you to go there again."

"Oh, Dad!" Nancy protested in dismay. "How can I help Ellen if I don't?"

"Well, don't go alone," he amended, flashing her an understanding smile. "You're all I have, Nancy. You're very dear to me. Don't forget that."

She hugged him and promised, then asked, "Do you think it would be unwise for Ellen to accept Mrs. Chatham's offer?"

"I'd say it would be foolhardy until we've checked the place thoroughly."

"I had hoped you might be able to tell me something about Rocky Edge, Dad."

Mr. Drew gazed out the window for several seconds. Then he said slowly, "It seems to me I do recall some trouble a few years ago at Rocky Edge. But that would have been before the Chathams bought it."

"Who owned it previously?" Nancy asked.

"I can't remember the name of the man," her father answered, "but I think he was an inventor and there was an unusual lawsuit against him, due to one of his gadgets. As soon as I can, I'll look into the matter for you."

"I wonder if there might be some connection between the gadgets and the strange things that happened today," Nancy remarked.

"I don't know. It seems to me Mr. Chatham was a friend of the owner and bought the place after the man died. Mr. Chatham himself passed away less than two years ago."

Nancy was silent a moment, then asked her father what she should tell Ellen.

"Advise her to stall," Carson Drew answered promptly.

Nancy decided that instead of telephoning Ellen, she would drive to Blackstone College the next afternoon. Ellen was to be in a recital and Nancy was eager to hear her sing.

She invited her friends Bess Marvin and George Fayne to go with her and they accepted. The two girls, who were cousins, often shared Nancy's adventures. Bess, blond and slightly plump, was a bit more timid than slim, tomboyish George.

"Oh, oh," Bess remarked as the three entered the college auditorium. "Nearly all the seats are taken."

"We'll squeeze in somewhere," Nancy declared cheerfully. "I see two places down front where the performers are seated."

She suggested that Bess and George go forward and take them. "I'll sit somewhere else. Introduce yourselves to Ellen Smith after the recital and tell her I'm here. We'll meet in the lobby."

As Nancy looked for a seat, she saw Mrs. Chatham, half hidden beneath an enormous hat, near the rear of the auditorium. There was an empty chair beside the woman. Nancy made her way to it.

"Are you saving this seat, Mrs. Chatham?" she asked, smiling.

The woman shook her head. The next moment, recognizing the newcomer, she beamed at Nancy as if they were old friends. Thus encouraged, Nancy began a conversation which she adroitly steered to a discussion of Rocky Edge. The widow mentioned its previous owner, Silas Norse.

"He must have been an interesting person. We've found several ingenious gadgets of his in the house," she said lightly.

Nancy casually mentioned her visit to Ship Cottage but did not refer to the secret panel or the man she had seen. She merely inquired if Mr. Chatham had collected the ship models.

"Oh dear no! They belonged to my first husband," Mrs. Chatham said with a pensive sigh. "He was such a good, kind man. It made me so sad to see those darling little boats in the house that I asked Mr. Chatham to move them to the studio."

"Do you go out there frequently?" Nancy queried. "To the studio, I mean."

"Almost never."

"I suppose it was built by your late husband?"

"No," the widow replied. "It was on the property when we took over the place. I judge it has been there for some time."

Nancy would have asked additional questions but just then the orchestra began to play. For an hour and a half she enjoyed the recital and was proud of Ellen Smith, whose vocal solos were the best numbers on the program and received the most applause.

"Do come and see me some time," Mrs. Chatham invited Nancy as she rose to leave.

"I'd love to," Nancy answered. "I'll try to drive to Rocky Edge within the next few days."

Just then Bess, George, and Ellen came up the aisle of the auditorium.

"Oh, Nancy!" Ellen exclaimed. "We've been looking everywhere for you."

She paused, slightly embarrassed to find herself face to face with Mrs. Chatham.

"My dear, your singing was marvelous," the widow gushed. "I had no idea you were so talented. I'll be happy to have you teach music to my Trixie. You *are* accepting the position?"

Ellen glanced at Nancy, seeking a cue to the proper response.

"I—I don't know what to say," she stammered nervously. "I want to think it over."

"I must know at once!" Mrs. Chatham insisted.

CHAPTER III

Fantastic Story

NANCY was afraid that since Ellen needed the money so badly she would accept the position immediately. She was greatly relieved, therefore, when the girl replied:

"I'm sorry, Mrs. Chatham, but I can't possibly give you my answer for at least a week!"

"Why, that's ridiculous!" the widow protested haughtily. "You can't expect me to keep the position open indefinitely."

The situation had become an exceedingly awkward one. Nancy spoke up.

"Mrs. Chatham, don't you think it would be difficult to find someone else who knows as much about music and who would be kind to Trixie?" she asked, hoping to gain time for Ellen.

Mrs. Chatham admitted that this might be true. She turned again to Ellen. "All right, I'll wait a week, but no longer."

"Thank you. I promise I'll give you my answer by that time," Ellen replied.

Without waiting to be introduced to Nancy's other friends, the widow left the auditorium.

"She's a pain," George remarked with a grimace.

"I certainly wouldn't want to work for her," Bess stated.

As the girls were about to say good-by to Ellen, she said, "Nancy, if you haven't any special plans, would you like to drive to my home and hear about the mysterious story Hannah Gruen spoke of? And I'd love to have Bess and George come too."

Nothing could have pleased Nancy more, and the other girls accepted eagerly.

"You mean you'll tell us on the way there?" Nancy asked.

"Not exactly. The secret really isn't mine to tell. It's my dad's."

Soon the group was on its way to the Smith home in Wayland. The three girls were very curious about the secret, but Ellen did not refer to the matter again.

"Do you commute to Blackstone College every day?" Bess asked Ellen presently.

"Oh, no," she replied. "I board at Blackstone."

When they reached Wayland, Ellen directed Nancy to the Smiths' small, old-fashioned house. As the car slowed to a stop, the girls saw a heavy-set man in his thirties, wearing a brown suit, hurriedly leaving the dwelling. His jaw was set and his eyes blazed. Without looking to left or right he jumped into a blue sedan at the curb, slammed the door, and shot away.

Ellen frowned. "I—I hope nothing has happened," she stammered, quickly getting out of the convertible.

Nancy, Bess, and George watched the rapidly disappearing car. Then they followed Ellen into the house and met Mrs. Smith. She was a pretty, white-haired woman in her late fifties.

"Mother, who was that man?" Ellen asked.

"His name is Rorke," Mrs. Smith replied, a note of suppressed excitement in her voice. "He came to see your father about a very important matter."

"Not the map?"

"Yes, but ask your father about the visitor."

The girls crossed the hall to a room which had been made into a combination studio and bedroom. Mr. Smith lay in bed, still recuperating from his accident. His eyes lighted with pleasure as Ellen introduced her friends.

"So glad to meet you all," he said. "Please sit down."

"What a charming room!" Bess exclaimed, her gaze wandering from the shelves of travel books to a large map of the world on one wall. "Are you interested in geography, Mr. Smith?"

"He's interested in finding a treasure island!"

Ellen answered eagerly. "Hannah Gruen thinks Nancy may be able to help us, Dad. She has solved lots of mysteries."

"Are you an expert at finding lost maps, young lady?" Mr. Smith asked, a twinkle in his eyes.

"I've had some success with them," Nancy answered, matching his teasing tone. "But I must say, all these hints of Ellen's about a treasure are intriguing."

"Do tell your story, Dad," Ellen pleaded.

The rugged-faced man brushed a strand of hair from his forehead, then began.

"First of all, I must tell you my true name. I'm known as Tomlin Smith, although Tomlin is really my last name. Years ago I added Smith, the name of the people who adopted me after my father's death.

"My mother died when I was fourteen. Father was captain of an ocean-going freighter, the *Sea Hawk*. He had followed the sea his entire life, and his father had too. After Mother's death he was determined to take care of my twin brother and me by himself, so he took the two of us aboard the freighter. We slept in his cabin and had the run of the ship."

"You must have visited many interesting places," George remarked.

"Only half a dozen ports," Mr. Smith said. "Except for a turn of luck, I'd have gone down to Davy Jones's locker along with my father."

"The ship sank?" Nancy asked, leaning forward in her chair.

"Yes, she went down in a hurricane. One of the worst on record. The seams of the old freighter cracked wide open. Every pump was manned by the crew but the ship was doomed. No one knew that better than my father."

"What did you do then?" Bess queried. "Take to the lifeboats?"

"I'm coming to that part in a minute. When my father realized that the old ship wouldn't hold together much longer, he called my twin brother John Abner and me into his cabin. Knowing he might never see his sons again, he told us our grandfather once had hidden a treasure on a small uncharted island in the Atlantic. He had left a map showing its location. My father tried to find it but never could.

"He took a parchment map from the safe," Mr. Smith went on, "but instead of giving it to either of us, he tore it diagonally from corner to corner into two pieces. 'You're to share the treasure equally,' he said, 'and to make sure of that I am dividing the map in such a way that no one can find the buried chest without both sections.' "

"Then what happened?" George asked as Mr. Smith paused.

"John Abner and I were put into separate lifeboats, and I never saw him again. A sudden explosion ripped the ship from bow to stern before

Father was ready to leave. He went down with it.

"Along with six sailors I landed on a small island. We lived there a year before we were picked up and brought to the United States. I tried without success to learn what had become of my brother, or where any relatives were, and finally I was adopted by a family named Smith."

"What became of your section of the map?" Nancy inquired. "Was it lost?"

"No," replied Mr. Smith. "All these years I've kept it, always hoping to find my brother and hunt for the buried treasure. For a long time I had plenty of money and thought little about ever needing any. But now—"

The man looked wistfully from a window, while there was an awkward pause.

"Even if we should find the other half of the map," Mrs. Smith said with a sigh, "we wouldn't have any money to look for the treasure."

"It would give me more satisfaction," her husband remarked, "to learn what became of my twin brother. As for the treasure, he or his heirs would be entitled to half of it."

"We won't worry about them just yet," said Ellen, trying to cheer her parents. "You see, Nancy, my father looked up every Tomlin he could find. Maybe his brother changed his name, and since he didn't look like Dad, nobody would think of the two being related. The map would be the only clue."

"May I see your half?" Nancy asked.

Mr. Smith requested his daughter to bring the paper from the top drawer of a desk on the second floor. Presently she returned with a piece of yellow parchment. Eagerly Nancy bent to examine the curious markings.

"Right here is our treasure island, as I call it," Tomlin Smith indicated, "but as you see, the name has been torn off. All that appears on my half is 'lm Island,' which isn't much help."

Nancy studied the parchment half map for a few moments, then asked Mr. Smith, "Would you mind if I make a copy of it?"

"Not at all," he answered. "Only I'm sure you can't make much out of it. As I told Mr. Rorke today, it's not worth a nickel without my brother's half."

"Was he the man who drove away in the blue car?" Nancy asked.

"Yes, he left the house just as you girls arrived."

"Mother said he came to see you about the map," Ellen declared. "How did he learn about it?"

"Mr. Rorke claimed he'd heard the story from the son of a man who was first mate on my father's sunken freighter—an officer by the name of Tom Gambrell. Rorke offered to buy my section of the map. Said he wanted it as a souvenir."

"You didn't agree to sell your half?" Nancy asked, afraid the answer might be yes.

"No, I told Rorke I wouldn't sell at any price," Mr. Smith said. "Even if the parchment is worthless, it was my father's last gift. I'll always keep it."

"I'm glad," Nancy said in relief. "Of course I know nothing about Mr. Rorke, but I didn't like his looks. Also, since you changed your name, how did he find you?"

"That's a good question," said Ellen's father. "I never thought to ask him. But he'll probably be back and I'll put that up to him."

"Did you show him your piece of the map?" Nancy inquired.

"Yes, I had Mrs. Smith bring it downstairs," Ellen's father replied. "But Rorke saw it only for a second; not long enough to remember what was on it, if that's what you're afraid of."

Nancy said no more and busied herself copying the torn map while the others talked about the recital. Bess and George spoke glowingly of Ellen's singing and her parents smiled proudly. Presently Mrs. Smith appeared with a tray of refreshments.

Soon afterward the callers rose to leave. Nancy carefully folded the copy of the treasure map and put it into her purse.

She smiled at Mr. Smith. "I don't promise to figure this out, but it will be good mental exercise and I'm eager to start working on some way to find your brother."

The callers said good-by and left. Nancy drove

toward River Heights. Presently they stopped for a crossroads traffic light. Directly ahead, waiting at the same intersection, was a blue sedan.

"That looks like the car we saw at the Smith place!" George exclaimed.

"It *is* the same one! The driver is that Mr. Rorke!" Nancy cried.

The traffic light turned green, and the blue sedan was away in a flash. Nancy's car was equally fast and kept directly behind Mr. Rorke.

"You're going to follow him?" Bess asked nervously.

"I'd like to find out more about him," Nancy replied. "It's my hunch he has a special interest in the Smiths' treasure map that he's not telling."

Bess and George were inclined to agree. As the man's car raced ahead and turned corners recklessly it was very evident that he was trying to lose Nancy. Twice Rorke glanced uneasily over his shoulder.

"He's knows we're trailing him," George commented. "But why should it worry him?"

"Nancy, do be careful," Bess cautioned, gripping the edge of the seat. "We're coming to a railroad crossing."

Signals warned of an approaching train. Knowing that it would be dangerous to attempt a crossing, Nancy stopped. The blue sedan, however, shot ahead onto the track.

CHAPTER IV

A Strange Lawsuit

Bess closed her eyes, expecting a crash. But the driver ahead crossed the tracks with only seconds to spare.

"He drives that bus of his as if the police were after him," George commented.

As the long freight train thundered past, Nancy looked between the cars to see if Mr. Rorke were in sight. But there was no sign of the blue car.

"We've lost him now," she declared gloomily. "I may as well turn back."

Nancy drove to River Heights and dropped George and Bess at their homes. In a few minutes she reached her own brick colonial house, which set back from the street and was reached by a curving driveway. Mr. Drew's sporty sedan rolled in right behind her.

"Hello, Nancy," the lawyer greeted his daughter fondly. "I came home early today—had a rather hard session in court."

Nancy and her father strolled through the garden.

"Dad, let's sit down here," she suggested after a few moments, indicating a stone bench. "I have something to show you."

"A letter from Ned Nickerson?" he teased. "Or is it from a new admirer?"

Nancy laughed. "Neither. It's something I copied today from part of a map of a treasure island!"

"Treasure island?" Mr. Drew repeated in disbelief. "You're joking."

"No, it's genuine, Dad."

Nancy handed the paper to him, then related everything she had learned at the Tomlin Smith home. Anxiously she awaited her father's comment.

"I don't like the sound of this Rorke fellow," the lawyer said. "He could be dangerous. I'd much rather help the Smith family in a financial way than have you concerned with a lost treasure that Rorke's also after."

"There's more than a map and treasure involved," Nancy told him. "Mr. Smith wants me to find his long-lost twin brother, John Abner Tomlin. He's heir to half the treasure their grandfather buried, and Mr. Smith insists they must share equally, as his father wished."

"That difficulty could be solved easily by putting half the money in a trust fund," Mr. Drew remarked. "But locating the treasure is a remote possibility."

"The half map Mr. Smith possesses appears to be authentic, Dad. My copy probably isn't good enough to convince you."

"I can't tell much from this," he admitted. "The parchment was torn in such a way that one can't figure out what any of the names or directions mean. Have you tried comparing it with an atlas?"

"Not yet, Dad. Let's do it now."

Carson Drew accompanied Nancy to his study and for some time they pored over several maps. When Hannah Gruen announced dinner, the lawyer was so engrossed that he was reluctant to give up the search.

"Old Captain Tomlin was a clever fellow," he conceded. "By tearing the map as he did, the shape of the island is destroyed, so now it's practically impossible to determine its location without the missing section."

"I'm glad you said 'practically.'" Nancy chuckled and led the way to the dining room. "You see, Dad, I mean to attempt the impossible. Monday I'll do some sleuthing at the public library."

Sunday morning the Drews went to church service, then spent the afternoon relaxing at home. Nancy kept thinking about the mystery and remarked to her father, "If the treasure is so hard to find, it could mean no one has dug it up yet!"

"Right!" Mr. Drew chuckled.

The following morning Nancy spent two hours at the library examining old atlases and historic records. Although the librarian permitted her access to some old and precious maps, she could find no chart which bore any resemblance to the scrap in her possession.

Disappointed, Nancy turned to business directories and biographies. She carefully studied the names listed.

"There's not a John Abner Tomlin Jr. among them," Nancy sighed.

Next, she consulted an old book on ships lost at sea. It contained a brief account of the sinking of the *Sea Hawk*. Captain Abner Tomlin, age forty-five, was in charge of the freighter. There also was a list of the officers and sailors who had shipped aboard. As Nancy carefully copied the names, she noticed there was no Tom Gambrell listed.

"That's point number one against Mr. Rorke," she decided, rising to leave.

Next, Nancy went to the newspaper office of the *River Heights Gazette* and asked if she might look through their files of old issues. Soon she was busy searching for stories concerning the Chatham estate. Without much trouble she found an article reporting the sale of Rocky Edge, after the owner Silas Norse had died.

"Now to find out if there are any items about strange gadgets there," the young detective told herself, turning sheet after sheet.

Finally her eyes lighted upon a startling headline:

BURGLAR STARTS LAWSUIT
Thief Injured at Estate Claims Damages

The story went on to tell how one Spike Doty had broken into the home of Silas Norse. As he was about to escape with valuable loot, he had been caught between sliding panels and injured rather badly. Though held for robbery, Doty had made a claim for damages.

"I wonder if he ever collected!" Nancy thought. "I'll bet he didn't because he was a trespasser!"

She hunted further and found a photograph and an article about the inventor himself. There were pictures of various rooms in his home, showing sliding panels, secret closets, and several gadgets. Nancy was on the point of deciding that Rocky Edge was no place for Ellen Smith when she read that Mr. Norse was planning to have all these things removed.

"But he forgot about the secret panel in Ship Cottage," she thought, recalling her adventure there. "I can vouch for that! And maybe Mr. Norse didn't remove some of the others!"

Nancy decided to talk with Ellen about her sleuthing so far. Upon reaching home she telephoned at once and was invited to come over to dinner and spend the night in the Blackstone dormitory.

When she finished the conversation, Nancy told Hannah the plans. "And tomorrow I'm going to the Emerson College dance with Ned, you know. It's the big year-end party of the Dramatic Club. I'm so sorry Bess and George couldn't accept Burt's and Dave's invitations. When the boys heard this, they decided to attend a fraternity convention, so I won't see them."

"I'm sorry too," said Hannah. "The girls would have been company for you on the long ride. By the way, Nancy, that new dress you're going to travel in hasn't been shortened yet. Suppose you put it on right now and I'll get the correct length."

While Hannah marked the new hemline with chalk, Nancy told her what she had learned at the library.

"I don't like the sound of any of it," Hannah remarked when Nancy had finished. "Ellen had better not go to the Chathams, and the Smiths ought to beware of that Mr. Rorke."

While waiting for the dress to be hemmed, Nancy did various chores around the house. Then she packed her suitcase and finally phoned her father to say good-by.

"Have a good time with Ellen and at Emerson, and be careful, dear," he cautioned her.

"Will do," she promised.

Nancy spent two hours at art school classes, then started for Blackstone, reaching Ellen's dormitory just before suppertime.

"Oh, I'm so glad to see you!" Ellen said warmly. "Come and meet my friends. By the way, would you mind going to my home tonight to sleep? We're giving an operetta here tomorrow and I've promised to bring over several things to use as stage props. And a couple of costumes."

"I don't mind a bit," Nancy replied. "We'll have a better chance to talk if we're alone."

Nancy thoroughly enjoyed herself at dinner and later at the dress rehearsal. It was after ten before she and Ellen got away and eleven when they reached Wayland.

"I imagine Mother and Dad have gone to bed," Ellen remarked as Nancy turned the car into the Smiths' street. "They seldom stay up late."

As she had surmised, her house was in total darkness.

"Do you have your key, Ellen?"

"Oh, I forgot it!" she exclaimed. "I'll have to ring the bell."

No one answered. After a long wait Ellen tried again, but still there was no response.

"They must be sleeping soundly," she commented.

"Let's try the back door," Nancy suggested. "If that's locked we may be able to get in through a window."

Moving quietly so that the neighbors would not be disturbed, the girls went around the house. Nancy halted suddenly, clutching Ellen's hand.

"Look!" she whispered tensely.

A tall ladder leaned against the house wall, terminating at an open window on the second floor. As the girls stared at it, a man's shadowy figure moved stealthily down the rungs!

CHAPTER V

The Stolen Parchment

"A BURGLAR!" Nancy whispered into Ellen's ear. "Don't make a sound! Maybe we can catch him."

Remaining motionless, the girls waited until the man had nearly reached the base of the ladder. Then, at a signal from Nancy, they made a concerted rush for him.

After the first moment of surprise he began to struggle. With one push he sent Ellen reeling backwards into a clump of dwarf evergreens. Nancy held on, but the muscular man was too strong for her.

"Let go!" he ordered harshly. "If you don't, I'll get rough!"

Headlights from a passing automobile momentarily focused on the struggling pair, and in that second Nancy caught a clear glimpse of the man's partially bearded face and angry eyes.

"I won't let go!" she defied him.

In the wild struggle the ladder was pushed away from the wall. It toppled, narrowly missing Ellen, and struck the garage with a loud crash.

"Help! Help!" screamed Nancy, hoping that her cry would awaken the neighbors.

Instantly the prowler clapped his hand across her mouth. Shaking free from her grasp, he lifted her bodily and threw her down on the grass.

Nancy fell so hard that the breath was knocked from her, but she struggled to her feet. By this time the man had run across the lawn and disappeared beyond a hedge.

"Are you all right, Nancy?" Ellen gasped, limping toward her friend.

"Yes, but it's too bad that intruder got away."

"Oh, I hope he didn't steal anything," Ellen said.

In the house next door lights were being snapped on. The upper floor of the Smith home suddenly was illuminated. Ellen's mother raised a window and called to ask what was wrong.

"Hello, Mother," said Ellen. "I'm afraid our home has been robbed. Nancy and I just tried to capture a man who was coming out of the house!"

"Oh, goodness me!" Mrs. Smith exclaimed.

"We couldn't hold him. Is Dad all right?"

There was no answer. The girls guessed that Mrs. Smith had run downstairs to her husband's room. A few minutes later she unlocked the back door. By this time several neighbors had arrived to find out the cause of the commotion. Nancy explained what had happened, and one man summoned the police. Ellen and Nancy found Mr. Smith in a state of nervous alarm.

"Probably my desk has been rifled!" he cried out. "I'm sure the parchment map is gone!"

"Now don't get excited, Tomlin," Mrs. Smith said soothingly. "Maybe the girls got here in time to prevent a robbery."

"If I were you I'd check to make sure," Nancy urged. "The man may have ransacked several rooms in your house."

While she and Ellen counted the silverware, Mrs. Smith hastened upstairs. In a few minutes she returned and one glance at her stricken face told the girls that the precious map was gone.

"I was afraid the map was what the prowler came for," Nancy commented. "Maybe that man Rorke sent him."

"That's what I call a low-down trick," Mr. Smith fumed. "Now who could that scamp be, and why should he want the map?"

"Obviously to obtain the treasure!" exclaimed Ellen. "Oh, Dad, the parchment *must* have genuine value! And to think we've lost it!"

"You forget that I made a copy of the original," Nancy reminded the others. "It's crudely drawn but fairly accurate and I have it with me."

Mr. Smith said gratefully, "You're a lifesaver."

To Nancy's embarrassment he introduced her

to the neighbors who had gathered on the front porch and told them how brave she and Ellen had been.

As soon as the police arrived, a Sergeant Holmes introduced himself and Officer Mentor. He asked the girls to describe the intruder. Ellen could remember nothing about him but his surprising strength. Nancy, however, not only provided the police with an excellent description of the heavy-set thirty-year-old prowler, but drew a rough sketch of his face.

Nancy had recognized the close resemblance between the intruder and the "apparition" of Ship Cottage but did not mention this.

"Say, you're something of an artist!" the sergeant said admiringly. "A good observer, too! This fellow looks like one of our old friends."

"Spike Doty!" the other policeman added, studying the sketch.

"The same Spike Doty who burglarized Rocky Edge a few years ago?" Nancy asked.

"He's the one. Has a record a mile long, and is wanted for another robbery."

Sergeant Holmes said, "He's a sailor, and a fairly good one when he's willing to work."

The officers went outside to make an investigation. Just before they left, Nancy walked out on the front porch. She saw a man and a woman dart from the side of the house and hurry to a car which had been parked up the street. The automobile was too far away for her to distinguish either the make or the license.

"That's queer," she thought. "I wonder if they were just curious bystanders or if they had some part in the robbery."

In the morning she and Ellen had breakfast about nine o'clock, helped with the dishes, and then drove to Blackstone College. They assisted in setting the stage for the operetta and had luncheon. At four o'clock Nancy said she must start for Emerson College to attend the dance with Ned Nickerson.

"I'm staying there only one night," she said to Ellen in parting. "On my way home I'll stop at Rocky Edge and investigate some more."

"Thanks so much. I do need a salary comparable to the one Mrs. Chatham offers so I can come back here next fall," Ellen said wistfully.

Nancy drove leisurely along a winding country road. A gray automobile followed some distance behind. She did not give it a second thought until she had gone several miles.

"Why doesn't that car pass me?" Nancy wondered.

Deliberately she slowed up, but the car behind also slackened pace. With increasing uneasiness Nancy remembered that she had the precious copy of Tomlin Smith's half map in her purse.

"It's time that I find out what's what!" she

thought. "We'll play a little game of hide-and-seek."

Again Nancy slackened her pace, turning into a paved side road. She felt certain that unless the occupants of the gray car were trailing her they would not make the turn. Watching in the mirror, she was alarmed to see the automobile leave the main road.

"I am being followed," she thought anxiously. "And they're gaining on me, too!"

By this time the gray car was so near that she could see two persons in the front seat, a man and a woman. Nancy recognized them as the couple who had hurried out of the Smith driveway the night before! She tried in vain to read the license plate which was covered with mud. Gradually, so as not to reveal her concern, Nancy speeded up but was unable to lose her pursuers.

"They mean business," she thought grimly. "If I don't lose them quickly, they'll probably try to stop me when we come to the first lonely stretch."

Directly ahead was a dirt road which Nancy knew led to the town of Hamilton, two miles away. Without hesitation she turned into it, even though she realized it would take her away from Emerson.

Another burst of speed put her far ahead of the pursuing car. Nevertheless, as she entered the town of Hamilton she saw that the man and woman had not given up the chase.

Nancy looked in vain for police headquarters.

"I am being followed!" Nancy thought anxiously

Finally she parked in front of the bus station and ran inside. Entering a telephone booth, she called Ned Nickerson at Emerson College and told him of her predicament.

"You stay there until I come," Ned advised. "A bus leaves for Hamilton in fifteen minutes. If I hurry I can catch it. Whatever you do, don't give that couple a chance to approach you."

"I'll be safe enough until you get here," Nancy said to reassure him. "There are several people around and I doubt the couple would try anything out in the open."

Even as she hung up the phone, the gray car parked some distance behind her own. Uneasily Nancy sat down in the waiting room. Recalling that she had failed to leave a copy of the half map with Mr. Smith, she took a notebook from her purse and began to sketch.

Nancy became so absorbed in her work that she did not glance up until a woman sat down beside her. The newcomer was about thirty-five years old, stout, and had a cold, steady gaze which rested on Nancy's notebook.

"She's the one who was in the gray car!" the young detective said to herself.

Getting up abruptly, Nancy thrust both drawings into her handbag and hurriedly left the bus station. A glance revealed that the woman's accomplice was waiting nearby, so she started walking in the opposite direction.

"I'll be safe if I stay within sight of other people," Nancy reasoned, clutching her handbag. "If
it's the half map they want, I must finish the second copy quickly and put it somewhere."

A block away Nancy came to a large department store. Turning into it, she made her way to
the third floor. She located a telephone booth and
closed herself into it.

"I'll be okay here for a few minutes," she
thought, opening her purse. "Now to finish copying the map."

She completed the sketch in less than five minutes. Realizing that both drawings could be stolen, Nancy came to a sudden decision. She sealed
her original sketch in an envelope which she addressed to her father, then discovered she had no
stamp.

"I'll mail it at the post office. I may be followed,
but I must take the risk."

Nancy hoped that she had not been observed
entering the store, but when she emerged from
the building, the woman and the man were waiting. As she walked hurriedly along the street they
followed in their car.

"They're afraid to approach me now," she reasoned, "but if I'm alone for a minute I'll have
trouble. I wonder if they're in league with Spike
Doty."

Nancy entered the post office, bought a stamp,
and mailed the map. She remained in the build-

ing for a few minutes, allowing herself exactly enough time to reach the bus station before Ned was due to arrive.

Her watch proved to be accurate, for as she came within view of the station she saw three buses coming down the street. With a sigh of relief she quickened her step and joined the crowd of passengers waiting to get on.

The farthest bus finally came to a standstill. Nancy caught a glimpse of Ned alighting from the last bus and waved to him.

As the passengers pushed toward the first bus, someone brushed against her. Nancy felt a slight tug on her arm. Startled, she whirled around in time to see a man running down the street.

"My purse!" she cried out. "My purse has been stolen!"

CHAPTER VI

Sudden Danger

AT Nancy's cry of distress a number of people turned around, but no one tried to stop the fleeing thief. He was soon out of sight. A policeman appeared on the scene and questioned Nancy about the purse snatcher.

"His car's over there!" she exclaimed, pointing. "And the woman with him—" Nancy stopped speaking abruptly. "Why—it's gone!" She felt sick over the turn of events.

"Suppose you tell me the whole story," the policeman said kindly.

Nancy did not wish to disclose the details of her recent adventure and its connection with the current mystery. She stated simply, "A woman and a man followed me here in a gray sedan. I believe he was the same one who snatched my purse. He's about six feet tall, sandy-haired, and very thin.

"The woman is about thirty-five, average

height, and rather heavy. She has light-brown hair and hazel eyes."

Nancy paused, then added, "I'd say the man is older than she is. They both wore navy-blue suits."

"Did you have much money with you?"

"Practically none. There were a few personal articles, though, that I hate to lose."

As Nancy was talking to the policeman, Ned Nickerson, a handsome, athletic young man, came through the group.

"Hello, Nancy," he greeted her anxiously. "What happened?"

"I'll tell you all about it in a minute," she promised.

Nancy thanked the officer for his help, then she and Ned went to a quiet corner of the waiting room where they could talk.

"Now tell me everything," he insisted.

When Nancy finished relating her afternoon adventures, Ned asked, "Do you have any idea what they are after?"

"This." From her dress pocket she removed a copy of Tomlin Smith's map and showed it to him. "When I was in the store's telephone booth, I transferred my money and this paper from my handbag to my pocket."

Ned studied the crude drawing. "It looks like a lesson in geography. Half a lesson at that."

"That's just what it is—half a map showing where a treasure is buried."

"Belonging to Captain Kidd?"

"I know it may sound fantastic, but this is a clue to an inheritance buried on some Atlantic island," Nancy declared.

Next, she told him the entire story of Rocky Edge, its eccentric owners, and the vanishing man in the music studio.

Ned grinned. "Guess I won't be seeing much of you for a while with two mysteries to solve—especially when you're off to some lonely island." Then, with a wide grin, he added, "Unless we go sailing for gold together!"

The two laughed and Ned glanced at his watch. If they were to reach Emerson College before dinnertime, they must leave at once.

"Do you mind delaying a few minutes longer while I buy a purse and a few things I must replace?" Nancy asked.

"Give you fifteen minutes," he conceded.

She completed her shopping, then they started off in Nancy's car. At the fraternity house, she was greeted by Mrs. Haines, the housemother, and several young women. All of them had been invited to spend the night.

As Nancy started upstairs to shower and dress for the dance, someone called out, "Telephone for Nancy Drew!"

"For me?" she asked in surprise, retracing her steps. "Maybe it's Dad."

The caller proved to be Ellen Smith, who spoke in an agitated voice.

"Nancy, I'm sorry to bother you," she apologized. "It's about Mrs. Chatham. She came to see me at college today and absolutely insists that I give her my decision about the position in three days. What shall I tell her?"

"I'll talk to Mrs. Chatham tomorrow," Nancy promised. "Don't do anything until I see you."

"I really can't afford to turn down the job."

"I understand," Nancy assured her. "Don't worry about it, Ellen. If it seems unwise for you to take the position, I'll try to find another one for you."

"Oh, I knew you'd think of something," the other girl said gratefully. "You're a darling."

After Ellen had hung up, Nancy decided to phone her home and tell her father what had happened. Hannah Gruen answered and said Mr. Drew was not there.

"I'm so glad you called," the housekeeper said, her voice unsteady.

"What's wrong? You sound upset."

"About half an hour ago a man phoned. He didn't give his name, but he had the most unpleasant voice!"

"What did he say?"

" 'Lay off the Tomlin matter or you'll be sorry.' Those were his exact words. Oh, Nancy, that warning was meant for you. And to think that I suggested you take an interest in the Smiths' problems!"

After a somewhat lengthy conversation Nancy convinced the housekeeper that there was no immediate cause for alarm. She did not mention the incident at the Hamilton bus station, knowing it would only add to Mrs. Gruen's uneasiness.

Later, as Nancy was dressing, she speculated as to who the strange caller might have been. Spike Doty or the purse snatcher? Finally she decided to forget both for the evening.

When Nancy descended the stairs in her striking white dress, she saw Ned's face light up with admiration. "Wow!" he exclaimed with a smile. "May I have the honor?"

"You may," Nancy replied.

The couple linked arms and strolled into the main dining room which was attractively decorated in the college's colors of purple and orange. Several of Ned's classmates gave Nancy an admiring glance and an exaggerated nod of approval to her escort.

After dinner there was an inter-fraternity dance in the gymnasium. Nancy thoroughly enjoyed herself. During an intermission Nancy noticed one of Ned's fraternity brothers walking toward them.

"I don't know him very well," Ned whispered. "He came to Emerson just this year. His name is Bill Tomlin."

"Tomlin?" Nancy asked.

"Why, yes, do you know him?"

"I didn't tell you, Ned, but the old sea captain had that same last name. They're probably not even distantly related but I must check every possible clue."

Bill Tomlin, pleasant and humorous, asked to dance with her. As they moved across the floor, she casually inquired if any member of his family had followed the sea.

"My grandfather's brother was a sea captain," he replied. "He had twin sons and I understand one of them was a sea captain. I don't know what became of the other brother."

Nancy tried not to show her mounting excitement. She asked, "Do you know if the captain is still living and where he might be found?"

Before her dance partner could reply, the music stopped abruptly. The bass drum thumped loudly and the chairman of the dance committee, Jeff Garwin, rose to speak.

"Your attention, please!" he said over the microphone. "I have an important announcement to make. The next event on our program is the presentation of a pantomime produced by members of the Emerson College Dramatic Club.

"As you all know, it is our custom each year to select an attractive young lady to preside over the event. She will wear the Festival Robe and Crown. After careful consideration by a committee of faculty and students, a choice has been made."

A hush fell over the audience as the announcer paused a long moment.

"Will Miss Nancy Drew please come to the stage," he said, smiling down at the girl.

The students clapped and whistled. Though startled, Nancy responded with poise and mounted the improvised stage. She donned a white robe, a golden paper crown, and accepted the seat of honor.

Lights were dimmed and the presentation of the pantomime began. It was impossible to tell who the players were, because they all wore black masks. Nancy thought she could identify Ned as a Black Demon, but before she could be sure, all the lights were suddenly extinguished.

"Hey, what's the big idea?" masculine voices called. "Is this part of the show?"

After several minutes of confusion the lights were turned on.

"I'm sorry for the interruption," the emcee said in apology. "Someone thought he'd play a practical joke, I guess."

"And steal the queen?" Bill Tomlin added, gazing toward the stage.

The draped chair which Nancy had occupied was vacant.

"Where is she?" Ned demanded, stepping forward in alarm and removing his mask.

The announcer's voice was unsteady as he

spoke. "No doubt Nancy Drew has stepped outside for a breath of air."

The explanation seemed to satisfy the audience, but Bill and Ned realized that Jeff did not believe this himself. The three hurried outside and began a search for the missing girl.

But by now Nancy was several miles away, a captive in a gray car which raced over the countryside. When the lights had been extinguished during the pantomime, a masked man, whom Nancy assumed to be one of the players, had glided to her side.

"Come with me!" he had commanded.

Thinking that it was part of the show, Nancy had obeyed. No sooner had she reached the hall than a woman appeared from behind a screen of palms. The pair were the same couple who had trailed her to Hamilton and snatched her handbag! They gagged Nancy and hustled her into the rear of a waiting car. The man jumped into the driver's seat.

"Don't make a move or try to escape," he rasped as the woman removed the gag. "Just hand over the map and you won't be harmed."

Nancy squirmed sideways on the car seat, peering at the woman who gripped her arm.

"So it was you who switched off the lights," Nancy remarked.

"Just hand over that map or I'll take it from you," the woman said.

"I have no map."

"Don't try to pull anything on us. You thought you were so clever removing it from your handbag this afternoon. Where is it?"

"I'm not in the habit of carrying maps in party dresses!" Nancy countered.

"All right, don't tell us!" the woman snapped. "But understand this. You're going to be our prisoner until we get it."

The threat filled Nancy with despair. She did not doubt the couple's intentions. If they should contact her father, he would turn over his copy of the map to insure her release.

Nancy set her jaw grimly. She must think of some way out of this situation!

CHAPTER VII

Ghosts

THE automobile was approaching a traffic light. Nancy decided that if the signal turned red she would make a desperate attempt to escape. First she must distract the woman's attention.

"It would be very foolish of you to hold me prisoner," she said in a firm tone of voice. "Especially since the original map has been stolen."

"We know all about that," the man answered.

"Perhaps you engineered the theft," Nancy said coldly.

"Not on your life! I overheard Tomlin Smith tell about the map and the duplicate you made of it. You've got it!"

The woman added, "You sneaked it out of your purse this afternoon!"

"Are you sure I was the one who removed it? Maybe your friend can explain what happened to it. Why don't you ask him?" Nancy suggested.

The man slammed on the brakes to keep from passing through the red traffic light. Angrily he glared over his shoulder at Nancy.

"What are you trying to do? Stir up trouble?" he demanded. "I don't know what you're talking about. I never took that map from your pocket-book."

"Your conscience seems to be bothering you," Nancy said.

"Fred, if you think you can double-cross me—" the woman shouted. "If you have—"

"Oh, shut up, Irene!" the man bellowed. "You make me tired!"

"You're working with Doty and leaving me out!" she accused him, her voice rising to a shrill pitch. "You want to get all the money for your-self and cut me out!"

With the two absorbed in their quarrel, Nancy knew this was her opportunity to escape. It was a long light and in a moment the traffic signal would flash green.

Nancy tore herself from the woman's viselike grasp and jerked open the car door. She tumbled out onto the ground, tripping over her white robe, but picked herself up and began to run.

"Stop her, Fred!" Nancy heard the woman shout. "Don't let her get away!"

Nancy was frantic. On either side of the high-way were deep ditches and high fences separating her from open fields. She kept running but knew that if her agile captor took after her on foot, she would be caught. A second later a car's headlights flashed behind her.

"The kidnappers won't dare bother me with witnesses in the vicinity," she thought. "And maybe I can get a ride!"

Nancy knew that normally it was unwise to signal strangers for a ride, but in this emergency she must try to stop the approaching automobile! She held up her arms and waved them crossways. There was a squeal of brakes. The car drew up a few yards away.

"Don't stop, Henry!" cried the woman beside the driver. "Go on! You know you shouldn't pick up hitchhikers. Besides, this one's dressed up like a ghost!"

Nancy had forgotten about her costume. Fearful that the couple would not help her, she called out:

"Wait! I'm not a ghost! Please wait!"

To her great relief the driver obeyed. Nancy ran to the car. Without waiting for an invitation she climbed into the rear seat.

"Oh, thank you," she said, gasping for breath. "The people in that car back there tried to kidnap me. Drive on quickly, please!"

"What!" the pair exclaimed in astonishment, and the woman added, "Why are you dressed up like that?"

Nancy explained quickly, and noted with relief that the kidnappers were making no attempt to pursue her.

"You don't say!" the driver remarked. "I suppose the kidnapping was like an initiation or something?"

Nancy was about to explain but decided she did not want to cause the couple further alarm. Instead she said, "I'm just so glad you came by. Would it be out of your way to take me to the Emerson gymnasium?"

"I'd be glad to drop you there," the man replied.

Twenty minutes later Nancy was running up the walk toward the college building.

As she did, someone called from behind a clump of bushes. "Nancy, is it you?"

She recognized Ned's voice and said, laughing, "Yes. Did you miss me?"

"Don't be funny. We were worried sick," said Bill Tomlin, who was with Ned. "What happened to you?"

"I was kidnapped. Ned, it was the same couple who followed me this afternoon. But we must keep the whole thing quiet."

"You mean you're not going to notify the police?" Ned demanded disapprovingly.

"No, not until I've talked to Dad. For now we must pass off my disappearance as a joke."

The boys frowned at each other, then Ned spoke. "Jeff Garwin went inside a minute ago to call police headquarters. I suppose you want me to try to stop him."

"Please do, Ned," Nancy replied. "I don't want any publicity."

While Ned hurried into the building, she and Bill Tomlin walked at a more leisurely pace. Nancy related the highlights of her harrowing experience. Then she told Bill of her search for the missing Captain John Abner Tomlin. "Can you give me any clues?"

"Captain Tomlin died when I was very young. I really don't know much about him or his twin brother. My father could tell you a lot more."

"I suppose your parents live some distance from here," Nancy commented thoughtfully.

"No," Bill said. "In Kirkland."

"Why, I'll be passing through there on my way to River Heights!"

"Then why not stop and talk to my father? He owns the Elite Department Store and no doubt will be in his office there."

"I hope he won't think I'm prying—"

"He'd be glad to see you," Bill declared. "I'll phone him and say you're coming."

Nancy was glad that Bill Tomlin had taken her curiosity so casually. She did not want to divulge any information about the Smiths or their possible inheritance.

When Nancy finally returned to the gymnasium, several young men and girls swarmed around her. She answered their questions, giving the impression that her disappearance was nothing more than a fun adventure connected with the pantomime. Her explanation seemed to satisfy everyone and once more the party got into full swing.

In the morning Nancy was awake early, eager to start for Kirkland. To her disappointment she did not see Bill Tomlin again, but Ned brought a message from him.

"Bill says his dad will be expecting you."

"Good," said Nancy as she stepped into her car. "I've had a wonderful time, Ned. Thanks a million for everything."

"I wish you could have stayed until after lunch," he complained good-naturedly. "Please don't take any shortcuts. Stick to the main roads and you won't be kidnapped!"

"You can depend on my obeying orders, sir." Nancy laughed. "And thanks for a grand time."

The trip to Kirkland took less than an hour and Nancy was certain that she had not been followed. Without difficulty she located the Elite Department Store and in a short while was escorted to Mr. Tomlin's office.

"Good morning," Bill's father said cordially, motioning her to a chair. "I understand you're interested in the Tomlin family history."

"Yes, I am. Friends of mine are trying to trace some lost family history. May I ask you a few questions?"

"I'll do my best to answer them."

Nancy inquired about Captain Tomlin, the third in his family to follow the sea. The store owner confirmed that the man had died many years ago while on a voyage to Japan.

"He was Captain John Tomlin and was a cousin of mine," he remarked. "A wonderful man. I thought a lot of him."

"Did he have a middle name?"

"I'm sure he had one but it has slipped my mind at the moment."

Nancy went on, "Your son told me he had a twin brother."

"Yes," Mr. Tomlin replied. "I don't know whether he's dead or alive."

"Did Captain John Tomlin leave a widow and children?" was Nancy's next question.

"He married but had no children to my knowledge. I've never heard what happened to his wife. She disappeared after his death."

"What was Captain Tomlin like?" Nancy queried. "Did he have any hobbies?"

"Yes, he enjoyed collecting things—rare sea shells for instance. I still have one he gave me. I've kept it all these years."

Mr. Tomlin opened a desk drawer. After hunting through a pile of papers, he brought out a small colorful sea shell.

"This is called a Lion's Paw," he said, offering it to Nancy. "It's a type of clam found in East Indian waters. It's Latin name is Hippopus Maculatus!"

"It's very pretty! Did the captain have other hobbies?" Nancy asked.

"He was considered an authority on old songs of the sea. He could sing dozens of them."

"Then he must have had a good voice," Nancy commented. She was interested in this piece of information; it might be a clue.

Everything she had learned seemed to confirm her idea that Captain John Tomlin was Tomlin Smith's missing brother John Abner. Feeling that she owed Bill's father an explanation for asking so many questions, she mentioned her theory to him.

"I should like to meet Tomlin Smith," he said. "I wonder if the two were identical twins."

"I don't believe so. As far as I know there is no resemblance between them."

"Somewhere at home I have a photograph of Captain Tomlin," the store owner said thoughtfully. "Would that be of any help to you?"

"Oh, yes. Mr. Smith should be able to identify the picture."

"Then I'll mail it to you if I can find it," Mr.

Tomlin promised. "Just write your address on this pad."

Nancy was elated by the successful interview, feeling that she had taken a long step toward solving the mystery about the owner of the other half of the map. As she walked lightheartedly through the store toward an exit, she decided to phone Bess and went to a booth.

"Hi, Bess!" she began. "I'm on my way to Mrs. Chatham's estate, but Dad doesn't want me to go there alone. Could you and George meet me there in half an hour?"

"I'll be glad to come," Bess answered instantly. "I'll call George."

"This is what I'd like you to do for me," Nancy said. "I'm going to investigate the music studio but I don't want Mrs. Chatham to know it. Could you both keep her engaged in conversation?"

"Will do," Bess promised. "Please be careful."

After chatting for a moment longer, Nancy left the store. She drove on toward Rocky Edge, arriving ahead of her friends. As she glanced up the road, wondering how long they would be delayed, she was startled to hear a shrill scream. The cry had come from the area near the building which Trixie called Ship Cottage.

Nancy sprang from her car and dashed toward the spot. Emerging from among the oak trees, she caught a glimpse of the little girl. Trixie Chatham was running away from the studio, her hair blowing wildly across her face.

"Ghosts! Ghosts!" she screamed. "I saw 'em! They're in the cottage!"

The child did not see Nancy nor hear her soothing voice as she called to the little girl. In panic Trixie scrambled through a hedge, straight into the path of an oncoming car!

CHAPTER VIII

Nancy Investigates

INSTINCTIVELY Nancy darted after the terrified child. She seized her by the hand and jerked the little girl from the roadway just as the automobile whizzed by.

"Let me go!" Trixie cried, trying to pull away. Then, seeing who her rescuer was, she relaxed slightly. "Oh, it's you," she said.

"What's the matter, Trixie?" Nancy asked gently. "You were almost run down by that car."

The little girl began to sob, her thin body shaking. While Nancy was trying to comfort her, another car approached and drew up alongside the road. George was driving; Bess sat beside her.

"What's wrong?" Bess asked, stepping from the car. "Has Trixie been hurt?"

"No, she's all right," Nancy answered, "but she had a narrow escape. Something frightened her and she ran into the path of a car."

"What was it that scared you, Trixie?" George asked.

Trixie moved nearer Nancy, away from the other two girls.

"It—it was a ghost," she answered, her voice trembling. "A great big one with horrible eyes! It glared at me from the window of the Ship Cottage!"

"Oh, Trixie, you don't really believe that!" George laughed. "There are no ghosts."

"Then what was it I saw?" the child demanded. "There's something big with horrible eyes hiding in there!"

Nancy spoke up quietly. "I'll tell you what we'll do, Trixie. You run along to the house with Bess. George and I will go to the music studio and take a look around."

"Maybe that thing will hurt you," the little girl said anxiously.

"We'll be careful. You go with Bess."

Somewhat reluctantly Trixie allowed herself to be led up the path. George and Nancy turned in the opposite direction, walking swiftly to the studio.

"Trixie didn't imagine that she saw glaring eyes watching her," Nancy declared, lowering her voice. "The first day I came here some very strange things happened while I was inside the building. That's why Dad doesn't like me to come here alone."

"You think someone may be hiding there?"

"It's possible. Before Ellen accepts work with Mrs. Chatham we must investigate this place thoroughly."

Cautiously the girls circled the quaint small building. They saw no one and heard no unusual sounds.

Nancy tried the door, expecting to walk right in as she had done the first time, but to her surprise it would not open.

"That's odd," she remarked in a puzzled tone. "The studio was unlocked when I was here before."

"Perhaps we can get in through a window," George suggested, testing one on the front of the house.

She could not raise it nor any of the others.

"I wonder if I should ask Mrs. Chatham for the key," Nancy mused. Then, answering herself, she said, "Why not? She can always refuse."

The two girls hurried to the main house, where they found Bess seated on the porch with Mrs. Chatham. Trixie was playing on the steps with a white cat and laughing shrilly at its antics.

"Can't you please be quiet?" her mother asked irritably.

"You always say that. 'Be quiet; don't do that!' If Daddy were alive, I'd have fun."

"Trixie!" Mrs. Chatham shouted. "Not another word or you'll go to your room." The child subsided into silence.

Nancy felt sorry for Trixie, knowing how upset the child had been. She was certain that Mrs. Chatham did not know about the unusual happenings at Ship Cottage. To confirm this theory, Nancy casually asked the woman who used the small house.

"Why, no one," Mrs. Chatham replied, surprised at the question.

"You never go there yourself?"

"Almost never. I've been reluctant to stir up old memories."

"You keep the studio locked, I suppose?" Nancy inquired.

"Usually I do," Mrs. Chatham replied. "For a while I left it unlocked thinking Trixie might like to play there. But she refused to step inside!"

"Did you ever ask her why she dislikes the place so much?"

"It would do no good," Mrs. Chatham said. "She has a very vivid imagination and tells outlandish stories."

Nancy was inclined to believe the woman had no idea that Trixie's misbehavior might result from a feeling of loneliness. If her mother did not believe her and the servants were not kind to her, the child did indeed need a friend. Ellen Smith could be just the person!

"You mentioned the other day that your first husband collected ship models," Nancy remarked after a moment.

"Would you like to see the collection?" Mrs. Chatham inquired politely.

"Yes, I would."

"I'll get the key," Mrs. Chatham said, rising.

Trixie remained at the house while her mother and the three girls went to the studio. The widow unlocked the front door, pushed it open, and stepped inside. The girls followed.

Nancy's eyes roved about the dusty room. Nothing appeared to have been disturbed since her last visit. There was no sign of either an intruder or an open panel in the wall.

"What charming little ships!" Bess exclaimed as she examined the model of a sailing clipper on the mantelpiece.

While her friends were talking to Mrs. Chatham, Nancy seated herself at the piano. Hesitatingly she touched the keys. The notes sounded clear and loud, echoing in the room.

"That's certainly strange," she mused.

Turning around, she asked Mrs. Chatham if the piano had a secret spring which at times prevented it from being played.

"Goodness, no! Why do you ask?" The woman laughed. But a moment later she said, "It's possible your question may be far more to the point than I first thought. The inventor who lived here might have installed some kind of gadget."

"Then the piano was here when you took over the place?"

"Yes, it was. Nothing has been changed. In fact, this building never has been used."

"You haven't found any secret panels?" Nancy inquired eagerly.

"Not here, but there is one in my bedroom. It serves no real purpose. Once Trixie got behind it by accident, and has never wanted to come into my room since."

Nancy decided to tell Mrs. Chatham about her strange experience in the studio. The woman was upset about the man behind the sliding panel. She was greatly relieved when the girls offered to search the room for hidden springs, secret doors, or mechanical gadgets. The trio industriously began looking for a movable section in the walls.

"I'll go outside and see how the exterior of the building compares in size with this room," George said.

Bess and Mrs. Chatham followed. Nancy resumed her investigating. First she turned up the corner of a rug which lay under the piano. To her surprise she found several wires which evidently ran down one leg of the instrument through the rug and the floor.

"There must be a switch to turn the piano off

and on," Nancy mused. "I wonder where it is."

Another search of the walls revealed nothing.

"The switch must be controlled from a spot back of a secret panel!"

Nancy decided to go over each section of the wall reflected in the mirror, moving her hands along the wall an inch at a time. A wooden peg which seemed to secure the wide panel to the sheathing drew her attention. As she fingered it, Nancy felt a slight movement. Between the boards she could see a tiny crack of space.

"I've found the opening!" she thought jubilantly.

Nancy pushed and pulled, increasing the gap only a little at a time. Then suddenly the woodwork gave, sliding back easily. As Nancy turned to shout her discovery, she heard a shrill scream.

"Help! Help! Nancy!"

The cry had come from outside the building. Nancy had recognized the voice as George's!

CHAPTER IX

Shadow of Fear

DARTING from the studio, Nancy spotted George far up the path, pursuing a man whose head was bent low.

Quickly guessing that the fugitive had been caught prowling near the building, Nancy joined in the chase. In a moment she caught up with George, but the two were unable to overtake the fleet-footed man. By the time the girls reached the boundary of the estate, he was out of sight.

"It's no use," George said, halting to catch her breath. "We'll never get him now."

"Did you recognize the man?" Nancy asked. "Was he near the music studio?"

"I'd never seen him before. He just suddenly appeared out of the rear of the building. His head was lowered and I couldn't get a good look at his face."

Before Nancy could question George further, Mrs. Chatham and Bess hurried down the path.

"What happened?" Bess asked anxiously. "We heard the cry for help. Did one of you get hurt?"

"No, we're all right," George replied. "After you and Mrs. Chatham went off, the man apparently thought no one was here. He pushed aside part of the cottage wall and stepped outside. When he saw me, he took off."

"Goodness!" Bess exclaimed nervously. "There must be a secret passage connected with the studio. That man probably was listening to our conversation when we were inside. He could have harmed us!"

"I found out how to open that secret panel in the studio only a minute ago," Nancy said.

"You did?" Mrs. Chatham asked in astonishment.

"I'll show you. But first I want to see the hidden door George found."

George started down the path.

"I'll join you in a minute," Mrs. Chatham said, turning in the opposite direction. "I'm going to call the police. It frightens me that someone is prowling about the premises!"

George had no difficulty locating the concealed section. Nancy pushed against the wall and stepped through the narrow opening.

"This passageway must lead along the back wall to an alcove behind the piano," she called, her voice muffled. "Let's explore."

"I'm not as thin as you are, Nancy," Bess complained as she attempted to follow. "I'll never make it!"

"Then go into the studio and enter through the secret panel. I left it open. George and I are bound to meet you somewhere!"

Bess vanished around the building. The other two girls moved along the inner wall until they came to an unlocked door which opened into a small chamber.

"I can't see a thing!" Nancy declared. "We should have brought flashlights."

"Ouch!" George exclaimed. "This place must be lined with rock!"

Cautiously the girls groped their way toward the half-open panel ahead. They were glad when Bess pushed it the remainder of the way, allowing light to flood the gloomy space.

"What did you find?" she called.

"Boxes and lots of other things," Nancy replied, gazing about her.

"Do you think it's a storage room?" George asked.

"Either that, or some thief's hideaway for loot," Nancy commented as she examined a large Chinese vase.

While the girls were inspecting two trunks, rain began to patter on the tin roof.

"Just listen to that!" Nancy said in dismay. "And I wanted to take a look at the footprints near the hidden door. Perhaps I can beat the storm. George, you stay inside with Bess. No sense in all of us getting wet."

Hastily Nancy looked about for a board or box lid to cover the prints but could find neither. She ran back through the passage and outside. Footprints made by a man's large shoes were still visible.

The rain descended heavily as Nancy took pencil and paper from her purse and rapidly drew an outline of one footmark. The toe of the shoe was very wide, and the rubber heel had left a peculiar star-design imprint.

"The marks are nearly washed away now," Nancy thought ruefully. "But at least I have a sketch."

She closed the secret door and scurried into the studio. Ten minutes later Mrs. Chatham arrived with a supply of umbrellas, but insisted that the girls stay at the cottage to see the police. Presently their car pulled up in front.

The two officers questioned Mrs. Chatham and the girls regarding the trespasser. Unfortunately George's description of him was sketchy. The only tangible clue was the footprint which Nancy had made.

"This should be of some use to us," one of the policemen declared, pocketing the drawing.

Before leaving, the officers inspected the hidden chamber. Mrs. Chatham readily identified many of the articles as the property of her first husband.

"At least I have a sketch of the intruder's foot-prints," Nancy said to herself

Some she did not recognize but assumed they must have also belonged to him.

After the police had gone, Nancy asked thoughtfully, "Is it possible that Mr. Chatham knew of this hiding place and stored goods here without your knowledge?"

"Yes, but I don't see why he wouldn't have told me." Mrs. Chatham paused. "Oh, I do hope nothing of John's has been stolen. It would break my heart to lose anything belonging to him."

Tears glistened in her eyes as she lifted a miniature ship, similar to those which the girls had seen in the studio room. For the first time Nancy felt herself warming to Mrs. Chatham. No doubt her strange actions resulted from grief and loneliness.

The question that troubled Nancy most was, Who was the mysterious fugitive and was he hiding loot on the premises or taking articles away?

"But how did he learn of this place?" she wondered.

As Nancy mulled over the matter, she absently raised the lid of a leather-covered box. She stared in surprise and delight. Inside, carefully wrapped in tissue paper, were many large, rare sea shells.

"Mrs. Chatham, did your first husband collect these?" she asked breathlessly.

"Yes, he did. He loved the sea and everything connected with it."

"You never mentioned your first husband's last name," Nancy said, waiting eagerly for the answer.

"Why, I thought I did. His name was Tomlin— John Tomlin."

"Tomlin!" Nancy could hardly believe her ears. "Then he may be related to Tomlin Smith!" she added, her eyes dancing with excitement.

"Tomlin Smith?" the widow repeated. "Who is he, may I ask?"

"Ellen's father! Mrs. Chatham, do you have a photograph of John Tomlin?"

"Unfortunately, no."

Nancy revealed everything she knew about Mr. Smith's quest for his missing twin brother but did not mention the map. She also related the story she had heard from Bill Tomlin's father.

"My husband had a fine baritone voice," Mrs. Chatham declared. "He loved songs of the sea and collected them."

"Everything tallies with the information given me by Bill Tomlin's father! Without question your first husband was related to the Tomlin family in Kirkland. The two men were cousins. Now if only I can prove a relationship to Tomlin Smith! Did your husband have a middle name?"

"If so, he didn't mention it. At no time did my husband tell me much about his early life," Mrs. Chatham added.

"He never spoke of his father?" Nancy asked, fingering a large pink shell.

"No. You see, we were married after knowing each other only two weeks. John settled me in a lovely little cottage, furnished it beautifully, and then set sail but he did not return."

"Was his ship lost?" Bess inquired sympathetically.

"My husband was taken ill and died on a voyage to Japan," Mrs. Chatham explained, her eyes misty.

The widow revealed a few additional facts but none of great value. Her husband, she said, had been ten years older than she and frequently had spoken of himself as a "son of the sea."

"That might mean his father had been a captain too," Nancy mused. "Tell me, Mrs. Chatham, did your first husband leave any papers or letters?"

"Several boxes were brought to me some time after his death. I received a small amount of money and an insurance policy. I'll confess I read very few of the letters, for they seemed to be old business ones and I wasn't interested. I was too heartbroken to care. But I saved every one of them. They should be somewhere in this studio. I asked Mr. Chatham to bring them here."

"I'll look right—"

At that instant a fearful shriek cut the air. The group was electrified for an instant, then Nancy made a dash outside.

"Moth-er!" came in terrified tones from somewhere to the right.

"Trixie!"

Nancy dashed off, with Mrs. Chatham, Bess and George close on her heels.

"Where are you?" the child's mother called.

There was no answer!

Frantically the group ran to left and to right, shouting Trixie's name. Suddenly a muffled sound reached Nancy's ears. She stopped short to listen.

The child was crying and saying, "I want to get out! I want to get out!"

Almost directly in front of her Nancy saw a yawning hole in the ground. She peered down. Indistinctly she could see a figure.

"Trixie!" Nancy gasped. "Are you hurt?"

"I'm okay. Where's my m-mother?" came the sobbing voice from below. "Please h-help me out!"

The child had fallen into a dry wellhole.

Nancy lay down on the ground and stretched one arm into the chasm. She could not reach Trixie.

"I'll get a ladder," Nancy said reassuringly. "Don't be frightened."

By this time the others had come up. Mrs. Chatham, hearing that her daughter was unharmed, alternately laughed and cried. In a few minutes George located the gardener and he brought a long ladder.

"I want Nancy Drew to come down," called Trixie as the man started to descend.

"Nancy, do you mind?" Mrs. Chatham asked.

"Not at all."

As Nancy began the climb, the woman snapped at the gardener, "Hoskins, how do you account for this uncovered hole? You are supposed to have charge of the grounds."

"Mrs. Chatham, I had no idea this hole was here. Probably it was grown over and—"

Nancy heard no more for she had reached the bottom rung. Trixie, her knees slightly scratched, impulsively hugged her rescuer and scrambled up the ladder. Nancy quickly glanced about. To her right was an opening to a tunnel. The young sleuth wanted to investigate it but decided that right now she had better hurry to the top of the well. Mrs. Chatham stood there hugging her daughter.

Nancy said mysteriously to Bess and George, "Very interesting place down there. I'll be back in a minute." She headed for her car. When Nancy returned, she held her flashlight.

Bess shook her head. "Don't tell me you've found something in that hole!"

"Uh-huh. Want to come along?"

"George, you go," Bess shivered in reply.

Excited over this latest development, George followed her friend into the dark pit. Nancy swung the beam of her light around the opening of the cavern. It was fairly wide and about six feet high. Cautiously the girls walked in for several feet to a point where the tunnel turned abruptly. As Nancy's light exposed the cavern beyond, they stared open-mouthed. Across one wall and on the ceiling flickered the shadow of a weird, forbidding shape.

CHAPTER X

Valuable Property

THE flashlight focused on a large dugout beneath the silhouette. In the center stood a strange-looking contraption, rusted and crumbling with age.

George broke the silence. "It has dials. Looks like an old oil burner."

Nancy did not reply. She pointed to an envelope attached to the unwieldy object. Printed on the envelope was a warning:

HIGHLY EXPLOSIVE
DO NOT TOUCH

"In that case," George put in quickly, "let's get out of here."

Nancy tugged her friend back, saying, "Wait a minute. You don't really believe this thing will explode, do you? Obviously it has been here a long while and—"

"*Mm*," George murmured warily. "Nevertheless it could go off."

She gulped as Nancy beamed the light through a decayed section, then said, "Well, Miss Detective, what next?"

"Two things. First, I've been wondering how the machine got here. I thought there might have been a door connecting this tunnel with the main house. But since there is none, the machine must have been constructed in this dugout," Nancy declared. "The only person who would have masterminded such a project was Silas Norse."

"I agree," said George. "What's the second thing?"

"The envelope."

Carefully Nancy removed the dusty envelope from the mechanism and opened it. A letter inside was headed: *List of Inventions in House and Grounds of Rocky Edge.* About ten were mentioned, revealing all kinds of strange gadgets secreted on the place, including the secret panel and piano in the music studio.

At the bottom was a description of Norse's machine, which he called his "greatest achievement." Many of the words were in German and the girls understood little of it. But the last line read:

" 'In this spot it has harmed no one yet.' "

Nancy stopped abruptly, saying, "There's a break here in this note with a short penciled sen-

tence. 'It will never harm anyone. I cannot finish
my work. I am too ill. Silas Norse.' "

"We'd better tell Mrs. Chatham about all of
this," George urged. "She'll want to have this
machine dismantled completely and see that all
the other gadgets are removed for the safety of
Trixie, herself, and the people who work on the
estate."

Nancy agreed. As the two started toward the
ladder, she said, "One thing I want to do right
away. Advise her to take Trixie away from here
until the place has had a thorough investigation."

When the girls emerged, Bess was waiting for
them. "You must have found a gold mine," she
said, adding almost immediately, "Mrs. Chatham
took Trixie back to the house, but said she'd return to the studio alone."

"Shall we go there?" Nancy suggested. "We'll
tell you and Mrs. Chatham what we found."

After Nancy had located the gardener and made
sure that he covered the hole with heavy planks,
the trio headed for Ship Cottage. Mrs. Chatham
was busy searching through some boxes which she
had carried from the windowless secret chamber
into the main room.

"Nancy and George stumbled upon something
unusual in the well," Bess told her.

Nancy related the whole story and produced the
inventor's letter.

Mrs. Chatham was both surprised and alarmed.

"I never dreamed such things were here!" she exclaimed. "If I had known, I wouldn't have stayed."

This was Nancy's chance to make a suggestion. "Until Rocky Edge can be thoroughly searched, don't you think it might be wise to take Trixie away on a vacation?"

"You're right. I wish we could go somewhere far away," Mrs. Chatham replied. "But I detest travel by automobile. And planes—well, I think the most relaxing way to travel is by boat."

Nancy had not intended to tell Mrs. Chatham about the treasure map in Tomlin Smith's possession until the relationship between him and the woman's first husband was established. Suddenly it occurred to her that should this be the case, Mrs. Chatham might propose an expedition to the mysterious island.

"Would you enjoy a trip to a treasure island?" she inquired with a smile.

"Are you joking?" the woman asked.

When Nancy had finished the amazing tale of the Tomlin twins' inheritance, Mrs. Chatham declared with enthusiasm, "If the missing half of the map can be found, I'll finance the entire trip. Nothing would please me more than to have you, Bess, George, and Ellen join us."

Bess's eyes popped at the generous invitation and she and George thanked the widow.

Nancy said, "Ellen will be thrilled! At the first opportunity I'll tell the Smith family the wonderful news." Then she added ruefully, "Finding the map is our only problem—"

"I just remembered," Mrs. Chatham interrupted, "that John did say we might go treasure hunting together. At the time I'm afraid I really didn't take the idea very seriously."

Nancy said eagerly, "That almost proves the relationship of the two Tomlins! And if that's so, then your husband must have had the missing portion of the map. Maybe it's—"

"In the box of papers I've been looking for!" Mrs. Chatham finished excitedly. "This detective work is new to me, but I'm trying to catch on."

Suddenly Nancy disappeared into the dark chamber.

Mrs. Chatham called after her, "Oh, Nancy, I've been all through there. I'm sure the box is gone. Maybe it was stolen."

But the young detective was unwilling to give up. She beamed her flashlight into the corners of the narrow room. Bess and George watched from the panel entrance.

Finally Nancy stooped to move a pile of small oriental rugs. "What's this?" she murmured.

Against the wall where the carpets had lain was a rectangle of wood which did not match the adjoining panels. As Nancy pushed against it, the section opened inward, revealing a small, dark recess.

"Another secret hiding place!" she called out.

Her two friends dashed to Nancy's side, Mrs. Chatham at their heels. With mounting excitement, Nancy thrust her arm into the opening.

"I've found something!" she cried out, and a moment later brought out a tin box.

"That's it!" Mrs. Chatham exclaimed. "That's the missing box!"

As Nancy unfastened the lid, she hoped they had at last found the long-lost half of the map. But the metal box contained only two objects—a small key and a bankbook. The name of the depositor was John Tomlin. Nancy had hoped it would be John Abner Tomlin. The bank was in New Kirk, a seacoast city, and there was a large sum of money on deposit.

"No doubt this key unlocks his safe-deposit box in the same bank," George put in.

"I must go to New Kirk at once," the widow declared.

Nancy spoke up. "You may have some trouble at the bank. You'll probably need proper identification and notarized papers. Why not discuss the situation first with my dad?"

"Yes, yes. I mustn't lose my head."

When Mrs. Chatham had calmed down sufficiently, Bess observed, "I've been wondering about this recess in the wall. I don't recall that it was included in Silas Norse's list of places where his inventions were."

"It wasn't," Nancy confirmed, "but that doesn't

necessarily mean Mr. Norse did *not* put it in. From the appearance of his weak handwriting, indicating poor health, I doubt that he made a record of all his work.

"I do have another idea, though," she went on. "Perhaps the man that George spied coming out of the concealed opening knows about the missing map!"

"What!" her listeners chorused.

"It's only a hunch but he may have stolen it from this box. Furthermore, he must have hidden the box here, not Mr. Chatham. Obviously Mr. Chatham did not know the contents of this box. If he had, he certainly would have told his wife."

Nancy's conclusions stunned Mrs. Chatham.

George tried to comfort her by saying, "We're used to Nancy's whizbang brain. I suppose, Nancy, you can tell us the thief's name, too." She grinned.

Nancy laughed. With a twinkle in her eye, she replied, "I might make a guess. I'll bet he's Spike Doty!"

She told of the old newspaper account of how Spike Doty, the burglar at Norse's mansion, had sued the inventor. She also mentioned that the police had deduced from her drawing and description that the thief at Ellen's home was Spike.

Before anyone could comment, Trixie came to the doorway of the studio. "Mother!" she called loudly. "There's a man and a woman at the house. They want to talk to you."

"Did they give you their names?" Mrs. Chatham asked.

When Trixie shook her head, the widow excused herself and went quickly to the house. Her daughter did not follow. Instead Trixie entered the cottage and peeked into the secret chamber where papers and objects had been carefully sorted. To keep the child from touching the articles, Nancy diverted her attention by saying:

"How would you like to play a magic piano?"

"A magic piano?" Trixie repeated, her eyes opening wide. "Where is it?"

"Here in the studio." She led the little girl to the instrument.

After Trixie had seated herself and played a few notes, Nancy turned off the control switch. Silence.

The child laughed. "How do you do it? Show me, please!"

Nancy smiled at the word "please," so different from Trixie's usual manner. As Nancy was showing her how to operate the switch, Mrs. Chatham reappeared.

"Nancy, I'd like you to come to the house and meet Mr. and Mrs. Brown. They have an interesting story which may shed some light on the matter of the missing map."

Excitedly Nancy followed Mrs. Chatham up the

winding path. A car Nancy did not recognize stood in the driveway. Mr. and Mrs. Brown sat on the porch.

The couple stared in astonishment as Nancy approached. The man said something to his companion, then both dashed from the porch and into the automobile.

"Well, what do you think of that!" Mrs. Chatham exclaimed indignantly.

Nancy had sprinted toward the man, but he was too quick for her. Before she could reach the car, it sped down the driveway.

"Why did they run away?" Mrs. Chatham asked, puzzled.

"Because," Nancy announced, "they are the couple who kidnapped me from Emerson College!"

CHAPTER XI

Clue to a Treasure

THE automobile had pulled away so swiftly that Nancy barely had time to jot down its license number. She ran into the house to call the police, thinking a patrol car might be able to capture the kidnappers.

With Mrs. Chatham hovering at her side, Nancy quickly reported what had happened, then hung up the phone. She turned to the widow.

"Please tell me what you know about the Browns."

"They introduced themselves as Mr. and Mrs. Fred Brown, and said they were trying to find the widow of Captain John Tomlin. They claimed to have known him well before his death."

"Did they question you about the map?" Nancy asked.

"They hinted that Captain Tomlin had told

them a great secret before his death and warned me to be on my guard if I were his widow."

"On guard?"

"It seems that an unscrupulous man—they wouldn't give his name—is determined to get hold of a valuable paper belonging to my first husband."

"Of course they referred to the map!"

"I thought so but pretended otherwise. The Browns advised me to leave Rocky Edge before the man might threaten or harm me. I told them I wanted a friend to hear their story before I made any decision. I didn't mention your name."

"My sudden appearance must have given them a great shock," Nancy commented.

"I wonder how much they really know about the lost map," Mrs. Chatham said.

"Probably not much. They may believe you have it here. Either they're working with that man who hid in the studio, or else they hope to outwit him and get it themselves."

Mrs. Chatham walked nervously to the French window and gazed into the garden.

Nancy said, "I suggest you hire guards. The Browns may sneak back and search for the map."

Mrs. Chatham promised to attend to the matter directly.

"Do you feel we should give up the proposed trip to New Kirk?" the widow asked as she walked with Nancy to the convertible.

Nancy replied quickly, "Considering what has happened, I think it's very important to learn the contents of your husband's safe-deposit box."

"Then I'll see your father as soon as I can," Mrs. Chatham declared.

After saying good-by, Nancy picked up Bess and George and said she wanted to go home via Wayland and stop at the police station.

"I'd like to talk to the chief, but not on the phone from here. Mrs. Chatham is too upset."

Nancy told the girls about the mysterious couple who had come to call and finished just as she reached the police station. There was no news of the Browns, but the chief confirmed Nancy's suspicion that the one clear footprint recently made by the intruder at the Rocky Edge studio belonged to Spike Doty.

"Spike first appeared locally while a seaman on a river steamer. After a prison sentence for burglary he was released and went to New York. We lost track of him. But we'll keep looking for Spike and the Browns, too."

On the way back Bess and George picked up their car. When Nancy reached home she found a special-delivery envelope from Bill Tomlin's father. He had enclosed the faded photograph of a man about thirty dressed in a sea captain's uniform.

"What a good clue!" she thought. "I must show this to Mr. Smith and Mrs. Chatham."

Nancy gave her father an account of her recent adventures, describing her abduction by the Browns and their unexpected appearance at Rocky Edge. She ended by asking permission to accompany Mrs. Chatham to New Kirk.

"You may go, but only on the condition that I talk to Mrs. Chatham first," the lawyer replied.

That evening Nancy mulled over the strange developments in the case. "Where do the Browns and Spike and Rorke fit into the picture?" she pondered. "Are they working together or separately?"

When Nancy finally went to bed she dreamed of a heavy-set man with evil eyes peering at her from behind various objects. In this fantasy she seemed to be standing on a high revolving platform. Regardless of which direction it turned, she kept seeing the same terrifying man in different costumes. Nancy awoke and sat up.

"What a nightmare! I can see that face yet!"

She realized that her mind had played a trick on her. The face in her dreams was that of the man on the ladder at the Smith home. The cruel, beady eyes and bearded face were those above the brass-button "apparition" which had haunted the Ship Cottage at Rocky Edge.

"Why, that's a clue!" she thought suddenly. "Why didn't I think of asking Trixie before?"

Leaping from bed, Nancy ran to her desk and

switched on a light. She seized a crayon and sketched the leering face she had seen in her dream.

"Now I have two pictures to show," she thought, "the photo to Mrs. Chatham and this sketch to her daughter. Trixie's identification would be double proof that Spike Doty is the ghost of Ship Cottage."

Nancy's opportunity came the next morning. The widow phoned that she and Trixie would call on Carson Drew at his office. Nancy said she would be there too.

She at once showed the faded photograph to Mrs. Chatham, who quickly recognized the captain as her first husband. "Yes, that's John. Of course he looks younger than the way I knew him."

Nancy said she would show the photograph to Tomlin Smith on her next visit. She then offered to take care of Trixie while Mrs. Chatham and Mr. Drew talked. Nancy led the child to an anteroom and took the crayon sketch from her handbag.

"I have a picture to show you," Nancy said. "This is a drawing I made last night."

The child gave a muffled shriek!

"It's that same ghost!" she cried. "Take it away, please! Even the picture scares me!"

Nancy hugged the little girl and spoke soothingly to her. In a moment Trixie's fears were gone. Soon Mrs. Chatham and Mr. Drew came out of his private office.

"Everything is arranged," the widow declared happily as she turned to Nancy. "Your father prepared the papers I'll need in New Kirk and made an appointment with the bank's president. Nancy, you're to go with me."

"Wonderful!" Nancy exclaimed, flashing her father a grateful glance. "When do we leave?"

"In two hours, if you can be ready."

"I can be ready in fifteen minutes." Nancy laughed. "How about plane reservations?"

"I made them by phone," Mr. Drew put in.

"Did you hire guards to watch your home?" Nancy asked Mrs. Chatham.

"Yes, two men are there."

Nancy looked at Trixie, then drew the woman aside. "Perhaps Ellen Smith could come to your house and take care of Trixie while we're away."

Mrs. Chatham was pleased at the suggestion. Fortunately Nancy was able to reach Ellen by phone. She said she would gladly stay with Trixie. Ellen could barely contain her excitement when told of Mrs. Chatham's generous invitation to go on a cruise in search of the treasure island.

Then she said, "About Trixie, I'll have to leave tomorrow afternoon."

"We'll be back by that time," Nancy replied, then hung up. "Mrs. Chatham, it's all arranged."

The grateful woman relayed the news to Trixie, who was delighted.

After the Chathams had gone, Mr. Drew turned to his daughter. "Besides Ellen, have you told anyone else about going to New Kirk?" he asked.

"I discussed it with Hannah. That's all."

Mr. Drew nodded approval. "I've advised Mrs. Chatham to keep the reason for her trip a secret."

"You think someone may follow us?"

"I doubt that, but it's better to be cautious," her father said. "The Browns have demonstrated their intense interest in the map, Nancy. That's why I want you to be careful."

"I will, Dad. And now I have something for you."

She handed him the crayon sketch of the Ship Cottage "ghost" and told him of Trixie's positive identification.

"I'll tell the police," he offered, studying the face. "I hope Trixie was sure and not just frightened by the sinister-looking face."

"She is very bright," Nancy replied. "I believe we can depend on her. Well, I must hurry to catch the plane!"

Aided by Mrs. Gruen, Nancy quickly packed an overnight bag and changed into traveling clothes. A short time later she and Mrs. Chatham were winging toward New Kirk. At the end of a speedy but uneventful trip, they checked into a hotel and then proceeded to the bank.

No sooner had they entered when Mrs. Chatham began to display signs of nervousness. While she and Nancy waited to see the president, the widow fingered the legal papers Mr. Drew had given her.

"Now what was it your father told me to say?" she asked in panic. In the same breath she continued, "Won't you do the talking, Nancy?"

"I'll be glad to if you wish, Mrs. Chatham."

Nancy had only a few moments to glance over the material before she and Mrs. Chatham were ushered into the private office of Mr. Dowell, the president. Nancy made a simple presentation of the case, offering proof of Mrs. Chatham's identity. She also gave the man a letter requesting the opening of Captain John Tomlin's safe-deposit box.

"For a long time we've tried to locate Captain Tomlin or his heirs," Mr. Dowell said. "Rentals on the box have accumulated, you know."

"I'll be glad to pay whatever amount is due the bank," Mrs. Chatham said. "May we look at the contents today?"

"I fear that will be impossible," the banker answered. "However, if we find your papers in good order, it's possible the box can be opened tomorrow in the presence of someone from the surrogate's office."

After making an appointment for nine o'clock

the following day, Nancy and Mrs. Chatham returned to the hotel. Despite their disappointment, the two thoroughly enjoyed the evening at a fine restaurant.

At bedtime Nancy was summoned to the telephone. Mrs. Chatham, who had been calling her home, said Ellen Smith wished to speak to her.

"Oh, Nancy," Ellen said in a strained voice, "please don't stay away any longer than you have to. I didn't want to frighten Mrs. Chatham, but her place is terribly spooky, with creepy shadows in the garden. Twice I've called to the guards but no one answered. I don't believe they're even on duty."

For the sake of Mrs. Chatham, Nancy kept calm. "Ellen, why don't you ask Hannah Gruen to come over? Dad has to be away tonight and tomorrow, I know, so she's alone. Please do that."

The girl promised, relief in her voice. Nancy went to bed but found it hard to sleep and was awake early. She hoped Mrs. Chatham's business could be attended to at once and an early return made to River Heights. When the two reached the bank, Mr. Dowell greeted them cordially and presented an official from the surrogate's office.

"The box will be opened without further delay," he assured them. "I've arranged for an inheritance tax man to be here this morning. He'll list the contents for tax purposes."

He personally conducted Nancy and Mrs. Chatham to an underground room and sat at one end of a long table.

The tax official directed Nancy and Mrs. Chatham to sit at the far end of the table. Then he and the bank official sat down with the box before them. As the government man raised the lid, the bulky papers that filled the box crackled. He picked up the top envelope and exclaimed, "Hm! What's this? . . . 'Clue to a Treasure'!"

CHAPTER XII

Triple Alarm

"THAT must be it," Nancy thought, trying to control her mounting excitement. She and Mrs. Chatham exchanged looks of apprehension. They hoped the official would not ask questions about the treasure. Both were quickly relieved when the men merely glanced at the enclosed sheet, put it back, and went on to examine the rest of the papers. Finally the contents were listed. Nothing was taxable. At length Mrs. Chatham and Nancy were left alone.

"Thank goodness!" Mrs. Chatham murmured in relief. "Now we can look in that envelope. Surely it must contain the missing map."

With trembling fingers she took out the contents.

"It's a letter," she said, unable to hide her disappointment.

"Is it signed by Captain Tomlin?" Nancy asked.

"Yes, this is his handwriting."

Did the letter tell what became of the missing treasure map? Nancy wondered.

Her voice vibrant with emotion, Mrs. Chatham read the entire note aloud. In it her first husband revealed details of his early life never before disclosed to her, including the fact he had dropped the name Abner because he did not like it. There were other facts sufficient to prove that he and Tomlin Smith were twin brothers.

"So that part of the mystery is solved!" said Nancy.

The letter concerned itself mainly with the inheritance originally secreted by Captain Tomlin's seafaring grandfather.

"Listen to this!" Mrs. Chatham exclaimed as she came to a particularly significant paragraph.

" 'All these years I have kept the torn section of a treasure map given me by my father. Fearing theft I made a copy of it. Only a month ago, this very copy was stolen from my cabin, unquestionably by a member of the crew.' "

"What is the date of the letter?" Nancy asked as the widow paused to catch her breath.

"It was written only a week before my husband's death. He continues:

" 'I have taken the original map and hidden it on the *Warwick*. This map, if combined with the section in the possession of my missing twin brother, will lead to the discovery of our grand-father's great treasure.' "

"That doesn't add up!" Nancy exclaimed. "Wasn't the *Warwick* the name of the vessel your husband sailed?"

"You're right, Nancy, it was."

"Then how could he have removed the parch-ment map from his own ship and still have hidden it there?"

"Perhaps he meant he hid it somewhere in an-other part of the vessel—away from his cabin," Mrs. Chatham suggested.

"That doesn't seem likely," Nancy said, shaking her head. "No, I'm sure Captain Tomlin never would have risked having the original found by members of his crew. Especially after the copy had been stolen."

Mrs. Chatham furrowed her brow in bewilder-ment as Nancy went on, "Apparently he thought you would understand where the map was hid-den."

"I haven't the faintest idea!"

Nancy was silent for several moments as she re-read the letter. Then suddenly her face bright-ened.

"I get it!" she exclaimed. "Captain Tomlin owned the ship models you have at the studio on Rocky Edge, didn't he?"

"Yes. He had many of them custom-built."

"And they were sent to you from the ship after his death?"

"Yes."

"Among the collection was there a replica of the *Warwick?*"

"Oh dear! I can't remember," Mrs. Chatham said. "There were so many of the little boats. I sold a few of them."

Nancy was worried. Mrs. Chatham might have sold the *Warwick!*

"You think my husband hid his half of the map in a model of the *Warwick?*" the widow asked.

"Doesn't that seem reasonable?" Nancy replied.

"Oh, it does!" the woman cried in despair. "And to think I may have disposed of it unwittingly! I'll have no peace of mind until we find out. We'll take the first plane home," Mrs. Chatham decided instantly.

The two were soon en route to River Heights. Aided by a strong tail wind, their plane arrived ahead of schedule.

They hailed a taxi and rode to Rocky Edge. As the cab rolled through the open gate, Nancy observed that no guards were on duty.

"Shouldn't at least one of the special detectives be stationed at the gate?" she inquired.

"They aren't detectives," Mrs. Chatham replied. "My gardener knew two strong men who were out of work, so we gave them the job. I'm sure they're around here somewhere."

Shortly the taxi pulled up in front of the main house. As Nancy and Mrs. Chatham stepped out, a servant rushed up to them.

"Oh, Mrs. Chatham," the young woman said, puffing, "what are we going to do? What are we going to do?" she repeated hurriedly. "I'm so sorry, so very sorry."

The widow put a comforting arm around the girl's shoulders and tried to remain calm. "Now tell me what the problem is," she said. "No one's had an accident I hope."

"No, no," came the sobbing reply.

Mrs. Chatham's face grew stern. "Well, then tell me what's going on," she said, raising her voice abruptly.

"Trixie is missing!"

"What!"

"Your daughter is missing. We can't find her anywhere."

The words ringing loudly in her ears, Mrs. Chatham made no response. She stumbled up the porch steps to a chair.

Nancy had been silent, not wishing to interrupt the woman's conversation with her employee. But now she inquired if Ellen Smith and Hannah Gruen had left.

Tears trickled down the young woman's face. She answered, "They both went away right after lunch. Miss Smith had to leave because of a singing lesson. And your housekeeper, Miss Drew, left because she couldn't get anything to eat. The cook resented her being here and wouldn't even make her a sandwich, much less let her into the kitchen to fix her own meal."

"Where are the guards?" Nancy asked.

"Oh, they got better jobs, so they left."

Nancy coaxed the girl to tell as much as she could about Trixie's disappearance.

"She's been gone close to two hours," was the reply.

Mrs. Chatham spoke up. "Have you searched everywhere? Over the cliff—and down by the river?"

"Yes, Madam, everywhere."

Mrs. Chatham seemed relieved by this statement. "Then Trixie has run away! Well, this isn't the first time. She'll come home."

"I don't wish to alarm you, Mrs. Chatham," said Nancy, "but I'm afraid she may have been kidnapped."

The widow gasped. "Then we must call the police at once!"

As the child's mother started toward the house, Nancy followed closely. When they entered the hall both noticed a sheet of paper lying near the telephone.

"What's this?" Mrs. Chatham asked, picking it up.

At a glance she saw that it was a ransom note.

Written in a bold scrawl was the alarming message:

If you want to see your kid again have this amount ready when our messenger arrives. Do not notify the police or you'll be sorry.

At the bottom of the paper was a request for thousands of dollars.

"Oh, no!" Mrs. Chatham groaned.

For a moment Nancy thought the woman was going to faint but she managed to steady herself and sat down.

"I don't want to pay the money," Mrs. Chatham stated, then said, "But what will happen to Trixie if I refuse?"

"Please don't worry about that—at least not yet," Nancy said, studying the ransom note again. "The kidnapping could be an inside job."

"I don't agree with you," Mrs. Chatham returned with conviction. "While my servants may be careless, they're all dependable. Whoever left this note here did so without the knowledge of my employees."

Nancy tactfully withheld her own opinion.

"I think I should call the police," Mrs. Chatham said nervously.

"Please wait until we've had an opportunity to search the grounds thoroughly," Nancy advised. "I have an idea."

Without explaining her hunch, Nancy hurried from the house. She ran down the path, a question burning in her brain. *Was Trixie a prisoner somewhere on the estate?* Perhaps in Ship Cottage with its secret room and sliding panels?

Cautiously Nancy opened the door of the music studio and peered inside. The room was vacant, but on a chair lay a child's hair ribbon.

Nancy groped for the peg which opened the secret panel. As the wall slid back slowly she was almost certain she heard a movement in the dark chamber.

"Trix—" she started to call.

At the same moment a hard object struck Nancy and she blacked out.

CHAPTER XIII

Tracing the Warwick

WHEN Nancy Drew opened her eyes, the room was spinning. A little girl, her mouth gagged with a white handkerchief, was staring down at her.

"Trixie!" Nancy murmured weakly and slowly got to her feet.

She removed the handkerchief and the child began to sob. "Oh, I didn't mean to hit you!"

"*You* hit me? But why and how?"

In bewilderment Nancy looked at the cords binding the child's ankles and hands which were crossed in front of her. She unknotted them as Trixie answered:

"I thought you were that awful man coming back. So when you opened the panel, I knocked this big stick off the shelf. It fell on top of you."

She pointed to a croquet mallet lying on the floor.

"Trixie, who put you in here? Tell me quickly."

"That horrid ghost you drew a picture of!"

"And he brought you to the cottage?"

"No, I came by myself," Trixie admitted. "I didn't think the ghost would bother me since the guards were around."

"How did you get in?"

"With the key. I saw where my mother put it after she locked up the place."

"Then what happened?"

"I was playing the piano when that bad man— the ghost—grabbed me. I couldn't yell 'cause he put his hand over my mouth. He tied me up and carried me in here."

She gulped and started to cry again but Nancy gave her a comforting hug. Hand in hand they walked back to the house. Mrs. Chatham was so relieved to see her daughter she barely listened to Nancy's explanation of what had happened to Trixie.

When the excitement had subsided, Nancy mentioned the ransom note. "I wonder why the messenger hasn't come yet. I should think the kidnappers wouldn't lose any time sending someone over here, Mrs. Chatham."

"You're right, Nancy. I'll call the police right away so they can capture him."

"Perhaps," Nancy said, "the man has been here and already left."

Seeing the woman's confused expression, she explained, "Whoever was sent to get the money from you may have spotted Trixie and me outside, and knew the game was up. Please don't worry any more, Mrs. Chatham. Get a good night's rest and in the morning, if it's all right, I'd like to resume the search for Captain Tomlin's map."

Police were stationed at the house and the cottage. In the morning they reported to Nancy, who had stayed overnight, that no one had shown up.

She and Mrs. Chatham went to the studio to examine the various ship models. Each bore a small brass plate with a name engraved on it, but the *Warwick* was not there. Moreover, a thorough examination of the miniature ships did not reveal a single hiding place.

"Mrs. Chatham, how many did you sell?" Nancy asked.

"About ten or twelve," the woman said. "I listed the purchasers."

"You did?" Nancy cried, her spirits reviving. "And the names of each model?"

"I don't remember about that. Perhaps I can find the record book."

Mrs. Chatham returned to the main house, and within moments came back with a small black book.

"Apparently I didn't write down the names of the ship models," she said, glancing through the book. "Only the prices paid and the eleven purchasers."

"Was Captain Tomlin's vessel very well known?" Nancy asked.

"No. It was a small ship and rather old."

"Then a model of it would be less likely to command a high price. I'm tempted to start our investigation with the purchasers of the least expensive ones."

They noted that a man named J. K. Trumbull had paid the lowest price. His address was given as Hope, a small city about twenty-five miles away. But to Nancy's disappointment his telephone number was not listed in the directory.

"I'll have to drive there and try to find Mr. Trumbull," she declared. "Maybe Bess and George will go with me."

When the girls were informed of the trip, both were eager to accompany Nancy. The cousins packed a picnic lunch and were waiting when she drove up in front of the Marvin residence.

Within an hour the trio arrived in Hope and began making inquiries about J. K. Trumbull. A local shopkeeper finally directed them to a white frame house. Its owner was a short, curly-haired man.

Introductions were exchanged and Nancy asked, "Mr. Trumbull, I understand you purchased a ship model of the *Warwick*. Is that correct?"

"Yes." He paused. "Say, are you the one who

advertised in the paper saying a good price would be paid for the *Warwick?*"

"Why, no," Nancy replied, surprised.

"Do you still have that paper?" George asked the man quickly. "And was there a name signed to the ad?"

"No, I threw it away days ago," he answered. "To your second question, there was no name, just a box number. I didn't need to know it because I have no intention of selling the model."

The girls' hearts sank at Mr. Trumbull's statement. Nancy explained that they were trying to recover the model of the *Warwick* for Mrs. Chatham, whose first husband had sailed the original vessel.

"May we borrow the model?" she asked. "We believe it contains a clue which may help solve a mystery for Mrs. Chatham."

"What sort of clue?" Mr. Trumbull inquired, his interest aroused.

"I can't tell you, for I'm not sure myself."

He remained silent a moment, studying the girls. Then, to their relief, he smiled broadly.

"I thought you just wanted the little *Warwick* to sell at a profit. Now that I see otherwise, you may have the ship for exactly what I paid."

Nancy gratefully gave him the sum. With her two friends she delightedly carried the model to the car.

"We'll drive out of town and then examine the model," she proposed.

Unnoticed by the girls, a sedan which had been parked across the street followed only a short distance behind. The occupants had observed the three leave the Trumbull house with the *Warwick*.

"Nancy Drew would never buy a ship model unless it has something to do with the parchment map!" the woman was saying to her husband. "If only we can get our hands on it! I'll bet it's the *Warwick*!"

"I have a feeling this is going to be our lucky day," the man replied. "The advertising trick didn't work, but now we have Nancy Drew and the *Warwick* right where we want 'em!"

"Please be careful, Fred. Nancy has preferred a kidnapping charge against us and—"

"Listen, Irene, you worry too much," he retorted as he speeded up to keep Nancy's car in sight.

With no suspicion that they were being followed, the girls pulled into a shady lane. While Bess took the picnic hamper, Nancy and George examined the *Warwick*.

"If the map isn't in here, I'll be very disappointed," Nancy declared, her fingers exploring the ship's hull. "It must be, unless Captain Tomlin's letter meant something totally different."

"Can't you find it, Nancy?" George asked, with

growing impatience. Bess, silent, anxiously fastened her eyes on the little ship.

While the search was in progress, Fred Brown parked his car some distance away. Noiselessly he stole among the trees until he was directly behind Nancy's convertible. He listened closely to the girls' excited conversation.

"Look at this!" he heard Nancy exclaim. "A tiny door in the bottom of the ship!"

"Try it!" George urged.

"I can't seem to get it open," Nancy answered. There was a short pause, then she cried, "It's coming now! I feel something inside!"

"Is it the map?" Bess asked tremulously. "Is it, Nancy?"

"I'm not sure yet. Yes, it is! Or a copy of it. We've found the missing directions!"

The eavesdropper, still crouched behind the car, smiled with satisfaction. He nodded with even deeper satisfaction as he heard Bess suggest to Nancy that she replace the half map in the ship, so that they could eat their picnic lunch.

Nancy did not reply. She was thinking, "I wish we could start on that cruise right away!"

Bess exclaimed, "This excitement has given me a big appetite!"

"Let's carry the hamper over to a shady spot in the woods," George added, pointing. "It's too sunny here."

"There doesn't seem to be anyone around,"

Nancy said. "I suppose the ship will be safe in the car." She looked about, then set the model on the front seat. Picking up a Thermos jug, she added, "Bess, please lock the car."

"Sure thing."

Fred Brown quickly ducked behind a clump of bushes, spreading their leaves, to watch Bess's movements. She had trouble with one of the snap locks and called out to Nancy. But by now the other two girls had disappeared into the woods and did not hear her. She looked at the little ship.

"I'm sure it'll be safe," Bess told herself, and started off to join the others.

As soon as she was out of sight, Fred Brown crept from his hiding place. He stole around the car, opened the front door, and snatched the precious *Warwick!*

CHAPTER XIV

Sneak Attack

IN the meantime Nancy and her friends were enjoying the picnic lunch under the trees. Bess had reported the balky lock on the car door.

"I'll have to get it fixed," Nancy said, then smiled. "Don't worry, Bess. There surely aren't any thieves in this lovely place."

Bess reached for a second helping of potato salad. "Isn't it wonderful! We've found the map and it may lead to buried treasure!"

"Providing Mrs. Chatham doesn't change her mind about financing the trip," George reminded her cousin. "What do you think, Nancy? Will she go through with it?"

"Oh, Mrs. Chatham is very enthusiastic. If we succeed in piecing the map together, she promised to ask both of you, and also Burt and Dave if you like," Nancy added with a twinkle in her eyes. "And Ned, Ellen, and Bill Tomlin."

"Terrific!" Bess exclaimed gleefully. "Four couples. What a houseparty!"

"Four couples and Trixie," said Nancy.

It was growing late, so after Bess had consumed the last sandwich, the girls gathered up the picnic debris and returned to the car.

"I'd like to look at that map again," George remarked.

Bess, who was a few steps ahead, swung open the car door. She gasped in astonishment at the empty seat.

"Oh, no! We shouldn't have left the ship model in here!" she wailed.

"What's happened?" Nancy asked.

"Someone stole it while we were eating!" Bess exclaimed. "Nancy, will you ever forgive me?"

George eyed her cousin disapprovingly. "Think of all the hours we spent trying to find that map."

Nancy gazed carefully about the clearing but could see no one. The thief was gone.

In a tranquil voice she said, "Fortunately it's not too serious."

"Not serious!" Bess cried. "We lost the treasure and our wonderful vacation trip and you say it's not serious!"

Smiling, Nancy opened her handbag and displayed the missing section of the parchment map.

"I took it with me when we left the car," she explained. "As for the little ship, it's not a great loss."

"Nancy, I'm so happy I—" Bess laughed and cried, giving her friend an affectionate hug.

"There's only one thing that bothers me," Nancy said. "I can't recall the wording which was on the bottom of the *Warwick*."

"Wording?" George asked in surprise. "I didn't notice any."

"Neither did I," Bess declared. "What was it, Nancy?"

"I can remember just one word—'Little.' No doubt it will come to me when I study the two pieces of map at home."

The girls had made only a casual inspection of the parchment, for even in a strong light the writing was difficult to make out. Nancy was eager to return home so she could look at it under a magnifying glass.

"Shall we start for River Heights?" she proposed. "We have a long drive ahead of us."

"And make no attempt to trace the person who stole the ship?" George asked in surprise.

"It wouldn't do any good. We don't have a single clue," Nancy replied. "Let's head back."

After loading the picnic hamper into the car, the three girls crowded into the front seat. Out of habit, Bess reached for the button lock and pressed it down. "It does work!" she exclaimed. George frowned at her cousin but refrained from making a comment.

"On second thought," Nancy interposed, "I'd like to stop and talk with Ellen's father. I have a photograph to show him and he'll want to hear the good news about the map." She turned in the direction of Wayland.

Mr. Smith was saddened to learn that his brother was dead. He readily identified the picture, saying, "John looked exactly like my dad at the same age."

Mr. Smith expressed great pleasure over the recovery of the long-lost section of the precious map and stared at it eagerly. "This *is* my brother's torn piece," he declared positively. "Now if only I had my own half!"

"Just as soon as I get home," said Nancy, "I'll compare this with my copy of your section."

"Has Mrs. Chatham actually promised to pay for the expedition?" Mrs. Smith inquired. "I don't like to think of her spending so much money on something which may turn out to be a disappointment."

"Mrs. Chatham wants to do it," Nancy assured her. "The trip will not only be an expedition but a vacation for her and Trixie."

Before leaving the house, the girls learned that the police had not caught the thief who had burglarized the Smith home. Although Nancy did not need the stolen parchment, she feared that Spike Doty might get to the buried treasure first.

That evening her father voiced a similar opinion.

"After what happened to the model of the *Warwick* you must be on your guard more than ever," he warned her. "The Browns and the others have demonstrated their ruthlessness. They will not give up, Nancy, until the fortune is theirs."

For a couple of hours she and her father studied the two sections of map, fitting them together and trying to decipher Captain Tomlin's writing. Directions for reaching the southern Atlantic island were fairly clear, but one vital section of a word was missing.

"It would be part of the island's name," Nancy commented ruefully. "Plainly it says, 'Little —lm Island', but it's easy to see more letters appeared on the original."

"Little Island as a clue means nothing," Carson Drew remarked, glancing up from an atlas.

"Mr. Smith said the island was uncharted," Nancy reminded her father.

"That was a long time ago," Mr. Drew replied. "No doubt it's on the big maps today. Anyway, I'll take another look at all the islands. Here's one. Little Palm—"

"That's it!" Nancy cried out. "Little Palm Island!"

"How do you know? How can we be sure? In this expedition a wrong guess could prove to be very costly."

"I'm not guessing, Dad. The name was carved

on the bottom of the ship model which was stolen from my car today."

"Then everything seems to be cleared up," Mr. Drew declared in satisfaction. "If Mrs. Chatham gives her approval, we can charter a ship."

Upon learning that the lost half map had been recovered, Mrs. Chatham was even more enthusiastic than Nancy had dared hope.

"By all means have your father engage a captain," she instructed. "And invite the Smith family and any friends you wish. We'll have a marvelous time."

Nancy telephoned to Bill Tomlin, Ned, Burt Eddleton, and Dave Evans. They all instantly accepted and in a whirl of excitement Nancy began to plan her cruise wardrobe.

On Monday her hopes were suddenly deflated by her father. "I'm afraid there's not a single charter boat available now," he announced at lunch.

"Oh, Dad!" Nancy exclaimed. "Are you absolutely certain? How about a plane?"

"I've tried everywhere and everyone. No chance. I'm sorry, Nancy."

"But the Browns or Spike Doty may get to Little Palm before we do and find the buried fortune!"

That afternoon Carson Drew made several more unsuccessful attempts to find a suitable yacht. The few that were offered to him were either too large or much too small.

"Remember, dear, the thieves don't have Captain Tomlin's section of the map," Nancy's father said encouragingly.

"No," she agreed. "But don't forget that a copy of it was stolen by a member of the crew." She reminded him of the letter found in the New Kirk bank.

Days went by and Nancy chafed at the delay. She made frequent trips to Rocky Edge to discuss the situation with Mrs. Chatham. Ellen had finished school for the year and come to the estate as piano teacher. Already Trixie was much better behaved.

One afternoon the child was not in sight when Nancy arrived. Ellen ran down the walk to meet the young detective, who sensed at once that something was wrong.

"Trixie has disappeared!" Ellen cried. "I'm sure she has been kidnapped again!"

CHAPTER XV

Detective in Disguise

HAD the kidnappers dared to abduct Trixie Chatham a second time? Nancy could not believe they would be so foolish.

"Maybe Trixie has only wandered away," she suggested.

"Oh, I hope so," Ellen said. "Mrs. Chatham isn't here and I'm very worried."

"Did Trixie talk about going anywhere today?" Nancy asked.

"Why, yes, she did. She spoke of going to see you. Of course I didn't pay much attention. I told her you would be coming over but—"

"Suppose she tried to walk to River Heights? She'd definitely get lost!" Nancy exclaimed. "Come on. Hop in my car."

The two girls had expected a long search, but to their surprise they spotted Trixie a few minutes later walking along the road. Beside her was a middle-aged man in a sea captain's uniform.

"I hope that isn't Spike Doty!" Ellen exclaimed nervously.

"I think not," Nancy replied, easing on the brakes. "I can't imagine who he is."

At a closer look Trixie's companion seemed to be quite pleasant. The child herself explained the situation and introduced the man as Captain Stryver. She had seen him walking past the estate and noticed that his uniform looked like those she had seen in pictures of men on ships. Trixie had followed him to talk about boats.

"I didn't mean to take the child away from her home," the man apologized, his weather-beaten face creasing into kindly wrinkles. "We've been gabbing a little about ships."

"He has one called the *Primrose!*" Trixie exclaimed, seizing Nancy's hand.

"I don't own her," the captain hastened to correct. "Mr. Heppel, my employer, is her master."

"Is the *Primrose* for rent?" Nancy asked.

"Mr. Heppel has had a lot of bad luck the past year. I'm sure he'd be glad to rent the *Primrose*. Not a prettier yacht afloat. She's tied up in New York now. I'm just here visiting my daughter."

Nancy and Ellen asked many questions, and soon were convinced that the ship was well worth an investigation. They liked Captain Stryver, and tactfully inquired if his services could be obtained for a voyage to an island in the South Atlantic.

"I know that area like a book," he said. "Nothing would suit me better than a cruise in those waters."

After talking with Captain Stryver for nearly half an hour, Nancy learned that Mr. Heppel was coming to Wayland the following morning to talk to the captain. She asked to meet him.

"Come to my daughter's house at ten o'clock." He gave Nancy the address.

Since Trixie had been responsible for calling the *Primrose* to their attention, neither Ellen nor Nancy felt like scolding her for wandering off. The girls brought Trixie home.

Carson Drew was pleased to learn of the *Primrose* and Captain Stryver. He went with Nancy to call on Mr. Heppel the next day. The man was willing to rent his yacht for a fair sum. Pictures of it and a maritime commendation convinced the Drews of its seaworthiness.

"You'll have no problem with Captain Stryver at the wheel," said Mr. Heppel. "He's honest and dependable," the owner declared, and the deal was concluded. The captain was promptly engaged and given the task of selecting a crew. Happy about the assignment, he left for New York.

Nancy's preparations for the trip were at their height later that morning when she received a telephone call from Chief McGinnis of the River Heights police force.

"We have a lead, Nancy," he said. The chief

was a long-time friend of the Drews. "Spike Doty's address." He rattled off the number and name of the street. "It's a rooming house."

"That's in the worst district of town," Nancy commented.

"A couple of our men are down there now," the chief said. "Dressed like town hoods. They're waiting for Doty to appear."

"Are you sure he still lives in that apartment house?" Nancy asked.

"The landlady verified it but said he hasn't been to his room since night before last."

"I'd like to take a look around myself."

"If you want a police escort—"

"Oh, no. I don't want to scare Doty off or be too conspicuous. As a matter of fact—" She stopped speaking. "I'll be okay. Thanks just the same."

Not wishing to reveal over the phone a plan she had suddenly thought of, Nancy assured him she would take no chances and said good-by. She went to her room and from the rear of her closet pulled out a dark-colored dress that was out of style, a pair of old brown shoes, and a bottle of gray dusting powder for the hair.

"I hope this'll work," she said to herself. "Too bad Hannah and Dad aren't here so I could tell them my plan."

Quickly she changed clothes and brushed some of the powder into her hair, giving it a gray tinge.

She combed it to give a scraggly appearance. Fully disguised, Nancy posed in front of the full-length mirror in the hall.

"Well, Mrs. Frisby, are you ready to do some housecleanin'?" Nancy asked her reflection. Could she trap the thief in this disguise? A broad grin spread across her face as she answered, "Give me a broom and I'll sweep Doty into jail!"

In a short while Nancy was on her way. She parked her car in a nice neighborhood several blocks from Doty's rooming house. Then, hunching her shoulders and lowering her head, she walked the rest of the distance. An untidy landlady answered her knock.

"What do you want?" she bellowed, glaring at the old woman before her.

A crude letter holder hung on the wall. Chalked onto it were several names and room numbers. Doty's was 22.

"I come t' clean up Mr. Doty's room," Nancy announced. "Kin I start right now? Just tell me where you keep everything and open his door, please. I'll be in and out in a jiffy."

The red-haired woman looked surprised but led Nancy up the sagging stairway. "All the cleaning stuff's in the closet down the hall. His room's over there. Door's always unlocked. I can't figure that guy. He's been out for almost two days and wants his room cleaned. For who? The mice?"

Without waiting for an answer, the landlady

Could she trap the thief in this disguise?
Nancy wondered

started downstairs, leaving Nancy alone. The young sleuth opened the door to Spike Doty's room. It was shabby and contained only a desk, a bed, and a chair, all piled with old newspapers and torn envelopes. She pretended to straighten up the room, hunting through the papers for a clue to any accomplices of Doty's or to his whereabouts if he had left town.

"What if he has gone to Little Palm Island!" Nancy frowned at the possibility.

As she continued to "clean up," a car stopped in front of the apartment house, but she was unaware of this. Fred and Irene Brown, somewhat disguised, alighted. They presented themselves at the door and inquired about Spike Doty.

"For someone who's not around he sure gets enough visitors," the landlady said irritably.

"Who else came here?" Fred Brown asked quickly.

"The cleaning woman for one. Look, I'm getting tired answering questions. Doty's not here. That's all I know."

"We do hate to take up your time, but could we talk somewhere in private?" Mrs. Brown inquired with exaggerated politeness. "We're Mr. and Mrs. Fred Brown."

As she spoke, a young man brushed past them and started upstairs.

"Wait a minute, fella. You don't live here," the landlady shouted after him.

"I'm visiting a friend," he called back, without turning around.

The annoyed woman threw up her hands in disgust and shook her head, then turned to the couple. "In here," she said and led them into a small living room.

The Browns asked a few more questions. "This cleaning woman you mentioned, do you know how we can get in touch with her?" the man asked.

"You won't have to go far. She's still upstairs."

At that moment Nancy was about ready to give up what was proving to be a fruitless search.

"A wasted afternoon!" she admonished herself. "I'd better do a little cleaning before the landlady comes barging in. Or before Doty returns!"

She had just folded the last newspaper when the knob began turning and the door creaked open.

CHAPTER XVI

A Hoax

"NED! What are you doing here?" Nancy cried in astonishment.

"I spotted you when you parked your car. In that get-up I knew you were up to something and decided to find out what it was," Ned answered quickly. "But I didn't want to interrupt your sleuthing so I stayed behind a distance. Listen, Fred and Irene Brown are downstairs," he added as a knock came at the door.

"Hey, what's going on?" the landlady asked, stepping inside. "I thought you said you were visiting a friend." She glared at Ned, who did not answer.

The woman turned to Nancy. "There's a man and his wife downstairs who want to see you—I don't know what about!"

Nancy squeezed Ned's hand, signaling him to watch her. Without saying a word to each other, they followed the landlady to the first floor.

As she turned into the living room, Nancy and Ned quickly sidestepped her, dashed outside and got into his car. As they shot away from the curb, Nancy turned to look back. The landlady, anger in her eyes, was flailing her arms wildly at Mr. and Mrs. Brown and shooing them down the front steps.

"Guess she didn't like them either," Nancy thought.

Ned drove Nancy to the spot where she had parked the convertible, then waved good-by, saying he would see her later.

Nancy went directly home, and after removing her disguise, glanced through the mail which had been delivered earlier. There was a letter from her Aunt Eloise but most of the envelopes contained advertisements. One, however, was addressed to her in pencil and had been mailed the day before. The message inside had been scrawled on a sheet of cheap tablet paper. It read:

> Dear Miss Drew: I tuk yer boat
> cus I need money but I can't sell it.
> You can hev it back for a few bucks.
> It says somethin important inside.
> Don't tell the cops and come alone
> on foot to 47 White Stret.

Nancy read the message a second time, then ran to the kitchen to show it to Hannah.

"This practically shatters one of my best theories!" she declared. "I had a hunch that the ship model had been stolen by Fred and Irene Brown. This note seems to prove I was wrong."

"It appears to have been written by a young or poorly educated person," the housekeeper commented as she looked at the misspelled words. "He signs himself Ted." After a pause Hannah asked, "What will you do, Nancy?"

"I don't know. Strange I didn't notice anything carved inside the *Warwick* model." She paused a moment. "It's a long distance to White Street, but this note says to come on foot—"

"Nancy, I can't permit you to walk through that area!" Hannah Gruen exclaimed.

"I'll take the car," Nancy said. "And maybe I won't have to go inside the house."

Mrs. Gruen did not approve of the mission and begged Nancy to be careful. The young detective was well on her way to White Street when it occurred to her it was odd that Ted knew her name and address.

She had no intention of walking into a trap and made up her mind she would not enter the house. Instead, she would insist that the ship model be brought to her.

As Nancy pulled up before Number 47, a shabby, old-fashioned house, she saw a boy with a sharp, taut face seated on the porch. Evidently he had been expecting her, because he quickly came to the car.

"Are you Ted?" she asked, trying not to seem unfriendly.

"That's me," he answered gruffly, "but you was supposed to come on foot. You want the boat?"

"Yes I do, Ted. May I ask why you stole it from my car?"

"You kin ask all you want but I ain't givin' no answers," the boy retorted saucily. "The boat's upstairs."

"You must bring it to me."

"Grandma won't let it go without the money," the boy said stubbornly. "She's sick in bed and we need the cash. If you want to see the ship, you gotta come upstairs."

Nancy was in a quandary. A chance to obtain the needed information on the exact location of the treasure might be lost! Reluctantly she climbed up a flight of worn stairs through a dark hall to a wood-paneled bedroom.

"Grandma, this is the girl," Ted said by way of introduction.

He disappeared, closing the door behind him. Nancy was startled by his sudden departure but tried not to show alarm. She attempted to reassure herself that nothing seemed amiss. The *Warwick* was in plain sight on the table beside the bed.

"How much money you got on you?" the elderly woman asked in a squeaky voice, her face half hidden under the covers.

Nancy opened her purse and pulled out several bills.

A gleam of satisfaction lit up the old lady's eyes as she reached for the money. "The ship's yours. Only promise you won't make trouble for Ted."

"Very well," Nancy consented, and turned from the bed to lift the model from the table.

Instantly the elderly woman threw off the covers and leaped from bed. Irene Brown!

Simultaneously, Fred Brown appeared from inside a closet and tried to pin Nancy's arms behind her. As she struggled violently, the ship crashed to the floor.

Although Nancy fought with all her strength, she was no match for her assailants. In a moment they held her fast.

"The clever Miss Drew wasn't so smart this time!" the man gloated, taking a handkerchief from his pocket to gag her.

Securely bound, Nancy was shoved through a closet with a concealed door which connected with an adjoining vacant house. She was seated at a table and told to write a letter to Hannah Gruen. Nancy was to request that the piece of map found in the ship model be sent to her at once.

"Don't try to get away with anything in this letter," Fred Brown threatened.

In despair, Nancy slowly composed the message. She knew she could not include anything that would indicate her true predicament. There was just one faint hope of outwitting the sinister couple. Accordingly she wrote:

> *Please give bearer the copy of the*
> *map found in the ship model.*
>   *Nancy*

"Perhaps if I concentrate very hard, I can get a thought wave to Hannah, so she'll make a copy—but not an exact one," Nancy told herself. "It's my one hope."

Unknown to Nancy, Mr. Drew and Ned already were alarmed over her long absence from home. Informed by the worried housekeeper that Nancy had gone to the White Street address, they set off in Ned's car to search for her.

"It isn't like Nancy to stay away so long without any explanation," the lawyer declared as Ned parked at the curb. "She may have walked into a trap."

As they rang the doorbell again and again Ned remarked that Nancy's car was not in sight. He knocked on the door several times but received no response.

At last Mr. Drew became impatient. Trying the door and finding it unlocked, he entered with Ned close behind.

"Why, this place is deserted," he observed as they looked into the empty first-floor rooms. "We do have the correct address, I hope."

"This is it all right. How about upstairs?" Ned asked, leading the way this time.

The first door confronting him opened into the bedroom where Nancy had been taken prisoner. Before them was an overturned chair and lying beside it the broken model of the *Warwick!*

"There has been a struggle!" Mr. Drew exclaimed, losing his usual calm. "Something has happened to Nancy!"

With increasing alarm he and Ned searched the entire house but found no trace of the missing girl. While Mr. Drew continued to look for clues in the room where the struggle had taken place, Ned went to question the neighbors. He returned with a discouraging report.

"I couldn't contact anyone, Mr. Drew. Must have rung four or five doorbells, too. The place next to this one is vacant."

"To the east or on the west side?" the lawyer asked.

"The east. It adjoins this room."

Mr. Drew had been fingering a small object which he now showed the young man. It was an ornamental pin from a dress.

"I picked this up from the floor of the closet," the lawyer explained. "I have a hunch it came from Nancy's dress and she dropped it as a clue. Ned, suppose you call Hannah Gruen and ask her if Nancy was wearing the pin when she left."

"I'll be back in a minute," Ned said, starting away. "Maybe Nancy has arrived home since we left."

Carson Drew was not so optimistic as he returned to his investigation of the closet. He found something which previously had escaped his attention. Although skillfully disguised with wallpaper, the back of the closet was made of wood instead of plaster. When he tapped his knuckles against it, there was a hollow sound.

"It's a door!" he exclaimed. "The pattern of the paper hides the outline!"

Mr. Drew pushed hard on the panel but could not budge it. Again and again he tried but to no avail.

He was mulling over the problem when Ned returned and reported, "The pin was on Nancy's dress. And she hasn't come home."

"There's no question about it, Ned. Nancy has been captured. I'm positive she was taken through this sliding panel to the next house."

"What!" Ned exclaimed.

"The panel has been locked on the other side. I've tried to get it open but—"

"Let's break it down," the young man urged.

"And tip off the kidnappers? No, I think we'd better proceed quietly," Mr. Drew answered. Just then he spied a small keyhole. "This is an ordinary lock," he said.

From his pocket he took a bunch of keys. One by one he tried them. The next to the last unlocked the door.

Never dreaming that her father and Ned were so close, Nancy remained alone in a tiny third-floor storeroom, ventilated by only one small window. She sat on an old wooden chair, gagged and tied so tightly her bones ached.

"If only something good would happen!" she thought unhappily. "What will Hannah do when she gets my note?"

At that very moment Irene Brown was ringing the doorbell of the Drew home. Behind the hedge her husband watched, pleased with himself. No one but the housekeeper was at home, he knew, and should she become suspicious, she could not call for help. He had just cut the telephone wire.

His wife greeted Mrs. Gruen pleasantly and said, "I have a note for you from Miss Drew. I don't know what it says, but she asked me to wait for an answer."

"Will you come inside?" Hannah asked.

CHAPTER XVII

Puzzling Paper

AFTER thoroughly searching the vacant house, Carson Drew and Ned were ready to give up. They had found no trace of Nancy.

"I was so sure she was here," the lawyer declared. He and Ned had reached the attic floor, which was dark and suffocatingly stuffy. "But maybe she was taken to another hideout."

"Listen!" Ned said.

They could hear a distinct scratching noise, as if someone were clawing against a plaster wall. Tracing the sound, Mr. Drew saw a door in a dingy corner of the room.

"Maybe she's in there!" he exclaimed, pulling at the knob.

Nancy, bound and gagged, stared in disbelief. Ned tore off the handkerchief while Mr. Drew untied her bonds.

"Are you okay?" he asked apprehensively. "You look pale."

"I'm all right," she assured him and her father, "but I'm afraid we've run into a real calamity."

"What do you mean?" Mr. Drew asked.

"The Browns made me write a note to Hannah ordering her to deliver Captain Tomlin's map to them."

"How long ago was that, Nancy?" her father inquired quickly.

"At least half an hour."

"Perhaps we can catch them!" Carson Drew exclaimed.

Leaving Ned to look for Nancy's car, he and his daughter drove home at top speed. Entering the house, they discovered Hannah Gruen down on her knees examining the telephone.

"Nancy, you're safe!" she exclaimed joyfully. "Oh, I'm so relieved."

"Did someone come here with a note from me?" Nancy asked anxiously.

"Yes, a woman. She left about ten minutes ago."

"That was Irene Brown!"

"I guessed as much, so I tried to call the police, but the telephone wires had been cut."

"You gave her the map?" Nancy asked.

"That was what you requested me to do," the housekeeper responded.

"Yes, I did. Oh, I can't blame you. You had no way of knowing that I didn't want you to carry out the instructions."

"All the same, I guessed it from the wording in your note," the housekeeper declared, ending the suspense. "I gave Mrs. Brown a map, but it will never do her and her husband any good. And it serves them right."

"Oh, Hannah, you're wonderful!" Nancy laughed happily and hugged her. "How did you manage to outwit her?"

"It was very easy. I knew you kept both sections of the map in your desk—Captain Tomlin's original and the copy of Mr. Smith's portion. I found an old piece of parchment in the desk and tore it diagonally. Then I quickly traced the original, leaving out many details and making several changes!"

"Mrs. Brown never once suspected?" Nancy asked, chuckling.

"No, she must have thought what I gave her was genuine, because she thanked me sweetly and went away."

"Hannah, you're as clever as any detective of my acquaintance," Mr. Drew said with a grin.

"I'm really grateful," Nancy added.

"There's just one thing that troubles me," Hannah said. "I copied the name of the island on the paper."

"Let's not worry about that," said Mr. Drew, "since you left out some of the directions."

While the housekeeper was preparing a late

dinner, Mr. Drew went to a neighbor's and called the telephone company to report the cut wire. A repairman was sent at once and within a short time the Drews' phone was back in service.

As they finished dinner the telephone rang and Nancy rose to answer it. She recognized Ned's voice.

"Hello, Nancy," he said, talking hurriedly. "I found your car. I'll bring it over as soon as I can. Right now I'm at the police station, and Chief McGinnis wants you to come at once."

"Now?"

"Yes. Fred and Irene Brown have been taken into custody. The chief wants an identification."

"Be there in a minute. 'Bye."

Nancy and her father went immediately to the police station. To their delight they learned that Ned had led the police to 47 White Street and aided them in nabbing the Browns when the couple had returned to release Nancy.

"May we talk with them?" she asked the police chief.

"Go ahead and good luck. We haven't been able to get a word out of either of them."

Mr. Drew and Nancy talked with the couple. They learned nothing from Fred, who denied the kidnapping of Nancy from Emerson.

"Forget it," he said. "It's the word of two against one."

Irene Brown proved to be less discreet. Nancy

played upon the woman's feelings by intimating that Spike Doty was in jail and had made damaging revelations which implicated the couple.

"Why, the double-crosser!" Mrs. Brown cried furiously. "He was the one who first learned about the fortune, and now he tries to throw all the blame on us!"

"Then you've been working with him?" Carson Drew asked quietly.

"Not any more."

"Rorke, perhaps?" Nancy inquired, watching the woman's face intently.

"Never heard of him," Irene Brown answered, but her eyes wavered—indicating to her questioners that she was not telling the truth.

"What did you do with the map you obtained from our housekeeper?" Carson Drew demanded. He had learned from the police that the paper had not been found in the Browns' possession.

"We sold it," Irene answered briefly.

"To Rorke?" the lawyer asked.

"Look, I don't have to tell you anything."

Realizing she had talked too much, Irene Brown fell into a sullen silence and refused to answer any more questions. Before leaving headquarters, Nancy and Mr. Drew again talked with Chief McGinnis.

"I'll have the Browns held without bail," the chief said. "Kidnapping is a serious charge."

Although the man and his wife were behind

bars, Nancy remained uneasy. Spike Doty and the mysterious Mr. Rorke were free and both were determined to get the Tomlin treasure.

"Have they learned the location of Little Palm Island?" Nancy wondered. "Are they on their way to it?"

She phoned Mrs. Chatham, who was as impatient as Nancy to get the treasure hunt under way. The widow telephoned Captain Stryver, urging him to speed preparations so that the *Primrose* could sail from New York as soon as possible.

"I can have her ready by tomorrow," he said. "If I had a little more time, though, I could be more selective about the crew."

"We can't afford to waste another day," the woman told him.

The next morning Carson Drew, the Marvins, and the Faynes said good-by to their daughters at the airport.

"Wish I were going along," the lawyer said. "Have a good time and bring home the treasure!"

"At least I'll get a good tan." Nancy laughed, squeezing her father's hand and kissing him.

The traveling group consisted of Mrs. Chatham, Trixie, the three Smiths, Bill Tomlin, and Nancy's special friends.

Bess's date Dave Evans was a blond, rangy, green-eyed boy who was on the Emerson football team. Burt Eddleton, George's friend, was also blond, but shorter and husky. He, too, played on the team.

With a grin Burt said, "A treasure hunt on a lonely island should have at least one pirate. I'm applying for the job."

Dave called, "I'll give you a patch for one eye!" The others laughed.

The trip to New York was fast. Taxis were hailed and the group headed for the dock and their first glimpse of the *Primrose*.

"Isn't she beautiful!" Bess exclaimed, gazing at the trim yacht.

As Nancy looked at the ship, her attention was diverted by a small piece of paper which had just blown from behind a crate on the dock. Wondering if it had been dropped by someone aboard the *Primrose*, she went over to pick it up. The next instant she stared in astonishment. A hand-printed message on the sheet read:

MEET YOU ON THE DOCK WEDNESDAY MIDNIGHT.

SPIKE

"That was last night!" Nancy thought.

Her friends, with the exception of Ned, were already going aboard and being greeted by Captain Stryver.

"Find something?" Ned asked Nancy.

She showed him the paper. "Wow!" he exclaimed. "I wonder who received this."

"Ned, I think we should tell the captain that Spike might have placed a bomb aboard or tampered with the machinery."

The two reported the incident at once and a thorough search was made. Nothing was found.

Although Nancy was relieved, she had an uneasy feeling that something was amiss. She would certainly keep her eyes open.

The *Primrose* was a comfortable, seaworthy craft which plowed through deep waves with scarcely a roll. Even so, Mrs. Chatham, a poor sailor, soon was confined to her cabin with a mild case of seasickness. Ellen and Trixie shared an adjoining stateroom.

Left mostly to themselves, Nancy, Ned, and the other couples thoroughly enjoyed the daylight hours on deck. The second night out they danced to records and held an impromptu entertainment. Bill Tomlin, a talented guitar player, was asked to accompany Ellen.

The young people would not let her stop until she had sung several selections. All applauded her loudly. Finally she begged off, saying she must put Trixie to bed.

"Come back soon," Nancy urged.

Trixie began to pout. "Ellen's my roommate. I want her to stay with me!"

Ellen merely smiled and promised a bedtime story, which Nancy was sure would put the child to sleep. A few minutes later Bill Tomlin slipped away from the group and followed Ellen down portside. Presently their voices, half-talking, half-laughing, could be heard against the sound of splashing waves.

The other couples strolled about the deck, enjoying the mild breezes and stopping to watch the moon's reflection ripple on the water.

"Nancy," said Ned, "since there's no trouble on the *Primrose*, I hope you'll forget about mysteries or treasure until we get to the island."

"It'll be won—"

"Help! He-e-e-lp!" a girl's cry interrupted Nancy's answer.

"That sounds like Bess!" Nancy exclaimed.

"It is!" Ned said. He pointed to a figure just surfacing the water.

CHAPTER XVIII

Treachery

In a flash Dave had jumped in after Bess. Ned rushed to a deck telephone to ask that the *Primrose* be stopped.

As the young people watched Bess and Dave swim toward the yacht, Captain Stryver and Mrs. Chatham came on deck.

"What's all the commotion about?" she asked.

"Bess went overboard," Nancy replied. "We don't know why."

In a few minutes the two swimmers reached the side of the *Primrose*. A rope ladder had been thrown down. Bess, shivering and her dress and hair limp, climbed up slowly. Dave followed.

Their friends plied them with questions. "Did you fall in?" "Were you pushed overboard?"

Bess's teeth chattered as she gratefully accepted a large beach towel from George and wrapped it snugly about her. Instead of answering immediately, big tears began to roll down her cheeks.

"Sit here," Nancy said, indicating a deck chair. "You've had a shock. Take your time and tell us what happened."

Bess said haltingly, "I asked Dave to get my sweater from the other side of the yacht. While he was gone, I rested my arms on the rail over there and suddenly it gave way. I screamed so you wouldn't leave me behind."

As Bess finished her explanation, Bill Tomlin arrived on the scene. He went to examine the rail. Finally he said, "This is part of a gate which wasn't latched properly."

George turned to Nancy, "Do you think it was a case of sabotage?"

Nancy frowned. "I can't get Spike out of my mind. He may have tampered with that latch before we came aboard."

The next day Nancy came on deck to find a tough-looking young sailor at the wheel of the *Primrose*. She did not like his appearance and recalled that Captain Stryver had been compelled to hire any available men.

"Good morning," she greeted him pleasantly. "I'm Nancy Drew. Your name?"

"Snorky."

"Snorky, have you seen Captain Stryver?"

"He's sick in his cabin," the man answered, a suggestion of satisfaction in his voice. He spun the wheel, bringing the yacht around slightly. "The mate's flat on his back, too," he added.

"How strange both of them are ill!" Nancy said to herself.

She walked aft. Meeting Ned, she mentioned the illness of the two officers.

"There's another mystery too," he said soberly. "We seem to have changed direction. I think I'll talk with Bill Tomlin. He's been charting our course since we left New York."

He was gone about fifteen minutes. When he rejoined Nancy, Bill was with him.

"I was right," Ned announced grimly. "Bill thinks we're off course. He has piloted motorboats all his life and studied navigation."

"I want to ask that guy Snorky a few questions," Bill said, and the three went forward.

Upon being questioned, the crewman took the attitude that guiding the *Primrose* was his responsibility, and not that of anyone else.

"We may be a little off course," he admitted, "but don't worry about it."

"Swing her back now," Bill Tomlin ordered sharply, "or we'll talk to the captain."

Angrily Snorky brought the bow of the ship around so the *Primrose* once more was heading south. No sooner had the trio moved away, however, than the sailor again altered the direction. Bill Tomlin, who felt the lurch of the vessel as it turned, became irritated.

"Please don't get into a fight with Snorky," Nancy pleaded. "Let's talk to Captain Stryver."

At once the young people went to his quarters. Barely able to sit up in bed, the officer listened in alarm to their story. He declared he would be topside in a few hours.

"I don't think we should leave Snorky in charge," said Bill. "He's taking us directly eastward."

"East!" the captain exclaimed. "I've got to get out of this bed!"

"No, you mustn't exert yourself when you're so weak," Nancy protested. "If Bill may have the chart, I'm sure he can check on our course."

"The chart's in my desk," the captain mumbled, sinking back on the pillow.

Bill found it and in a few seconds cried, "We're way off course!"

"I think Snorky is deliberately trying to delay us," Ned stated. "But no one else can be spared to take his place."

"I can steer the *Primrose*," Bill declared confidently. "There's nothing to it. Come on. We'll take care of Snorky!"

He and Ned went forward. There was a brief argument with the sailor. When he refused to give up the wheel, the boys bodily removed him and Bill took over.

The remainder of the day went along quietly, except that Snorky glowered angrily as he washed down the decks. All this time Nancy kept thinking of the note she had found. Was Snorky a friend of

Spike's? And had Spike arranged with Snorky to take the yacht on a wrong course?

Another thought came to her. She confided it to Bess and George. "Do you suppose he's responsible for the captain's illness? Maybe he bribed the cook to put something in his food."

The next morning Bill Tomlin was taken ill while at the wheel of the *Primrose*. His attack was a mild one, though, and he refused to leave his post.

Unknown to the others, Nancy and George kept an eye on the galley. They became well acquainted with the cook, winning the man's gratitude by peeling a large pan of potatoes. After they had talked with him for half an hour, the girls decided he had not connived with Snorky.

Nancy whispered to George, "Possibly Snorky engaged the cook in friendly conversation and waited for the chance to contaminate the food when the cook wasn't looking." George agreed.

Next, Nancy asked Ned to slip into the forecastle and hunt for a clue among Snorky's belongings. His possessions did not reveal anything suspicious. Ned ran his hand under the mattress of the sailor's bunk.

"Here's something!" he thought, holding up a small envelope.

It contained an odorless white powder. Ned felt certain that Snorky had used some of it to taint the ship's food. He reported his find to Nancy.

"I have an idea!" she said. "Wait here for me."

Nancy ran to the galley and grabbed a large salt shaker. She took a small plastic bag from a drawer, then hurried back.

"Ned, substitute this salt for the powder!" she said. "Put the white powder in this plastic bag. We'll keep it for evidence."

Taking her friends into her confidence, Nancy organized a watch over the galley. On the pretext of helping the overburdened cook, the girls even assisted in serving the meals. At lunch Ned complained his food tasted very salty.

"Snorky is sly," Nancy observed to George as they discussed the situation. "We'll have to tighten our watch. If we don't, I'm afraid something dreadful may happen before we reach Little Palm."

An unexpected change in the weather temporarily drove all thought of Snorky from everyone's mind. The barometer fell steadily and within a few hours waves were breaking over the decks.

Although weakened by his illness, Captain Stryver resumed command of the ship, relieving the weary Bill Tomlin. As the day wore on, the gale became worse so that everyone was driven below. Even the cook went to his bunk.

Nancy, however, grew restless. Deciding that Snorky should be watched, she went to look for him. The sailor could not be found, even after Ned and Bill had joined the search.

"Say, maybe he was washed overboard!" Bill said uneasily. "I'll ask the captain if he has seen him."

Nancy did not agree. Without telling anyone where she was going, the young detective went below to the galley. Before she reached it, the door opened and the missing sailor came out, carrying a box in his arms. He turned in the opposite direction without seeing Nancy.

"Now what was he doing in there?" she thought. "He must have had more poison powder for the food, and he's carrying away the good stuff for himself!"

Thoroughly alarmed, she started up the ladder, intending to warn her friends not to eat anything served. Nancy was midway up the rungs when the yacht gave a lurch.

She was thrown off balance. Unable to steady herself, Nancy toppled backwards, falling to the deck. Her head struck hard and everything went black before her eyes. When Nancy opened them, she was lying on a couch in Captain Stryver's cabin. Her anxious friends were grouped about her.

"You okay?" Ned asked, pressing a cup of water to her lips.

Nancy sat up, trying to recall what had happened. Her eyes roved from one face to another.

"What is it, Nancy?" Ned asked, sensing that something was wrong.

"Don't eat," she whispered. "Whatever you do, don't touch anything coming from the galley!"

Nancy told how she had seen Snorky stealing away from the ship's galley.

"He's trying to keep us from reaching Little Palm Island," she ended her story wearily. "Will you help me to my cabin?"

While Bess and George made Nancy comfortable in her bunk, Bill Tomlin and Ned sought the captain. The three of them searched the ship. They found Snorky hiding in the hold, presumably to avoid Stryver. The captain demanded a reason for his conduct.

"I wasn't within a mile of the galley," the man whined. "I was hunting in the hold for some extra clothes of mine."

Suspicious, Captain Stryver ordered another sailor to send the cook up with a sample of every dish of food which was to be served at dinner. Commanded to eat, Snorky sullenly obeyed, refusing only to taste a bowl of split pea soup.

"What do you know about this?" Stryver asked the cook.

"Nothing, sir. Snorky must have sneaked into the galley when I was in the dining room."

"Throw the soup overboard," the captain instructed the cook. "As for Snorky, we'll lock him up until we reach port."

A thorough search was made of his cabin. No evidence against him was found other than more of the sickening white powder. Nancy had hoped a clue involving him with Spike would turn up. None had, but she did not swerve from her original theory that Snorky was working with people interested in the treasure.

To everyone's relief, the remainder of the trip was uneventful. Late one afternoon the *Primrose* came within sight of Little Palm Island. Through binoculars it looked like a tiny crescent-shaped spot of green, its sandy shores lined solidly with gently waving palms.

The ship nosed her way cautiously ahead and at length dropped anchor a safe distance from the pounding surf. Captain Stryver, Bill Tomlin, and Ned decided to row ashore to make a preliminary investigation.

Anxiously those aboard the *Primrose* watched the little craft row away. A few minutes later a crewman came up hurriedly to the group to report that Snorky had escaped from the cabin where he had been locked up.

"He's nowhere on the ship!" the seaman added. "He must have jumped overboard and swum to shore."

"How frightful!" exclaimed Mrs. Chatham. "Now none of us will be safe!"

Nancy's uneasiness for the men in the rowboat increased. Captain Stryver's party might be attacked!

CHAPTER XIX

Impostor

To the relief of everyone aboard the *Primrose,* the small boat returned from the island in less than an hour.

"What's the report?" Nancy asked eagerly as Captain Stryver climbed aboard the *Primrose,* followed by Ned and Bill.

"This side of the island seems to be deserted," the captain replied. "We did find considerable evidence of digging, though."

"Oh dear!" Nancy exclaimed. "That means someone has reached the spot ahead of us! And Snorky has escaped!"

"What!" Stryver shouted, and went off to get more details.

Nancy said to Ned, "Snorky has probably joined Spike and maybe others on the island."

A few minutes later Captain Stryver came topside and said all the men except Mr. Smith would go back to the island in search of the fugitive.

"When it's safe for you girls to land, I'll let you know."

Mrs. Chatham, Mrs. Smith, Nancy, and the other girls remained on deck. Anxiously they watched the men go ashore, then vanish behind a fringe of palms.

Mrs. Chatham walked the deck nervously. "Oh, I wish they'd return!" she said over and over.

"Listen!" Nancy cried suddenly. "I thought I heard someone shout!"

"So did I!" agreed Ellen, who was standing beside her.

A moment later the watchers saw several men on the beach. Seizing the binoculars, Nancy adjusted them to her eyes.

"They've caught Snorky!" she exclaimed. "Another man, too. I think he's Spike Doty."

"Who's that in the white suit?" Mrs. Chatham asked. She had observed him join the group on the beach.

Nancy replied, "His big hat is pulled too low for me to get a good look at him."

As she watched intently Nancy could tell that the newcomer was arguing with Captain Stryver. He seemed to be ordering the *Primrose* party away from the island. This was substantiated by Ned and a sailor when they rowed back to the yacht a few minutes later.

"That Heyborn fellow in white claims he owns the island," Ned explained. "He won't permit us to land or to dig."

"But there's been a lot of digging on the island already," Nancy said in quick protest.

"He claims he knew nothing about it. We've caught Snorky, and that other guy in the blue jeans may be the one who robbed the Smith home," Ned declared. "I came back to get Nancy and Ellen for a positive identification."

The two girls set off for the island with Ned. Heyborn had disappeared before their arrival. One glance satisfied them that Snorky's companion was indeed Spike Doty.

Captain Stryver said, "Mr. Heyborn, the owner of the island, volunteered to look after the prisoners, but I declined the offer. I don't entirely trust him."

He lowered his voice when he saw the man in the white suit returning. Darkness was coming on, and although Nancy tried her best, she could not obtain a good view of the bearded man's face buried under a low-brimmed hat.

"Please let us search," Ellen pleaded. "It means so much to Mrs. Chatham and my family."

"Sorry, I can't allow that," he said irritably.

Ned and Ellen would have pressed the matter further but Nancy gave them a warning glance.

"I can see your point of view," she said to the owner. "We'll leave at once."

Her friends stared, aghast. A few minutes later, on their way to the yacht, they demanded an explanation.

"I wanted to throw him off the track," Nancy told them. "I don't believe he's the owner of Little Palm Island. He must be a pal of Snorky and Spike."

Ellen was thoroughly alarmed. "We must do something to stop him then. But what?"

"I have a little plan," Nancy said.

She proposed that a few of them wait until after dark, then steal back to the island and investigate.

"Where does Mr. Heyborn live?" she asked Ned. "He must have some kind of a house in the woods."

"It's a cabin," Ned replied. "We saw it from a distance while we were chasing Spike and Snorky among the trees."

"Then we should begin there," Nancy stated. "Maybe Bill will go with us."

Ellen, who was somewhat timid, did not care to be included in the adventure. Bill Tomlin, however, was enthusiastic.

"Nothing would suit me better than to round up that gang," he said.

In a short while the trio quietly launched a boat. With muffled oars they rowed to the beach as thick clouds scudded overhead, obscuring the moon.

"No sign of anyone around," Ned whispered as

the boat grated on the beach. "All the same, we'd better be on our guard."

After camouflaging their craft with palm leaves, the three moved stealthily through the tropical woods. Presently they came to a worn path which led them to a one-story building made of palmetto logs.

"That's the place," Ned told his companions. "Now what?"

"Somehow we must look inside," Nancy whispered to the boys. "I suspect that the real owner of the island may have been taken prisoner by the man who claims to be Heyborn. And I'll bet that the impostor is here, too."

Moving to the rear of the cabin, flashlights off, the three paused beside a window. Nancy pressed her face against the screen.

"Let me have your flashlight, Ned," she whispered. "I think a woman is lying on the bed, bound and gagged."

"Maybe it's Mrs. Heyborn," he replied.

Nancy flashed the beam, drawing in her breath at what she saw. A sleeping woman lay on the bed, her ankles tied together and chained to one of the posts!

Horrified, Nancy raised the screen and called to her softly. At first the figure did not stir. When the woman did lift her head from the pillow, she shivered in fear.

"Don't be afraid!" Nancy called in a soothing voice. "We're here to help you."

"Please! Please!" the woman pleaded pitifully. "My husband and son are prisoners, too!"

Ned hoisted Nancy through the window so that she could talk with less fear of discovery. He and Bill waited outside, keeping watch.

"Are you Mrs. Heyborn?" Nancy asked, and introduced herself.

"Yes," the woman murmured. "Two men landed here a few days ago in a boat. They accepted our hospitality, then made us prisoners. My husband and son are chained in another room. Oh, I hope they're all right!"

"What became of the boat? We didn't see it when we landed."

"Gone," Mrs. Heyborn revealed. "I heard one of the men—the others call him Spike—say it would return in a day or two with a lot more digging equipment."

After examining the woman's bonds, Nancy realized she could not hope to release her without the key to the padlock.

"I'll be back," she said in a comforting tone. "Then I'll get this lock off."

Tiptoeing to the window, she climbed out and rejoined Bill and Ned. She told them everything she had learned.

"We must capture the man who is impersonating Mr. Heyborn and get the key to the padlock

The sleeping woman was chained to a bedpost

from him right away. And, boys, the real Mr. Heyborn and his son are prisoners somewhere."

At the rear of the building was a screened porch which the young people had barely noticed. As they walked around the house they saw that a cot had been set up in the enclosure. A man was stretched out on it.

"That must be the impostor!" Nancy whispered to her companions. "If we're quiet, we can take him without a struggle!"

Making no sound, the three opened the door of the porch and slipped inside. Ned took a rope from his pocket and bound the man's feet. The startled prisoner, awakening, struggled to a sitting position. A beard lay on a nearby chair with a big straw hat and white coat.

"Mr. Rorke!" Nancy exclaimed.

He tried to break free, but Ned and Bill held him securely while Nancy tied his hands behind his back. The boys searched his pockets and turned the man's keys over to Nancy. She hurried to Mrs. Heyborn, freeing her, then her husband and young son.

The little boy grinned sleepily. "This is just like in a storybook," he remarked.

When Mr. Heyborn heard the entire story, he was amazed. He assured the young people that he would not interfere with the Tomlin treasure hunt.

"Dig to your hearts' content," he urged them generously. "My wife and I came here to enjoy a peaceful existence. And our son loves it. I'm a naturalist, connected with the American Museum, and have been studying the flora of the island. All I ask is the privilege of continuing my work without interruption."

With Spike Doty, Snorky, and Rorke captured, Nancy believed there would be no further trouble. A ship-to-shore telephone call was made to government officials, requesting that a boat be dispatched from the nearest point to take charge of the three prisoners.

On the way back to the yacht Nancy questioned Rorke. He admitted learning of the treasure from the son of the first mate of the *Warwick,* not the *Sea Hawk.* The man, now dead, was not named Gambrell. The mate had stolen Captain John Tomlin's copy of the half section of the parchment map, but had lost it. The only words he could remember on the paper, he had told his son, were "Pa" and "South Atlantic."

Rorke had discovered the whereabouts of the captain's twin brother, now known as Tomlin Smith. Accordingly, Rorke offered Ellen's father money for his section of the map.

At that point in the confession, the rowboat reached the *Primrose.* Nancy decided to wait until morning for the remainder of the account. Dawn was coming up and the adventurers needed rest.

Nancy fell into a deep sleep, but early in the morning she awakened with a start. From somewhere a young man's voice was calling, "Nancy Drew! Come out on deck! It's important!"

She quickly put on a robe and tiptoed to the door. No one was in the corridor.

"Did I dream I was being called?" Nancy wondered.

The summons was not repeated. Nancy went back to bed, but not to sleep. She had just begun to feel drowsy when she heard the summons again. This time the sounds seemed to come through the open porthole.

Once more Nancy got up, poked her head out, and looked to the deck above. The young sailor who had announced the disappearance of Snorky was leaning over the rail. He smiled down at her.

"I have an important note for you from Mr. Rorke. I can't bring it down because I'm on duty. Please come up and get it."

Intrigued, Nancy replied, "Okay."

As she quickly put on slacks and sweater, Nancy kept wondering what the note might say. Was it a further confession, a clue to the treasure, or perhaps a warning?

Bess and George had not awakened and she did not disturb them. Nancy hurried up the corridor and climbed the metal stairway to the open area above. The sailor was working at one of the big rowboats on deck near the prow. He was untying the heavy canvas tarpaulin stretched over it under the direction of a heavy-set crewman. Together they laid the canvas on deck.

"Good morning, miss," the sailor said. "This guy's got the note." He walked off and disappeared.

Nancy went up to the burly crewman. "You have a note for me from Mr. Rorke?"

"It's a message," the man replied. "He says to tell you you're goin' t' be punished for not mindin' your own business, Miss Nancy Drew!"

In a surprise move the sailor knocked Nancy down so that she sprawled on top of the tarpaulin. Before she could get up, he had pulled the canvas around her and now tied the ropes tightly.

"Help! Help!" Nancy cried, but the sounds were too muffled for anyone to hear.

Seconds later she felt herself being lifted up and then thrown. She landed in the water and began to sink!

CHAPTER XX

The End of the Quest

NED Nickerson's cabin was next to the one Nancy, Bess, and George occupied. He had also heard Nancy's name spoken, and the summons for her to come up on deck. At first he had thought little of it, but upon second thought it worried him.

Leaning out his porthole, he called to Nancy but there was no response. Alarmed now, Ned threw on some clothes and dashed up to the deck above. From a distance he could see Nancy being rolled into the tarpaulin and quickly tied up. Ned dashed forward but he was too late to keep the burly seaman from hurling her overboard!

"You rat!" he yelled at the man.

With a tremendous swing at the sailor's jaw he sent him crashing to the deck in a knockout punch. The next second Ned was poised on the rail, then he dived into the water.

Nancy was not in sight. Because of the weight

of the tarpaulin she had plummeted straight down. There was enough air inside it so she could breathe for a few minutes and Nancy struggled hard to free herself. But her attempts were futile. She knew now that she would die of suffocation rather than drown.

"Poor Dad!" Nancy thought. "And I promised him I'd be careful." Then, after praying a little, she added, "I don't want to leave Ned and Bess and George and Hannah, too—all the people I love!"

Suddenly Nancy became aware of something touching her. Within seconds the rope was untied and the tarpaulin was being unrolled. Then, as if a miracle had happened, she was free! Nancy was already holding her breath, and with an assist from Ned, she swam to the surface.

By this time Bess, George, Dave, and Burt had been awakened by the young sailor. Having thought over the episode of the note, he had begun to suspect trouble. The young people had rushed to the deck and were puzzled to find the crewman unconscious.

Just then two heads broke the surface of the water. The onlookers were aghast to see Nancy and Ned, now taking in great gulps of fresh air.

"They have on regular clothes," Bess commented. "What happened?"

Burt leaned over the rail. "Need a hand?" he called.

"Guess we can make it," Ned called back. "Get the captain. And put down the ladder."

Dave dashed off. When Captain Stryver arrived, the two bedraggled swimmers were back on deck. Nancy and Ned told what had happened and pointed to the burly seaman, who was just reviving.

The captain yanked the sailor, John Todd, to his feet and demanded an explanation. He said that Rorke had told him when he reached New York he was to go to a certain place and receive a large amount of money for "putting Nancy Drew out of the picture."

Under his breath Burt said, "And he's too dumb to know he'd be double-crossed and never get a cent."

Todd said the young sailor was innocent. He had been asked to summon Nancy because she knew him. He apologized profusely to Nancy and to the captain.

"Nancy," said George, as Todd was taken away, "you're shivering. Let's go and get some dry clothes."

"And a hot breakfast," Bess added.

A half hour later everyone gathered in the captain's dining room. In order not to alarm Trixie, Nancy had requested that no mention be made of what had happened. Conversation was all about the hunt for the treasure.

"I want to dig," said Trixie. She reached under

the table and brought out a small pail with a shovel. She kept looking into it and smiling. "I got a map," she said.

"May I see it?" Nancy asked.

"I don't want to show it," Trixie replied.

"Why not?" her mother asked. "And where did you get it?"

Trixie's lips began to quiver. On the verge of tears she answered, "From a drawer in Nancy's cabin."

Mrs. Chatham scolded her daughter. When the girl began to cry, Mr. Smith tried to quiet her by showing his copy of half the old map.

Nancy spoke up. "Don't worry. Trixie, you never could have found the treasure with that half map, even if it had been matched with the good half."

"What do you mean?" the little girl asked.

As everyone listened in amazement, Nancy explained. "When Irene and Fred Brown followed me that day and I was afraid they might steal the exact copy of Mr. Smith's half map, I mailed it to Dad at his office. However, before I did, I made another drawing of it, but I deliberately reversed all the directions. And that's the paper you have, Trixie."

Everyone laughed and George said, "Leave it to Nancy to outwit the schemers!"

The Smiths were eager to start the treasure

hunt. Ellen's father felt much better and insisted upon going. Digging tools were procured and the group set off in rowboats.

When they assembled on the beach of Little Palm Island, Nancy rearranged her figures on the half map to give the correct directions. Then work started near a large palm tree. Soon mound after mound of sandy soil had been turned up. No treasure chest was revealed.

A disheartening thought struck Nancy. Suppose the treasure had been dug up long ago and carried away!

She went off by herself, and using a compass, re-figured the directions. "What a goose I've been!" she scolded herself as she looked at the result. "We've been working at the wrong spot!"

She hurried back to tell the others and chose a different palm tree for the search. It stood on a beautiful knoll overlooking the rolling sea.

"I'm sure this is the place!" Nancy exclaimed, marking off a large rectangle on the ground.

Again the young people turned up the sandy soil and loose rocks. After fifteen minutes Ned's spade struck a hard object.

"Probably just a rock," he said, without much hope.

Turning up another spadeful of earth he bent to examine the object.

"This is no rock!" he shouted jubilantly. "I think we've found the treasure!"

The other boys rushed to help him dig. Presently the top of a rusty iron chest was uncovered. In another five minutes they were able to lift it from the hole.

"This seems too good to be true," Ellen said, tears of happiness in her eyes.

"Nancy," Mr. Smith spoke up, "you must have the honor of opening the lid."

"If you don't mind," she answered, "I'd rather you three Smiths do it. But the chest must be pried open with a crowbar."

Ned offered to do this and soon succeeded. As Mr. Smith raised the lid, everyone stared in stunned silence. Inside lay hundreds of gold and silver coins, jewelry and rich ornaments from all over the world. That the wealth had been the property of Ellen's great-grandfather, Captain Tomlin, there could be no doubt, for a stained letter addressed to his descendants bore his signature.

Mrs. Smith clasped her husband's hands in happiness, and Ellen exclaimed, "Dad! Everything's going to be fine from now on!"

Congratulations, handshakes, and thanks were exchanged. Everyone praised Nancy, who modestly reminded them, "Without Mrs. Chatham we couldn't have made the trip."

The Smiths, Bill Tomlin, and Mrs. Chatham consulted together, with the result that they presented a generous gift to the Heyborns, and similar tokens for every member of the expedition. Nancy received a beautiful jeweled bracelet, one of the fine pieces in the collection.

The chest was prepared for transfer to the *Primrose*. With such a precious cargo aboard, Captain Stryver was worried that the prisoners might get loose and make trouble. He tried to keep the news from them, but they overheard the excited conversations of the others. The three captives were furious, each blaming the other for their failure to obtain the treasure. Before the voyage home was begun, however, a government seaplane arrived and to everyone's relief took charge of the captives.

"How did the men get together in the first place?" the young people asked Nancy, who had heard the prisoners' confessions.

"When Rorke failed to buy Mr. Smith's half of the map, he got in touch with his old friend Spike," she explained. "To his surprise he found his partner had also heard the story from the *Warwick*'s first mate, and was working on it from the Captain John Tomlin angle."

As Nancy paused, George spoke up. "When Spike traced Mrs. Chatham, it was easy for him to snoop around Rocky Edge. He knew the place because years before he had robbed it."

"Spike hid in the house and in the studio," Nancy continued. "He overheard many things, and learned that Mrs. Chatham had a lot of money in a safe. When he needed some cash, he decided to kidnap Trixie for a sizable ransom."

George spoke up again. "But Nancy found her in time."

"The messenger was Snorky. He saw us leaving the studio and cut out quickly," Nancy put in. "Incidentally, he did steer the *Primrose* off course on purpose."

She went on, "Spike used the secret room in the studio to examine all the papers he could lay his hands on. When Trixie and I kept showing up, he tried to scare us away."

"Did he admit to stealing my half of the map?" Ellen's father asked.

"Yes. Rorke got him to do that. The arresting officers have it now."

"Where do the Browns fit in?" Bill Tomlin inquired.

"They were part of the ring, but didn't get along very well with the others," Nancy explained. "They thought they were smarter than Rorke and Spike. But Spike managed to get the wanted piece of map from them—at least the one Hannah made. She had copied the words 'Little' and 'Pa,' giving him the first word and part of the second in the name of the island, but she had misled him completely in the directions to the buried fortune.

"You know, Hannah Gruen really saved the treasure," Nancy added. "If she had given the right directions in John Tomlin's half map to the Browns, the buried chest might have been taken before we reached here!"

"But, Nancy, *you* really solved the mystery!" Ellen exclaimed.

"*Mysteries,* you mean," her father put in warmly. "After all, Nancy traced my brother, the map, the thieves, and the treasure!"

"Oh, please stop it!" Nancy declared, blushing. "I couldn't have done a thing without the help of every one of you, and especially Mrs. Chatham for engaging the *Primrose.*"

"Nonsense!" the woman replied. "This trip did more for me and Trixie than you'll ever know."

Nancy was happy about this, but at once began to long for another mystery. To her delight she was to encounter *The Clue in the Jewel Box* soon.

That evening when she and Ned were on deck gazing at the moon, he said, "Nancy, how about taking your mind off mysteries for a while and thinking of me instead?"

Nancy laughed mischievously. She gave a mock salute and said, "Aye, aye, sir!"

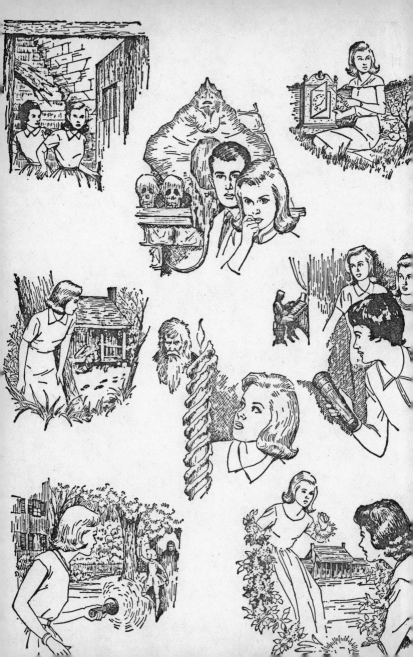